I0761279

# MURDER IN THE READING ROOM

Con Lehane

First world edition published in Great Britain and the USA in 2026
by Severn House, an imprint of Canongate Books Ltd,
14 High Street, Edinburgh EH1 1TE.

severnhouse.com



Cover and jacket design by Nick May at bluegecko22.com



*British Library Cataloguing-in-Publication Data*
A CIP catalogue record for this title is available from the British Library.

ISBN-13: 978-1-4483-1455-3 (cased)
ISBN-13: 978-1-4483-1916-9 (paper)
ISBN-13: 978-1-4483-1454-6 (e-book)



*All Severn House titles are printed on acid-free paper.*

Typeset by Palimpsest Book Production Ltd., Falkirk, Stirlingshire, Scotland.
Printed and bound in Great Britain by TJ Books, Padstow, Cornwall.

The manufacturer's authorised representative in the EU for product safety is Authorised Rep Compliance Ltd, 71 Lower Baggot Street, Dublin D02 P593 Ireland (arccompliance.com)

# Praise for the 42nd Street Library Mysteries

"A treat . . . Draws us in and keeps us firmly glued to the page"
*Booklist* on *Murder by Definition*

"Intriguing . . . Those with a taste for noir lite will want to check this out"
*Publishers Weekly* on *Murder by Definition*

"Fans and new readers will enjoy solving Ambler's latest puzzle"
*Booklist* on *Murder Off the Page*

"Atmospheric . . . Those who love New York City and libraries will be rewarded"
*Publishers Weekly* on *Murder Off the Page*

"Intense, thought-provoking"
*Library Journal* on *Murder in the Manuscript Room*

"Plot twists and multiple points of view add to a gritty, complex tale that weaves details of library work and references to crime novels throughout the story"
*Booklist* on *Murder in the Manuscript Room*

## About the author

**Con Lehane** is a mystery writer, living in Warrenton, Virginia. He is the author of the 42nd Street Library Mysteries, featuring Raymond Ambler, curator of the library's (fictional) crime fiction collection. He's also the author of three mysteries featuring New York City bartender Brian McNulty, historical PI novel *The Red Scare Murders*, and short stories published in *Ellery Queen Mystery Magazine* and *Alfred Hitchcock Mystery Magazine*.

Over the years, he has been a college professor, union organizer, and labor journalist, and has tended bar at two-dozen or so drinking establishments. He holds a Master of Fine Arts degree in fiction writing from Columbia University School of the Arts and has taught fiction writing at The Writer's Center in Bethesda, Maryland.

conlehane.com

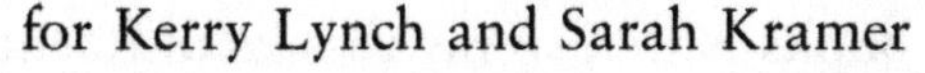

for Kerry Lynch and Sarah Kramer

# Author's Note

Editors make books better, so my thanks to Rachel Slatter for her brilliant editorial work on my last three books for Severn House—*Murder by Definition*, *Murder at the College Library*, and this latest entry, *Murder in the Reading Room*. My thanks also to Severn House for taking on the 42nd Street Library Mysteries, when the series was orphaned by its first publisher. Severn House's intrepid crew—copy editors, production editors, designers, book promoters, marketers and others behind the scenes—has done a remarkable job of bringing the books, which we are all justly proud of, into the world.

Sadly for me—because I will miss my imaginary friends—*Murder in the Reading Room* will be the final book in the series. Raymond Ambler has has enough of crime and criminals and will henceforth limit himself to quieter pursuits. It's always possible something will happen to change his mind, but for now this is goodbye—with tremendous appreciation—to his faithful readers.

# ONE

"Your phone number came up a couple of times on her cell phone. I thought that was interesting." Mike Cosgrove paused.

"She tried to call me last night?"

"Last night and again this morning."

Raymond Ambler felt a chill run through him. Something cold and hard clutched at his chest. He shivered.

"The homicide cop who caught the case remembered I knew you, so he tipped me off. I'm at the scene now."

"Robin? Robin Cartwright?"

"That's her. She had a key card of some sort from the 42nd Street Library in her purse." Mike's tone softened. "You wanna come over? . . . Not a lot to see. The crime scene unit's finishing up; they'll be gone by the time you get here."

The hotel was on the west side of Manhattan in what's called the Meatpacking District, the designation because the area had once been home to slaughterhouses and meatpacking plants. Like the rest of Manhattan, it had since gentrified. The Mystique Hotel, a three-story triangular structure next to the West Side Highway, a couple of blocks below the Chelsea Piers and overlooking the High Line, had survived gentrification, flourishing as what was termed euphemistically a short-stay hotel.

The hotel's operation was shut down during the crime scene investigation, so a dozen or so couples of varying shapes, sizes, ages, and ethnicities still milled about restlessly on the sidewalk alongside the hotel. The body had been taken away, along with any evidence, or any other sign that something had happened in the hotel.

Ambler didn't know why he'd come. The hotel room looked and felt like the boudoir of some femme fatale from a 1940s film. The bed, draped with a pastel purple satin bedspread, took up most of the room. The room itself was bathed in a soft purple light and the satin-covered bed was reflected from a large mirror on the ceiling. The one window, with a blackout shade, looked out on the High Line. A scent of something floral hung in the air; not thick enough to be cloying, but nothing that would remind you of summer in the park.

*What was she doing there?* Ambler kept asking himself. The short answer should have been obvious. But the obvious answer didn't fit the Robin Cartwright he'd gotten to know as a reader at the 42nd Street Library.

"Technically, it's an unattended death," Cosgrove said. "The uniforms called homicide because that's what they're supposed to do and because someone other than the deceased attended the death.

"She'd checked into the hotel with a man late that morning. Hotel security found her body a few hours later, after checkout time, the man long gone. My guess is the bastard smothered her with a pillow. You can't tell anything looking at the body. We have to wait for the medical examiner on the cause of death."

Ambler noticed the pillows were gone from the bed. Anything Robin or the man had brought with them had also been taken by the police as evidence. Nothing was left in the room that would suggest who visited it last. Still, he took in everything in sight, trying to make sense of what had happened. Something about the garishness, the unsubtle subtlety of the decor reeking of soulless sex, depressed him more than he already was depressed. *What was she doing there?*

Cosgrove watched sadly as Ambler took his inventory. "The enterprise here being what it is," he said after a moment, "the hotel doesn't use security cameras in the lobby. The guy had to show I.D. to register. But it's not like the desk clerk went over it with a magnifying glass. The precinct detectives will interview anyone who might have seen them arrive or the guy leave. We'll see what they come up with."

Ambler continued to inspect the room as if to imprint it on his memory, not really hearing Cosgrove, not really taking in what he looked at either.

"Why did she call you?" Cosgrove asked.

"I don't know; she didn't reach me. I'd been helping her with her research. She didn't leave a message, only said 'Damn!' when I didn't answer the second call."

"Why didn't you call her back?"

"I was too busy the first time, and then it got late. I just got back into the city this morning. I didn't see the second message until you called me."

"You were too busy to answer a phone call?"

"I was holding a baby who was crying. The second time I was rushing to get back and missed the call. I had no idea how important it was."

Mike raised and lowered his eyebrows a couple of times but didn't ask anything else.

The truth was he should have called her back. What he'd told Mike was both true and not true. He knew more about why Robin might have called him than he'd said. He should have known the call might have been because she was in danger.

Dr. Robin Cartwright had arrived at the 42nd Street Library a few weeks before, as a scholar in the library's visiting professor program. Blake Beasley, the director of the program, brought her to Ambler's crime fiction reading room shortly after she'd set up shop.

"Dr. Cartwright asked to meet you," Beasley had told him. "Dr. Cartwright, may I present Raymond Ambler, the library's resident scholar on all things murderous."

Ambler cringed. He didn't know Beasley well, but well enough to resent his chummy, condescending manner. He was one of the snobbish senior librarians who looked upon the crime fiction collection that Ambler curated in the same way the snobs in a family looked down on their poor relatives.

"Can a death that's been officially ruled an accident actually have been a murder?" she asked as soon as Beasley had left the room. Direct and straightforward to the point of bluntness, that's how she was. And he liked her for it.

He'd answered by gesturing with both arms to take in the hundreds of volumes on the shelves surrounding them. "I'd say a murder initially thought to be an accident would be a central element in dozens if not hundreds of the mystery novels written over the last century."

Dr. Cartwright dressed and carried herself like the mid-career college professor she was. Assertive but not overbearing, sure of herself in a well-mannered way, she was unruffled by Ambler's response. "In that case, I'm glad I'm not writing a mystery novel."

What she was writing was a book about deaths that had initially been suspected to be murders, but had been ruled accidental and the suspects cleared. "My book will focus on three cases in particular where I've studied the rulings and I'm convinced someone got away with murder."

Ambler wasn't surprised. "It's not so uncommon to get away with murder. You might even say it's likely that it happened in some of the cases you're looking into. But if the investigators at the time couldn't find evidence of murder, it will be a lot harder—maybe not possible after the fact—for you or anyone else to find evidence."

She had an answer for this, too. "If you were to go through my database, you'd find cases in which questions were raised and not answered, glaring omissions, contradictions, implausibilities."

Ambler shrugged. "Even so . . ."

She answered the question he didn't ask. "I've worked on this for a long time." She drifted off, dreamily, and spoke as if from a trance. "It's an academic project, that's true. I'm a sociologist . . . a criminologist." She met his gaze, her assertiveness wavering. "The truth is I'm obsessed with the idea."

"Why?" he asked, though he suspected she would have told him if he hadn't asked.

She hesitated. "It's personal, I'd have to say . . . Because of something that happened a long time ago when I was in college." She drifted away again but caught herself. "My best friend died in what the police said was an accident.

"But I knew—not in the sense I could prove it—but I knew it wasn't an accident. I was young. I didn't have the confidence to challenge powerful people who said I was wrong." She glanced at the book-lined walls. "The book is how I make up for not doing what I should have done then."

This was how it had begun. He should have realized her call at an unusual hour the night before might have been because she was in danger. He'd been around long enough to know you didn't go in search of a murderer—one who believed his crime was undetected—without risking the ire of the murderer you're stalking.

"That's absurd," Ambler had said, when Mike told him before they left the hotel that there was a good chance the coroner would rule the manner of her death undetermined. "Why would the man she was with run out and leave her if it was an accident? How could she suffocate herself?"

Mike had taken a last lingering glance around the hotel room—as if he might spot something the uniformed police, the detectives who'd caught the case, and the crime scene investigators had missed. "I remember a couple of cases like this—death by rough sex. Not exactly the same but close enough.

"Here you've got a quickie in a hot-sheet hotel. She's face down, her head buried in the pillows. He's . . ." Mike stopped. "You get the picture. I'm Irish-Catholic; I'm not going into detail on this. The guy's lost in the moment; his weight is on her back; she can't get her head out of the pillows. He thinks her writhing about is part of their gymnastics; she can't breathe; she can't talk or scream; she is smothered. He's a married man, a respectable businessman. She's dead. He can't do anything for her. His reputation—his life—is ruined if he's caught with his pants down in a hotel room with a dead woman. He panics and takes a powder.

"In one of the cases I'm talking about, the guy split. But we knew who he was, and he turned himself in before we got to him. The circumstances were different. It was a bondage thing. He pleaded to misdemeanor manslaughter. I think he served six months. The other case went to trial and the guy got off. The judge bought his lawyer's argument that it was an accident, so he walked."

"This wasn't like that, Mike . . . She wasn't like that. The phone calls I didn't answer, I swear, were to tell me she was in danger." He told the detective about the book Robin was writing. "You know as well as I do that someone poking around in a murder investigation risks getting themself killed."

Mike was skeptical. When wasn't he skeptical? "By one of the men she was investigating? Why would she go to a hot-sheet hotel with a man she's trying to prove is a murderer?" He shook his head. "It's a lot more likely to be what it looks like: heavy-duty sex gone wrong. An old boyfriend came into town. Or she found a guy she liked and wanted a quickie before she went back to those boring, dusty library books."

"Why the phone calls, then? Why did she call me in the middle of the night?"

Mike's typically steely eyes twinkled. "She might have been calling around, seeing who was available."

"Your hunch was the man she was with smothered her on purpose . . . murdered her."

Mike nodded. "There's that, too."

The ridiculous tragic irony that hit Ambler as he walked in a daze across 14th Street on his way back to the library, oblivious to the balmy early autumn afternoon, would be if Robin had become one of those murder victims she was studying whose death is ruled an accident.

Soon after he got back to work, Ambler, stunned and grieving over the loss of a colleague, called another colleague, now a former colleague and once—and he hoped future—lover, Adele Morgan. She answered after a long time, sounding harried. "I've just gotten Jennifer to sleep. I need to sleep myself. Are you coming up this weekend?"

Ambler was touched by the plaintive note in her voice. "I don't know." He told her what had happened. "Jennifer was crying and kicking while I tried to change her diaper. I was too frazzled and too nervous to answer my phone. It was a tragic mistake. I should have known she'd only be calling at that time of night if she was in trouble. I knew what she was doing was dangerous. Why didn't I answer or at least call her back?"

"The woman you were helping with her research project?" Adele's tone changed from plaintive to aggrieved. "And I suppose if the police decide she wasn't murdered you'll start investigating to prove she was . . . rather than visit your daughter?" Her voice could cut glass.

"They'll investigate even if they don't know if she was murdered. But not with the effort they'd put in if it was a murder."

"And you?" Her tone changed again and he heard tears in her voice.

"I don't know . . ." He waited through a long silence, knowing what he should say, what he should do.

"I need to sleep; I'm a wreck." No longer tearful, Adele sounded exhausted and exasperated. "The nanny is coming tomorrow for the first time . . . What if Jennifer doesn't like her? I start work in two weeks. I'll be away from her for the first time." Now he heard panic in her voice. The guilt he tried to keep under wraps gnawed at him.

When Adele's maternity leave ran out twelve weeks after Jennifer was born, instead of returning to work at the 42nd Street Library, she'd left her job and the city and moved to a small town in the far northern suburbs where she'd taken a job at the River City Free Library that would start when the baby was four months old.

She hadn't asked Ambler to come with her, and although they'd talked about the move, it was her decision alone. She did give him to understand, without actually saying so, that if he wanted to move with her and the baby, he'd be welcome.

Of course, he'd been torn. He'd spent his entire life in the city, not even leaving for college or graduate school. He loved his job at the library. His devotion to his life's work of building the crime fiction collection hadn't diminished over the years; nor, if he were honest with himself, had his fascination with the murder investigations that now and again fell into his lap.

And now, the mystery behind Robin Cartwright's death weighed on him. *Why was she in that hotel room and with whom?*

It was this bewildering behavior that, after the call with Adele, led him to visit the visiting professor reading room, where his friend—and she had become a friend—did her research, research he was quite familiar with. After their initial meeting, Robin had taken to stopping by the crime fiction reading room most days to talk about her ideas and discuss her findings.

The visiting professor reading room, on the second floor, housed about a dozen cubicles partitioned off from each other by flimsy half-walls; not elaborate, but the walls did give you a sense you could work undisturbed. In addition, a row of pigeonhole storage spaces lined one wall, where the readers stored the books and journals and whatever else they'd called up from the stacks. This way they didn't have to go to a call desk every morning to reorder their research materials.

No one was at any of the desks—not surprising on the afternoon on which one of the cohort had died mysteriously. Robin's laptop was on her desk, along with a loose-leaf binder she used as her research journal that she wrote in by hand. Some books and piles of Xeroxes were in her small cubby. Unlike a lot of readers, she wasn't worried about security breaches or much inclined to take measures to protect her research from prying eyes. She did worry about losing it though, so she kept a working draft of her book and the most important notes from her research journal on Google Docs. She'd given him access to the Google Docs document and he'd read and commented on sections of the draft and left her notes about detective novels she might want to read.

He knew that the handwritten journal in the binder not only contained work she'd backed up in Google Docs—research notes, references, a bibliography, and such—but was also a kind of personal journal, which she'd been keeping for a long time, where she recorded observations that had to do with her life outside of her research. He hadn't had occasion to look at the binder in the past and wondered if he should look at it now. Was it evidence in the police investigation? He wasn't sure. No one had told him not to touch Robin's things, so he put it in his bag. He'd put it back in her cubby when he'd read it.

* * *

Later that same afternoon, as he readied to leave for the day, he got a call from a detective at the 38th Precinct, who said he was investigating Professor Cartwright's death and asked Ambler if he'd come by in the morning to answer a few questions.

Ambler politely said he'd come with his lawyer. The detective, whose name was Lambert, said this would be fine, and to have the lawyer give him a call to set up the appointment. There was no urgency to the detective's request, nor did he seem bothered that Ambler would want a lawyer present at the interview.

Ambler called an attorney he knew from other encounters with the law.

"Levinson here," said David Levinson. If he had an office, Ambler had never seen or heard any evidence of it; David was always on his cell phone.

Ambler told him what had happened.

"May her memory be a blessing," Levinson said.

"A detective wants to ask me some questions tomorrow." He told the lawyer the detective's name and the precinct number.

Levinson didn't miss a beat. "You didn't murder her, did you?"

"No." Ambler didn't know if David was serious or joking.

"Just checking . . . I'll set something up for early afternoon." He paused. "You were right to call me. Cops tie you up in knots if you're naive enough to talk to them without a lawyer. By the time they're through, you're thinking maybe you were in the hotel room with the victim . . ." He stopped and theatrically cleared his throat. "You weren't in the hotel room with her, were you?"

"No. Of course not. I was upstate with Adele and baby Jennifer."

"Just checking."

David didn't chuckle and Ambler couldn't see his face, so he still didn't know if the lawyer was serious or trying to be entertaining. Ambler had known David for quite a while and still couldn't figure him out.

After the call, he closed up the crime fiction reading room and headed to the Library Tavern. On the short walk over to Madison Avenue, he felt a sudden chilling wind come up 41st Street from behind him. Darkness had snuck in early, as it did when autumn was waning and winter was coming on. Riding on the wind was a sudden realization of the emptiness of his life. For years, when he'd gone to his favorite after-work watering hole, he'd either walked over with Adele, met her there, or knew she'd arrive soon after he did.

Not only had Adele taken herself and the baby upstate, leaving a gigantic hole in his life, but his son and his grandson had moved out of his small apartment also, moving to the North Bronx; even his dog Lola had left for the open spaces of the North Bronx with the boys, leaving his once happily overcrowded apartment feeling as lifeless as a tomb.

He'd become the monastic self he'd been before they all showed up, the solitariness more painful now. Whereas before he met Adele, his solitariness had been a state of being—the way his life was, neither good nor bad—now the solitariness was the loneliness of missing someone. At least, he still had McNulty.

The bartender actually smiled when he glanced up and saw Ambler—he always looked up when the door opened but seldom smiled. "I was on the crosstown bus and saw you walking along 14th Street this afternoon. You were out of place. Why would you be there? I figured maybe with Adele out of town, you were up to no good. You weren't far from the old No-Tell Motel."

Ambler had had enough with suggestions of impropriety. "What were you doing on 14th Street?" he challenged him.

The bartender glanced over his shoulder, leaned toward Ambler, and lowered his voice. "I was actually up to no good. I spent a joyful morning with an old girlfriend whose philandering husband was out of town."

"My reason for being on 14th Street was as far as you can get from being joyful." Ambler told him about the murder.

"Sorry for your loss," said McNulty. "It's a shame. She was nice, a bit reserved but nice. It's not enough to say such a thing shouldn't happen to her. Such a thing shouldn't happen to anyone."

"I think she was murdered. But the cops might decide her death was an accident."

McNulty raised his eyebrows. "She was smothered. Maybe it was kinky sex."

Ambler was irritated. "I told you about the book she was writing. It's likely she rattled the wrong cage."

When he got home—a beer and a hamburger at the Library Tavern having served as dinner—he went to his laptop, signed onto Google Docs, and found Robin Cartwright's outline for the book. He began to glance through it, having no idea what he was looking for. Something that happened years ago might have come back to life to haunt her. But it would have to be something that happened recently that would tell him why she was at the Mystique Hotel and with whom.

He decided to look for the answer to that in the binder where she wrote her research notes and kept a kind of diary. He pulled the binder out of his bag and started with her latest entry. He'd work his way backward toward her arrival in the city a month before her death. If he didn't come up with anything this way, he'd go back and start at the beginning.

Before he'd gotten very far, something written a little more than a week before her death made his hair stand on end.

*After all these years (I wonder if he knows???), I ran into Preacher on the library steps. I almost died. I was shocked and felt so guilty as if I was trying to hide something and got caught (like the time when I was in high school and my mother found a box of rubbers I was hiding). But why my reaction? He couldn't possibly know about the book. And even if he did, I don't have anything to be ashamed of. He does! Still, I had a ridiculous urge to confess.*

*He couldn't possibly know about the book . . . Even though I'm certain of that, a voice in my head kept telling me: He Knows!! Yet when he asked about my life since the last time I saw him, it was clear he had no idea what I was doing in New York. And he obviously had no idea what I was doing at the library. He didn't even ask.*

*As charming and tempting as I remembered him, he took me for a drink and then dinner at the Library Tavern. Strangely—very strangely—we talked about everything, except that time. After a few glasses of wine, he began coming on to me—he can't help himself; he never could—and he's still very good at it. You look into his eyes and you're sure you're the only woman in the world for him. And still it was subtle, the same as back then, subtly so if I wasn't interested, he could pretend he'd not been coming on to me; subtly so we both could pretend it hadn't happened. For a moment, it made me sick that he thought I'd want to be with him again after what happened.*

*Yet, I hate to admit it even to myself, he still turns me on. Then I got an idea. I might have batted my eyelashes. I might have blushed. Devious is my middle name. I told him I didn't know what was happening to me; I didn't know what I was feeling. It was so amazing to see him. The way I said it, my sultry tone—I put my hand on his thigh; I gazed into his eyes—would lead him to think I wanted to see him again. I gave him my cell phone number.*

Ambler sat for a moment, stunned by what he'd read. First, that the Robin Cartwright he knew wrote it. But then, how well did he know her? He'd certainly never have thought of her dying in a short-stay hotel room. What he knew was the persona she presented to him in the library. Why should he be surprised she'd let her hair down after work? Scholar by day, vixen by night?

Whatever the case, he may have just read about her having dinner with the man who murdered her. Twenty minutes later, he got a second shock, from an earlier entry two weeks after she'd arrived at the library.

*What a crazy message, sent from an email address I don't recognize, and no name signed at the end: "I know what you're doing. I won't give in to extortion. I'll die first OR YOU WILL."*

*What could it possibly mean? I'm not extorting anyone. How am I supposed to stop doing something I'm not doing in the first place? The jerk's clearly got the wrong person, but it doesn't seem sensible to reply to a death threat from a psycho.*

*But what if it was meant for me, after all? Could one of the subjects of my book have discovered what I am doing? I don't see how they could have. Even if someone did, that's not blackmail.*

*I wonder if it's George, another attempt in his warped way to get back at me for the divorce. Scare me into going to the police and making a fool of myself. Or it might be some kind of internet scam. Maybe I should just delete it and hope that's the end of it.*

# TWO

"Of course, it's a threat," Mike said with exaggerated patience. "I'm not arguing." They were talking over breakfast at the Red Flame, a diner on 44th Street, not far from the library. It was a day off for Mike, but he was in the city anyway, so they met before Ambler went to work.

"Tell the guy . . . Lambert. Tell him about the threat. Tell him about her book. Tell him everything you told me." Mike studied his lox and onion omelet for a moment before turning his world-weary expression on Ambler. "If the M.E. rules it an undetermined death or, for all we know, a natural death, nothing you tell Lambert will get him to overrule the M.E." Mike gestured like he was shooing away a fly. "She made the point herself. The subjects of her book didn't know she planned to write about them—"

Ambler interrupted him. "We're not sure of that—"

Mike interrupted Ambler. "Even if one of them did know, it's clear from what she wrote she wasn't blackmailing any of them. She sounded frightened. Would she lie to herself in her own journal?" He waved away Ambler when he tried to get a word in. "And if I'm wrong about that—which I'm not—why in the name of all that's holy would she have shacked up with a man she was blackmailing, who'd threatened to kill her?"

"That's one reasonable way of looking at it," Ambler said calmly. "It's not necessarily the only way."

Mike snorted and then laughed. "It's that kind of a day anyway. I'm going for a root canal after this."

Ambler's meeting with Lambert proceeded along similar lines, except Lambert asked more questions than Mike about Robin Cartwright and her research. The only question the lawyer Levinson objected to was whether Ambler had been romantically involved with her.

Ambler gave his lawyer a dirty look—why couldn't he just say he wasn't?—but followed his advice.

"Did you think it strange that she was so interested in murders?" the detective asked.

Ambler wondered if the detective meant him also—a little weird being the curator of a collection of crime fiction? "Her friend in college died in what was called an accident. Professor Cartwright believed her friend had been murdered."

"Why did she think that?"

The detective was a big man—a big man among big men—the size of an offensive lineman—maybe six foot five; close to 300 pounds; his head, with a buzz cut, appeared to be the size of an ox's. He wasn't fat; he was big. Even Levinson was in awe of him. Yet he spoke quietly; if a tone of voice had manners, you'd call it mild-mannered. Ambler liked that he asked questions like someone who was curious, not like he had an axe to grind.

"She didn't tell me, but she wrote about the death in her journal . . . not at the time it happened but more recently, looking back on it, just the details—nothing about why it was or wasn't a murder. She said the book was a way of making up for what she should have done at the time."

Lambert took a moment to think over what he'd heard. "Did she have a personal connection to the other incidents she was writing about?"

Ambler saw a glimmer of light. "Not that I know of. She was focusing on three cases, including that of her friend's death; I do know that. Do you want to take a look at what she wrote? She called her notebook a research journal, but it's more than that. In some places, it's like a diary."

Lambert shook his head. "You know, I'd like to. Your collection sounds interesting also. I like to read mysteries when I have time, ones with cops in them. You ever heard of Ed McBain?"

Ambler said he had. "His real name was Evan Hunter, which wasn't actually his real name either. That was Salvatore Lombino; he had it changed to Evan Hunter. He wrote books as Evan Hunter and as Ed McBain, and a half-dozen other names as well . . . lots and lots of books."

"I only thought he was Ed McBain—the 87th Precinct. They're New York books but he doesn't call it New York; he calls Manhattan 'Isola.' There's no 87th Precinct in the city, either."

It was great that the detective liked Ed McBain, but this wasn't getting Ambler anywhere. He tried again to interest him in Robin Cartwright's book project and the threat she'd received. "The email threatened to kill her."

Lambert nodded ponderously. "An anonymous threat isn't so unusual. If it's followed up by someone getting murdered, though, that'd be different. She never reported the threat to the police, right?"

Ambler nodded.

"And she didn't know who threatened her?"

"Right. She wondered if it might be one of the three men she was writing about, though she didn't think any of them knew about her research. And, she said she wasn't blackmailing anyone."

"She was a college professor, right?"

"A sociology professor, a criminologist."

"Not someone you'd take for a blackmailer." He said this off-handedly, as if it didn't mean much. But since he said it, it must have meant something.

"One of the deaths she was looking into happened in the city about ten years ago." Ambler hoped this would spark some interest. Lambert didn't bat an eye.

"We got a squad does cold cases," he said. "Those are ones we didn't close. No one's looking into ones we did close. If someone came forward and confessed, or an eyewitness that didn't speak up at the time, someone might. Even then, it would need to be convincing. Screwballs come in all the time confessing to things. They killed Kennedy or John Lennon or Tupak Shukar. Anytime a murder hits the papers, we get a bunch of confessions."

The detective asked if Ambler knew who Robin might have been with in the Mystique Hotel. Ambler told him about the mysterious Preacher, the man from her past she'd run into recently.

This produced another set of raised eyebrows and, after a pause, another question. "Did she write about her ex-husband?"

"She did seem to consider if he might have sent the threatening email. Before I read that in her journal, I didn't know she was divorced." He realized Robin hadn't told him anything really about her personal life.

"Anyone she was involved with here in the city?"

Ambler weighed his answer. He thought she'd spent more time with him than anyone else. He didn't think this was the kind of involvement Lambert meant, though, so he didn't mention it. "As far as I know, only what she wrote in her journal about meeting a man she knew in the past and having dinner with him. This was maybe a week before she died."

"Did she give him a name, by any chance?"

Ambler shook his head. "Preacher. That's all. I thought this kind of strange. Why was she trying to keep his name secret?"

Lambert thought about that for a moment. "Could be that's what she called him, like I met Tom, Dick, or Harry for a drink." This satisfied him, if it didn't satisfy Ambler. He asked about people she knew at the library.

She was one of this year's cohort of visiting professors, Ambler said. He gave the detective Blake Beasley's name. "He's the director of the program. He'd know more about her than I do."

"What do *you* know about her?" Lambert asked in his mild-mannered way, as if they were talking about a mutual friend. It was a subtle but probing question.

"Not a lot." This was the truth. He didn't know about her life outside of her research project. He enjoyed talking with her when she stopped by the reading room, which was almost every day she was in the library. They'd talked about her research. They'd talked about true crime and mystery novels but not about themselves.

He hadn't told her about Adele or his son John or his grandson . . . or his new baby daughter. He hadn't known Robin had been married until he read it in her journal; had no idea if she had children; didn't know if she lived a happy life or a sad life. Of course, he knew now, hers was a tragic life.

"I took an interest in the book she was writing," he said. There was more to their connection than that; for some reason, he didn't have the words to describe it.

Lambert's eyebrows spiked. "Why was that?" His tone hinted that Ambler might have some explaining to do.

From the question, Ambler gathered Lambert didn't know his reputation among some cops who resented what they considered his having meddled in police business a few times in the past. These were the same naysayers who had it in for Mike Cosgrove because of a case Mike handled that unearthed a cover-up by some of New York's Finest.

"I helped her find a few books whose plots centered on deaths that looked like accidents but were discovered to be murders. We'd talk about similarities between those cases and the ones she was looking into. She wasn't so far off that accidents can be faked to cover up a murder."

Lambert swallowed what he wanted to say a couple of times before he said it. "We got about six unsolved murders on our plate right now, and that's in one precinct. Ask the detective bureau how many they got." He let this sink in. "I like the 87th Precinct books because the cops were like real cops trying to bring in the perp . . . not some lady from a bakeshop or some fat rich guy from France or somewhere outsmarting the cops." He let that sink in too. "This professor, she thought she was going to run down a murderer? . . . Lots of luck with that. And then she tried to blackmail one of them?"

"I told you she wasn't blackmailing anyone. Someone mistakenly thought she was. Very possibly the person who killed her. You should look into her emails. She didn't know who the sender was, but your tech experts might be able to track them down."

Lambert wasn't argumentative, but he took his own counsel; he wasn't looking for any wisdom from Ambler. "First off, we don't know she was murdered. If she was, the odds are it was someone she knew. She wouldn't have been in a hotel room with a stranger—"

Again Ambler interrupted. "She might not have gone there willingly."

Lambert opened his eyes wider and then narrowed them again. Whether this was agreement or disagreement, Ambler didn't know because he didn't say anything. After a short pause, the detective had a few more questions, all of them having to do with Robin's time in New York, none of them with the cases she was writing about, her journal, or the threatening email.

"If the medical examiner rules this a murder, I'll want to take a look at those notebooks, or whatever they are. We should get a preliminary report in a couple of days. I'll let you know."

"And if the ruling says the cause is undetermined?"

Lambert held out his hands, palms up, in a gesture of resignation. His expression was sympathetic but not apologetic. "We'll look into it."

Ambler had a hard time keeping his mind focused once he returned to work. He got a phone call from a rare book dealer shopping the papers of a best-selling thriller writer. The price he quoted was more than the library could afford—at the moment, the budget for crime fiction acquisitions wouldn't cover the cost of a newly released hardcover, much less a high-priced author collection—and Ambler didn't think much of the author whose papers the dealer was peddling anyway.

Nonetheless, getting rid of the dealer was no easy matter. Ambler's guess was nobody else wanted the collection either at the price he was asking. Yet the dealer sometimes had worthwhile collections, and Ambler didn't want to get on the guy's bad side. This meant spending longer than he would have liked on the phone listening to the praises of the author in question. Once he hung up, he went to find Blake Beasley. He wanted to talk about Robin Cartwright.

# THREE

Beasley was a nervous wreck. To look at him, you'd think someone had tried to kill *him*.

"What happened?" he asked before Ambler was even through his doorway. His eyes were wide with a kind of terrified wonder, like a child's eyes might open with fear and alarm watching a scary movie.

Not giving Ambler time to reply, he lowered his voice to a hushed tone. "Was there foul play?" He spoke hesitantly. "The newspaper didn't say . . . And what the hell is a short-stay hotel? It sounds—"

Ambler hadn't come to hold Beasley's hand. "The police are waiting for the medical examiner. Foul play is a possibility." He waited a moment. "What do you know about what happened?"

Beasley's eyes sprang open wider. "Me? What do I know?"

"Take it easy, Blake. You saw her every day. You talked to her, didn't you? Did she tell you she was afraid? Did she tell you she was threatened?"

Beasley took a deep breath and stared at Ambler, his head slightly cocked, as if Ambler might have said something nonsensical. "Why would she be afraid? Who would threaten her?"

Ambler sighed. "It would be better if you didn't answer every question with a question. The book she was writing could have exposed a murderer. That could lead someone to threaten her or worse, wouldn't you think?"

Beasley looked baffled. "Honestly, that never occurred to me. Professor Cartwright was writing a study of criminal behavior. Not an exposé. She isn't . . . wasn't . . . seeking headlines. Hers was an academic endeavor. Who would even be aware of it?"

"Would you please stop asking me a question every time I

ask you one? Someone did threaten her." He told a skeptical Beasley about the entry in Robin's research journal.

Beasley's eyes narrowed as his skepticism became suspicion. "Yes, she did tell us that she'd received a strange email, but it was obviously fake. I told her to delete it and forget about it. But how do you know what she wrote in her research journal?"

"She shared her research with me." Ambler was glad he'd already returned Robin's journal to the visiting professor reading room. "You have access to her notes on Google Docs as well, if I'm not mistaken."

"I do?"

Ambler rolled his eyes. "I'm not going to talk to you if everything you say is a question." Either Beasley was playing dumb or he really was oblivious. "I gave your name to the detective handling the case. He's going to ask you for the names of the other readers in the visiting professor program. Can you give them to me also?"

Beasley said he didn't have time at the moment to get the list and wasn't sure it would be appropriate for Ambler to be questioning the scholars in his program anyway. "They shouldn't be subject to a rude and intrusive interrogation from someone who has no business questioning them. I'll give the names to the police officer if he asks."

It was difficult—even for Ambler who eschewed violence in all its manifestations—not to want to smack Beasley's smug smile off his face. You had to wonder how he'd gotten by this long without someone taking a poke at him.

He was more competitive and devious than you'd think possible from a colleague. His manner, rather than collegial, was like the petty competitiveness you'd find from salesmen working on commission at a fly-by-night used car lot. He'd bet that when Beasley was a kid, he was a toady and a squealer.

After leaving Beasley in his cubicle, as he was crossing the reading room, he recognized one of the visiting professors whom he'd met at a welcoming reception for the new scholars a month or so before. He didn't remember his name but did remember that he was working on a monograph about Malcolm X's murder.

Most of the time he worked at the library's research branch in Harlem, the Schomburg Center. But he was probably following up some correspondence in Manuscripts and Archives. They'd chatted a bit at the reception because Ambler had never believed the official story on who killed Malcolm. The professor had had something to do with the exoneration of two of the men originally convicted.

He stopped by the desk where the man was sitting, reintroducing himself, hoping the professor would do the same, since he couldn't remember his name. No such luck. "I wonder if I could talk to you for a moment, if it's not an imposition," Ambler said.

The man glanced up, his dark eyes cloudy, as if he'd been awakened from a dream. "I'm always busy, and everything that interrupts me is an imposition." Harsh words, but he laughed after he'd said them, and stood. His standing up was a striking event because of his height; he towered over Ambler—maybe six-five or taller and broad shoulders—but moved slowly and a bit awkwardly as if in pain, reminding Ambler that . . . Jones, Thomas Jones, that was his name, had gone to college on a basketball scholarship.

"I imagine you want to talk about the death of our colleague," Jones said when they'd taken a seat on one of the stone benches up a flight of stairs, outside the Rose reading room amidst a throng of milling-about tourists. "I hardly knew her but I miss her."

His expression was brooding, reflecting a deeply felt sadness, his gaze sharing something with Ambler, as if he'd lost someone dear to him and expected Ambler's sympathy. "A life full of promise snuffed out, just like that. I've seen too much of it."

Although Ambler noted Jones's sadness, he was puzzled. "Why did you assume I wanted to talk about Professor Cartwright?" Realizing how abrupt the question was, he softened his tone. ". . . if you don't mind my asking."

Jones drilled him with a penetrating gaze; not angry but giving no quarter, a protective shield. "Because of who you are, and because of the circumstances—Dr. Cartwright receives a threatening email and a couple of weeks later she's dead.

Next thing, the library's resident expert on murder—if we're to believe Mr. Beasley—wants to ask me questions. It doesn't take a great leap of the imagination."

Again the unexpected from Dr. Jones. "You knew she'd been threatened?"

"She told us about it at our weekly tea not long ago. Ironically, she asked if she should take the threat seriously." He hesitated. "Beasley dismissed it as spam—said he'd seen emails like it before—and told her to delete it. She seemed inclined to follow his advice. I disagreed, but no one else did."

"Why?"

Jones looked at him curiously. "Why did I take the threat seriously?"

Ambler nodded.

He folded his hands under his chin. The hands were large but graceful, with long, tapered fingers. He'd have no trouble palming a basketball. "I grew up in Compton." He watched Ambler to see if he knew of Compton. Ambler did. "When someone threatened you, you'd best believe them and be ready.

"I got out of the hood because I played basketball better than most of the kids. Some of my friends played better than me; they didn't make it out. The ghetto stays with you. I don't threaten anyone. If someone threatens me, I believe they mean it." His tone was matter-of-fact, no drama.

Ambler didn't ask why none of his colleagues took the threat seriously. If you live a life of the mind, your environment—the university or college campus—is usually protected and safe. You don't expect that safety to be disrupted. You don't want to feel unsafe, so you act as though you are safe until you can't do otherwise.

"Was Blake Beasley at the tea?"

Jones hesitated. "It was his get-together. He presided . . . Actually, I remember distinctly he was there. He and Dr. Cartwright spent a good part of the time talking together." Jones tucked his finger into the collar of his shirt and tugged at it, as if the conversation made him uneasy. "I try to avoid campus gossip—or in this case library gossip—but the rumor was they'd become something more than colleagues."

"An affair?" Ambler sounded as shocked as he felt. Had he been so naive as to not recognize Robin had a side to her other than that of dispassionate scholar? You didn't go to a hot-sheet hotel with someone to compare research notes. With Blake Beasley? No! It couldn't be. Him?

"I don't suppose it's anything to be shocked by," Jones said, after watching Ambler's reaction with mild interest. "She was attractive and vulnerable, rebounding from a hurtful divorce. She wanted, you might say sought, the attention of men."

This news was confounding. Robin hadn't sought that kind of attention from him, had she? Later, he would recall mannerisms he'd noticed at the time but paid little attention to—her smiles, touching the back of his hand, laying her hand on his shoulder, leaning close to him when she sat down beside him at a table in the reading room, once resting her hand on his thigh for a moment as she sat down beside him. Thinking about her in this light, some of what she'd done might have been suggestive. He was too caught up in his own concerns—Adele and the baby—to catch on.

Jones gave him the names and contact information for his colleagues in the visiting professor program. They didn't have much to do with one another, he said; no collaboration on the projects they were working on. They saw each other at the weekly gathering—the tea Beasley hosted—and nodded when they passed in the hallway. Some of them might have lunch or dinner together; he didn't know.

"This is rare uninterrupted time for doing research on something important to us," Jones said, "so we're not careless with the precious time; we don't waste it in idle chatter. We're civil but—except for what I mentioned about Blake and Robin, which is uninformed gossip—we keep to ourselves."

Ambler was tempted to ask Jones for his take on Blake Beasley but decided not to. An assessment of character based on limited contact wouldn't mean much. Nasty people often have charming facades; dour and grumpy folk can have the softest of hearts. What Ambler needed from those he questioned, he'd learned over the years, was information. If Jones could tell him, for instance, where Beasley was on the morning of Robin's murder, that would be something.

On the other hand, Jones not having seen Beasley that morning, which was the case, didn't mean much. Ambler phrased his questions carefully. He asked about the daily routine of the visiting professors. Did they have a set time to be in the library? They didn't, but with few exceptions they all showed up when the library opened its doors in the morning, or shortly after, and got to work.

Was Beasley there to greet them each morning? Most mornings he dropped by at some point, but not so regularly that anyone would notice if he missed a morning or two. It was more likely they'd miss Robin if she weren't there, he said, but she was always there until . . .

Had Dr. Cartwright shared her research with her colleagues in the program? Not with him, Jones said. He couldn't speak for anyone else. "We know in general what others in the group are doing. There's a plan for some presentations of works-in-progress later in our stay. Ironically, Dr. Cartwright was to be first to present. If you want to know about her research, Blake would have read her proposal since he organized our applications and sent them to the judges. You'd have to ask him about that."

Ambler had already determined he wouldn't be asking Blake Beasley about much of anything. That Beasley had already lied to him was clear. He knew a lot more about Robin than he'd let on. The nagging question was why he'd done so. Picturing Beasley and Robin together in the Mystique Hotel grated on him, so he pushed the image out of his mind every time it tried to get in.

Later that afternoon, he paid a visit to someone he did trust: his boss, Harry. Harry was loth to speak ill of anyone, especially someone whom he supervised, which was the case with Beasley as well as Ambler. It was also likely—if not certain—that Harry wouldn't do anything to encourage or further another Ambler murder investigation, especially one so close to home.

"The poor woman." Harry's expression was mournful, his tone solemn. "You knew her quite well, didn't you?"

"I thought so, but I'm not so sure anymore."

Harry's eyebrows spiked. "She shared your unhealthy interest in criminal behavior. And now this . . . Hers was a bizarre accidental death, I understand. But still . . ." At this point he caught something in Ambler's expression and his face went rigid, as if it were plaster that had suddenly hardened. His eyes were glued to Ambler's face.

Ambler understood this reaction to mean Harry knew that Ambler was about to tell him his suspicions regarding Robin Cartwright's death.

"I don't believe you." Harry said this, despite Ambler not having uttered a word.

"We're waiting for the coroner—" Ambler started to say more but Harry interrupted him.

"The president's office has already received word that the death was probably accidental."

Ambler swallowed his surprise and irritation. Of course, that was how things worked in the city, in the country . . . for that matter. The elites get the news first, before the run-of-the-mill folks like him are told anything. They get a heads-up so they can get their story straight before they're asked any questions that might create discomfort.

"I didn't know they'd issued a report."

"I'm told the report will be issued later this week. President Ledyard called to let me know it was coming since Professor Cartwright's appointment was technically to my department and reporters might ask me questions."

"Murder can look like an accident."

"For someone like you, it might. Normal people accept what their eyes and ears tell them."

Rather than asking Harry about Beasley, as he'd intended, Ambler decided to wait for a calmer time. He went back to the crime fiction reading room and called Mike Cosgrove, who didn't know there was a preliminary report either. He said he'd find out and call him back, which he did a half-hour later.

"The M.E. reports deal with two things," Mike told him. "The cause of death and the manner of death. Your boss jumped the gun with his assumption. The cause of death was asphyxiation, as I thought. The manner of death was undetermined. Manner could be a lot of things. The guy's dead at the bottom of a tall building: jumped, fell, or was pushed? Accidental or purposeful? Purposeful by one's own hand, or by someone else's hand? Yesterday we didn't know the manner of death and today after the M.E. report we know the cause but still don't know the manner."

"So?"

"So we look into it."

"Great."

"Easy for you to say."

As always, when the days troubles weighed heavily on him, Ambler headed for the Library Tavern and his pal, bartender Brian McNulty. Before he'd finished his first beer, he'd brought the bartender up-to-date on what he'd learned about Robin's death since his last visit.

Not surprisingly, McNulty had his own take on things. "Young people these days are into choking as part of sex. Did the cops think about that?"

"I doubt it," Ambler said. "I certainly didn't think about it. She was smothered not choked."

"No matter. You said, asphyxiated; that's what it's called, 'erotic asphyxiation.'"

Ambler didn't know where McNulty was headed. "Is this something you've studied?"

McNulty's expression was a bit sheepish. "Not exactly . . . I spent some time with a young lady who considered herself sexually adventurous or, as she put it, 'uninhibited.' You might call her kinky. In any event, she tried to explain it to me. But I didn't get it. Then she tried to show me. She choked me while we were . . . grabbed me around my throat and squeezed until my eyes bulged."

He lowered his gaze. "I couldn't talk and she wouldn't let go, so I popped her one right between the eyes." He shrugged. "She liked that, too, and wanted to do it all again. She was very much into this 'do it again' idea. I came to my senses and decided I should stick to women more my age and temperament. I told her she needed to find a younger man . . . maybe a few younger men."

Ambler shook his head to clear it. Talking to McNulty was always a treat. "Let's put that aside for a moment," he said. "Robin was in here with a man at some point before she was killed." McNulty's raised eyebrows forced him to start over to avoid an argument. "Before her death, McNulty. Let's put it that way. She was in here for dinner with a man not long before her death."

"An older man," McNulty said. "Big guy. Pain in the ass. Acted like we worked for him . . . He sent his drink back. You'd think someone his age would know better than to insult the bartender. Not enough liquor in it, he told the server. He couldn't taste the bourbon. So I gave him a new one with less liquor in it. He was fine with that."

"You'd recognize him if you saw him again?"

"I'd pick him out of a crowd at fifty feet."

"Ever seen him before or since?"

He shook his head.

# FOUR

The following morning Ambler called Mike Cosgrove to tell him McNulty could identify a suspect in Robin's murder.

"Where do you get suspect? And who said 'murder'?"

Ambler nodded, though no one was nearby to see him. Another doubter. He should be used to it by now. "You said you'd be looking into it. I thought—"

"First of all, it's not my case; and second of all, it's not a murder investigation. It belongs to the 38 and they'll investigate."

"You told me the guy smothered her."

Mike was silent for a moment before he said, "You shoulda informed me anything I said would be used against me. That was off the top of my head. I was angry. Finding the body of someone who shouldn't be dead makes me angry. That the guy left her there made me angrier." He was silent again but Ambler knew he wasn't finished.

Cop through and through that he was, Mike had the belief—maybe he didn't have it any longer, but he'd started out with it—that nabbing the killer and putting him away made the fact of the murder easier to take because justice had been done. Ambler had not found this to be true. He regretted a death as much after the killer was caught as he did before; putting the killer away provided no satisfaction.

Mike believed in the criminal justice system he was part of, despite its shortcomings. He was one with his fellow workers and would circle the wagons when criticism—deserved or undeserved—came at the cops from the outside. Despite his friendship with Ambler, a gulf remained.

"No matter my hunch, I'm not going to say she was murdered without evidence. Maybe you can. If it was up to me—which it isn't—I'd treat the case as a murder investigation until something told me different. Maybe the guys in the 38 will approach it that way, too. Maybe they won't. I'm not going to tell them how to handle their case. Why don't you give it a try?"

Ambler caught the sarcasm.

Mike's tone became more subdued. "The guy who caught the case, Lambert, he's a good cop. If there's something there, odds are he'll find it. If you decide to take a closer look at some things—that research she was doing, her diaries or whatever they were—and come up with something, he's not going to turn you away."

This was at least a bit of encouragement. "I don't suppose Lambert would keep you in the loop . . . and you could tell me what he's come up with or where he's looking."

Mike's long-suffering sigh. "That's not going to happen, Ray. Anything that's public, I'll let you know."

That wasn't much but it would be something. The newspapers weren't going to pay attention for more than a day or two, unless it became a murder investigation. He wasn't sure what Lambert would do. He should at least follow up on the email threat. That was something the police should know how to do. He didn't. The cops might be able to track down the blackmailer, too, if there was one.

The precinct detectives might do these things. But they might instead concentrate on what Robin had done and who'd she seen in the days before her death, which should include the man McNulty saw her with. Lambert seemed most interested in the ex-husband—who Ambler hadn't known existed—which made sense. Suspecting the ex-husband always made sense.

He should have asked Mike about surveillance cameras on Madison Avenue. They might have picked up the man Robin had dinner with at the Library Tavern. So he might actually follow up on Mike's sarcastic suggestion and give Lambert some advice.

Not advice really. Tell him McNulty could identify a man Robin was with not that long before her murder. He might even suggest Lambert have the bartender take a look at surveillance video of Madison Avenue, if McNulty could remember which evening, and if it hadn't already been deleted.

Before he left the library for the evening, he went back to the visiting professor reading room to pick up Robin's loose-leaf binder again. He wanted to go through it once more. He'd only skimmed it the first time he'd looked, and there would undoubtedly be things he'd missed. He probably wasn't authorized to take it, but it wasn't library property, and it wasn't likely anyone would be looking for it until the police stepped up their investigation. In any case, who would he approach to ask for permission? Beasley? Hardly.

But the binder wasn't where he'd left it in her cubby, or anywhere else in the reading room. So he went looking for Beasley after all, to find out what had happened to it. No surprise, Beasley was no help.

"I didn't know she had a loose-leaf binder. I don't snoop through our readers' belongings."

"You don't have to snoop to know she had a research journal. What did you think she was doing here? She had a file on Google Docs and she had a binder she kept here in the library."

Beasley scratched his head. "I don't remember. Even if I knew where it was, I wouldn't tell you. We're not supposed to touch anything. There's a police investigation."

"Who told you that?" Everybody knew what was going on but him. Could the police have taken the binder? If Beasley knew, he wouldn't tell Ambler.

"Harry," he said smugly.

Arguing with Beasley was like being in fifth grade again. Ambler resisted the urge to smack his colleague, left Beasley in his cubicle, and sought out Harry, who not only didn't know where Robin's binder was but said he didn't know such a thing existed.

"I know it existed. I saw it," Ambler said. "If the police took it, they would have told you. Someone might have stolen it."

Harry's eyes grew wide, enormous pools of blue behind his glasses. "Who? Why?"

"A murderer. To get rid of incriminating evidence."

"Murderer? I thought—"

"You were wrong."

Harry blinked three or four times rapidly, something he did when he was befuddled. "A murder investigation? That's not what President Ledyard said."

"It's in the early stages." This was playing loose with the truth, but Ambler felt he was justified. "They call it an undetermined death investigation."

After another few minutes of back and forth over what the investigation might mean, he asked Harry to arrange a meeting with the visiting professors.

Harry grimaced as if he were in pain. "Why ask me? Ask Blake to do it."

"For one thing, he wouldn't do it. He's done everything he can to not help, including lying to me. For another, I don't trust him. It may be in his interest not to help me."

Harry folded his hands across his ample midsection and leaned back in his chair with his scandalized schoolmarm expression firmly in place. "I don't believe Blake would lie to you."

"You think I'm lying?"

Harry's eyes widened again. "Of course not."

"One of us is."

Harry stretched out his arms in supplication. "Now Ray, I don't think you lied. You could be mistaken. You could have misunderstood. Blake is . . ." He was at a loss for words.

"I don't know what his reasons might be for putting up roadblocks, so I'll give him the benefit of the doubt." Ambler wasn't going to talk about his suspicions. Even Beasley didn't deserve to have unsubstantiated accusations hurled about. That didn't mean he couldn't hurl some substantiated ones.

"You know damn well he's a conniving, brown-nosing, backstabber, and you wouldn't trust him as far as you could throw him either. Everything he says and does is self-serving."

Ambler's criticism of his colleague wounded Harry to his core. A former Jesuit, who'd reluctantly left the priesthood years before, he'd brought with him most of his priestly virtues.

It was against his nature to harshly criticize any of his charges. “I never knew you had such antipathy toward him.”

“I hate his guts,” Ambler said, realizing as soon as he’d said it that he’d gone too far.

“Whose guts do you hate?” Benny Bevone, one of the library aides and a pal of Ambler’s heard the imprecation as he was passing Harry’s office with another library aide, so he stopped. The other aide took a look at Ambler and Harry and kept going.

Discord in his ranks threw Harry for a loop. “Satan’s,” he said to Benny, reverting to his Jesuitical instincts. “Ray hates Satan and all his wiles.”

Ambler laughed. But Harry was right in a way. He didn’t like anyone who used their wiles to get over on someone else, be it Satan or Blake Beasley. Little did he know—though he should have known—that the off-hand, thrown-out phrase, “I hate his guts,” would come back to haunt him.

“You were talking about Blake,” Benny said. “Don’t pretend you weren’t. Everybody hates the guy’s guts. A pompous asshole—”

“*Benny!*” Harry was beside himself. The Manuscripts and Archives division was devolving into anarchy.

Benny was undeterred. “He thinks he’s the lord and the library aides are serfs. No one wants to work with him. You’d do us all a favor if you fired him.”

Harry’s face was red, his cheeks bulging. “Enough! We’re not having this kind of bickering and profanity directed against our colleague. Stop this now.”

Ambler wanted to placate Harry so he said, “I didn’t mean what I said, Benny. I was letting off steam.”

“Well, I meant what I said.” Benny was adamant. “I was going to ask for a new assignment anyway. I like working with those readers—the visiting professors. They’re really smart. But Beasley’s too much. He’s—”

Ambler didn’t let him finish. “You’re the research assistant for the visiting professors? Why didn’t I know that?”

“The Invisible Man syndrome,” Benny said. “No one notices us. They think they fill out a slip and the books show up on their desks, like opening a computer file.”

"I'm an idiot," Ambler told himself. To Benny he said, "We need to talk. I'll buy you a beer after work."

"OK . . . Can we plan how to get rid of Beasley?"

"I want to talk about a loose-leaf binder."

Hoping for a truce, Harry told Ambler he'd invite the visiting professors into his office the following day for an informal status meeting to discuss their concerns and questions. If Ambler wanted to talk to them about Dr. Cartwright's death, it would be reasonable enough. He could ask a few—a very few—questions.

Later that day at the Library Tavern, Benny and Ambler talked about the visiting professors. "They're like a lot of the readers in the library—living in their own heads. They're nice enough, but you get the feeling sometimes the soul has left the body."

He'd especially liked Robin Cartwright. "I was really sad she died. She always made it a point to talk with me. I knew she was talking with you, so I told her we were friends. She was excited about that and wanted to know about you. She said you didn't talk about yourself.

"I told her how you'd saved me when the cops wanted to arrest me for something I didn't do. She was thrilled that I'd been a murder suspect and told me about the book she was writing. She talked to me like I might actually have a brain. The others act like I'm a branch line of the conveyor belt that brings up the books."

For some reason, Benny sitting on a barstool looked like a kid perched on a stool at a soda fountain; gleeful, as if his mug of beer were a chocolate malted. "She wanted to know how I came to be a murder suspect and what it felt like." He waited while some memories caught up with him. "I didn't mind telling her how it happened. But I didn't like remembering what it felt like to be hauled in by the cops and having to get a lawyer and all that."

He looked up at McNulty who'd been standing in front of them for a moment or two. "You remember that?" he asked the bartender. "You got me the lawyer."

McNulty chuckled. "Levinson. You're probably still paying off his bill."

Benny laughed, too. "It wasn't too bad." He nodded toward Ambler. "But it would've been if Ray hadn't gotten me off."

"And you met your girlfriend," McNulty said.

"My wife now." Benny beamed like the kid with the malted.

"I wouldn't be so smug." McNulty's expression was dour as usual. "Marriage ain't what it's cracked up to be. Why buy the cow if you can get the milk for free?"

"Bullshit, you were married, McNulty."

"That's what I mean. Once was too much." He almost cracked a smile. "I'm pulling your leg, Benny. You're a lucky guy . . . I'm waiting for Ray to follow in your footsteps." He cocked his head toward Ambler. "I'll miss you when you move upstate."

"Who said I'm moving upstate?"

"Everyone but you knows you are."

"Who's everyone?"

"Me," said McNulty.

Back to business, Ambler told Benny about Robin's missing loose-leaf binder.

Benny turned serious. "Some nights she took it home with her. Most nights she left it in her cubicle or in her pigeonhole locker. I noticed it because most readers use laptops for everything now. I hardly ever see a binder like that anymore."

"It was there after her death. I saw it in her cubby this morning. And then it wasn't there this evening when I came back."

"Someone took it?" Benny squinted and wrinkled his forehead, rethinking what he'd said. "I guess that's obvious . . . So you wanna know who."

"You have any idea?"

"No." He waited a moment. "I suppose you want me to see if I can find out."

That was exactly what Ambler wanted him to do.

"So. We're working on a case together?"

Ambler spoke hesitantly. "You could say that . . ."

"I did say that." Benny brightened. "I'm your inside guy."

It took Benny until a half-hour before lunch the next day to find the research journal.

"It was on a shelf in the stacks near the woodworking shop," he told Ambler as he handed him the binder. "The only thing on the shelves that didn't have dust on it."

The stacks under the Rose reading room were mostly unused the past few years, abandoned in favor of the newer stacks under Bryant Park. But the carpentry shop was still there. Most people didn't know the library had its own workshop in the stacks, where carpenters built and repaired the oak reading tables and chairs. Ambler knew about it but still he was surprised. "How did you come across the binder? What were you doing down there?"

Benny as usual dressed stylishly—Bensonhurst stylish from another era, that is: purple shirt, silver sports jacket, skinny black dress pants, and shiny, pointed, black dress shoes. "What do you think I was doing there? Looking for the binder."

"Why there?"

"I was methodical. I looked everywhere."

Benny left the binder with Ambler, who browsed through it during lunch, noticing as he did that pages were missing from the journal. The pages weren't numbered, but in at least three places a page would be followed by a page that had no relation to what preceded it. He didn't have time to go through the entire journal and debated keeping it. He thought to take it home when he left work, but decided instead to try to provoke a reaction by returning it to its rightful place. For this, he enlisted Benny again.

"While you're dropping off the material the readers ordered from the stacks, stick it back in Robin's cubicle. Try to do it when most or all of the visiting professor readers are in the room, and especially when Beasley is there. But don't let anyone see you put it back. They won't be paying much attention to you, right? If you could hang around until someone notices it, that would be great."

Benny eyed Ambler skeptically. "How am I supposed to do that? Pretend I have a flat tire on my delivery cart?"

"You'll think of something. Start a conversation with one of the readers."

What Benny did was mix up some of the call slips and give

the wrong books to a couple of the readers. "I do that every once in a while for fun," he told Ambler. "so I can watch them try to straighten things out. Most of the time they accuse each other of screwing things up. They fight over the stuff like kids in a sandbox."

It wasn't likely he'd find out anything by doing this, Ambler knew. But he also knew that disrupting the order of things can create a chain reaction that reveals something that wouldn't have come out otherwise. In this case, Benny told him that evening as he was leaving work, it was Blake Beasley.

"The star of the show," Benny said. "He saw the binder when he was leaving the reading room. He did a double-take but pretended he didn't and then looked around to see if anyone saw him. He started to leave—his hand was on the doorknob—but changed his mind and came back as if he'd forgotten something.

"Then he tried to get a better look without letting on that was what he was doing, so he sort of stalked it, like a hunter stalking a rabbit, looking over his shoulder every other second." Benny chuckled. "When he got pretty close and was straining to get a better look and pretending he wasn't, I got up near him and said pretty loud, 'Hey, Blake!' He jumped about a foot off the ground and dropped the files he was carrying."

"Was anyone else interested in the binder's return?"

Benny shook his head. "No one paid any attention, even during Blake's pantomime show. After I called his name, he looked back and forth between me and the notebook a couple of times. I could tell he wanted to ask if I put it there, or hoped I'd tell him about it on my own. At the same time, he pretended he hadn't noticed it. I looked at it and at him but didn't say anything."

Benny had the self-satisfied look of someone expecting a commendation. "What next?"

"I don't know." Ambler felt like Snidely Whiplash twirling his mustache. "I think we'll give Beasley a day or so to see if he might do something stupid."

"He's trying to cover his trail?"

"You'd think that."

Benny narrowed his eyes, which were slits to begin with. "Why did he take the notebook and then put it back?"

"We don't know for sure he took it. If he did, it was to remove some of its contents."

Benny eyes widened again. "Why would he do that?"

"I don't know." Ambler spoke absently because he was deep in thought. Clearly, he had missed something his first time through the binder. Among the Xeroxes of newspaper and magazine articles, and of excerpts from books written on cases similar to the ones she was pursuing, she had kept her personal observations, which would include anything that had to do with Beasley—if she'd written anything about him; and now, if she had, they were gone.

"If he was hiding it, he could have done a much better job. Someone would have found it in the stacks sooner or later. Why didn't he burn it or throw it in the river or shred it?"

"He took what he wanted out of it." A surge of anger hit him out of nowhere—at Beasley or whoever took pages from Robin's journal; at himself for not holding onto it when he had the chance; at his inability to understand what anything meant, at whoever murdered Robin, at the cops and the rest of the world for not realizing she was murdered.

"He didn't care if someone found the binder after he took the pages he wanted. But he would've been smarter to put it back himself . . . *unless he hadn't finished.*" He said this calmly, the rage gone as fast as it had arrived.

"What did he take? Did Robin think he was going to kill her and wrote it in the notebook?"

Ambler held up his hands to quiet Benny. What he'd said was unfounded. Beasley snatching the binder and taking some of its contents—if in fact he did—might make him a suspect. But even that didn't prove him a murderer.

"You want to know why Beasley has been acting strangely. You want to know for sure if he took the binder. You want to know what he took out of the binder and why he took it. All those are things I'd like to find out too, but right now we don't know the answers."

He held Benny's gaze for a long moment. "You've been a

big help with this. But you can't tell anyone what you found or what we think it might mean. No one. If Harry or the bosses above him get wind of us accusing Blake of anything—without a trunk full of evidence—you'll be working at a library in Staten Island, and I'll be curating a collection of fishermen's diaries in the Sheepshead Bay Library."

It required that Ambler basically deputize Benny as his partner to convince him he couldn't say anything about what he'd learned.

"Don't worry," Benny vowed. "They can rip out my fingernails and I'll still keep my trap shut."

Ambler worried.

# FIVE

The meetings with the visiting professors took place the following morning in Harry's office. He'd emailed each of them with a specific time, telling them he wanted to answer any questions they might have concerning the death of their colleague.

Ambler didn't believe he'd find a murderer among them; not impossible but improbable. Nor did he know what any of them might tell him that would be helpful. Yet someone might know something he didn't know, and this might tell him what to do next. Even though he could think of a half-dozen things he *might* do, he sure as hell didn't know what he *should* do.

The first interviewee was Edith Murphy, a woman of a certain age who taught history at an Historically Black College in Atlanta, where years before she'd been a student activist during the sit-in days at the birth of the civil rights movement of the 1960s. If the word "distinguished" needed a personification, Professor Murphy could handle it. She spoke precisely, was reserved without being aloof, as well as warm and collegial.

"Dr. Cartwright and I often—I wouldn't say regularly—ate lunch together, taking our sandwiches or salads on one of these beautiful autumn days to a cafe table in the park. She was quite engaging, interested in the work I was doing, more knowledgeable about the Second Migration than I expected. She is . . . was . . . a sociologist, of course, but still."

The professor told them about the book she was working on—for some years, it appeared—and how pleased she was to have access to the resources of the New York Public Library to perhaps finally finish it. Like other professors Ambler had known, Dr. Murphy would, at the drop of a hat, describe the scholarly project she was working on in great detail—certainly more detail than Ambler cared to hear about. Harry's eyes had glazed over after the first two minutes.

After what seemed like hours, Ambler snuck in a question when the good professor paused for emphasis. "Were you interested in Dr. Cartwright's work as well?"

Ambler realized asking the question might be impolitic—suggesting he wasn't interested in the migration of Black Georgia sharecroppers to Bedford Stuyvesant in the years during and after World War II—which wasn't exactly the case. But he was, after all, trying to determine if a murder had taken place, and some things took precedence.

The professor took the question in stride. She smiled. "We are here to talk about Professor Cartwright, aren't we? Once you get an historian talking about her work, you might never get a word in edgewise." She laughed good-naturedly.

"Ray is asking about Dr. Cartwright's death," Harry said, "because the circumstances are a bit cloudy . . . it's not clear how exactly she died, who she was with. He . . ." Harry hesitated. "He . . . and I . . . thought she might have said something, or you might have observed something unusual in her behavior recently."

"Did she seem worried or afraid?" Ambler asked.

Professor Murphy's attention heightened. "Robin had come in contact with a man from her past. I wouldn't say she was fearful after the encounter. Rather, I'd say she was intrigued because of the coincidence, and strangely excited."

"Coincidence?" Ambler kept his voice steady, despite his quickening interest.

"He was the subject of one of the cases she was reviewing . . ."

Ambler recognized that the professor had developed the habit some intellectuals have of pausing for long stretches in the middle of what they're saying. Ambler did this himself sometimes—pausing in the middle of a sentence—when he thought of something related to what he was talking about and wanted to follow through on the thought lest he lose it. Aware of this, he kept quiet and waited.

"You are familiar with her work . . ." Whether this was a question or a statement, it was directed to Ambler. She didn't wait for his response. "Yes. I'm sure you were. She mentioned she relied on your expertise in the area of unsolved murders."

"I wouldn't say I was an expert, but we did talk about her work." Ambler wasn't being modest; he believed what he said. "This man . . . from her past . . . did she tell you his name?"

"Not his name. You're aware, I assume, that the names she used in the proposal and in the draft she was working on weren't the actual names." This was a question phrased as a statement.

He wasn't aware this was what Robin did—and he didn't understand why he wasn't aware of it or why she'd do that. "These were actual cases," he said. "She'd need the actual names to do the research. All of the research materials she collected—news articles, court transcripts, notes from anyone she interviewed—would have the correct names. So why disguise the names in her manuscript?"

"I surmised it was because she might show her work in progress to others and wanted to protect her subjects' privacy until she was sure of her facts. She would be the only one with access to her notes and research materials, so no need for such precautions there."

Unless someone steals your research journal, Ambler said to himself. Returning Robin's binder to her cubbyhole no longer seemed like such a good idea. What if someone took it again and didn't put it back this time? It might be best to retrieve it when he finished with the professors.

"Did she talk to you about her husband?"

"Ex-husband." The professor was quick to correct him. "He left her for one of his students. He'd married Robin when she was his grad assistant. She grew older and his tastes didn't. So he started over with a younger woman—she was just nineteen. Robin was bitter. Fortunately, they had no children."

"Was she afraid of him? Had he been in contact with her recently?"

"I would say no on both counts." Dr. Murphy scrutinized both Harry and Ambler, as though she were assessing them for a task she wasn't sure they were up to. "Is your concern about her death that you suspect she was murdered?"

Harry started to say no and then almost said yes; tongue-tied, he could no longer meet her friendly but penetrating gaze.

Ambler had no hesitation. "Do you?"

Professor Murphy didn't flinch. "Something out of the ordinary took place. She was young enough, attractive, and she was lonely and vulnerable. I think a man could have taken advantage of her. If you suspect something sinister about this mystery man from her past . . . I would join you in the suspicion.

"Something in her manner when she talked about him made me think of the naughtiness otherwise proper young girls exhibit when a bad boy makes a play for them. They're intrigued, flattered. He's a boy they know they should stay away from because he's dangerous, though that's the very thing about him that attracts them."

The next interview Ambler expected to be perfunctory. He'd already spoken with Thomas Jones, who most likely wouldn't have anything to add to what he'd said then. But Jones wasn't to be dismissed so easily. After a few questions and answers, he said, "I think we have something in common, Mr. Ambler."

This got Ambler's attention. He'd had a stray thought while Jones repeated most of what he'd said initially that the professor was holding something back, but on second thought he had dismissed it. Now it appeared he shouldn't have. He waited.

"I believed the threatening email sent to Dr. Cartwright should be taken seriously when no one else did. You believe she was murdered when no one else does. Why do you suppose we're the outliers?"

Ambler didn't get where Jones was going with this. He hadn't actually said to Jones he thought Robin was murdered. It was interesting that Jones thought he had. He thought to set the record straight on what he'd said and not said, but decided to hear the man out instead. "So we have in common a suspicious nature. Anything else?"

Jones spoke softly, his tone making clear he wasn't trying to get over on Ambler. "What I meant is we both feel a sense of responsibility, for reasons of our own, to Robin's memory.

I don't know why you do. But I owe her a debt. She's largely the reason I was awarded this fellowship. I could tell you about all that, but it's not important at the moment."

Ambler thought it was important, if only because Jones hadn't mentioned it before. He'd said he didn't know her very well. So when Jones suggested they talk later in the day, Ambler arranged to meet him after work at the Library Tavern.

Next up, C.R. Spaulding was an amiable, cheerful, and engaging young professor from a SUNY college upstate, who was writing about the historical journey—his term—that tobacco and baseball had taken together, using the resources of the library's George Arents tobacco collection. The book was his ticket to gaining tenure, he told them. "I'm an aficionado of all things popular culture, and the bulk of my scholarly activity is online." He noticed what must have been perplexed expressions on his questioners.

"You know, TikTok, WhatsApp, Instagram, podcasts, ezines, blogs? I'd hoped my activity and expertise in social media and my podcasts would ensure my tenure; the students are crazy about what I do." His expression became downcast for the briefest of moments. "Those media don't sit so well with my senior colleagues, of whom there are many. So I told them I'd write a book—still popular culture, but *a book*." He brightened.

He said the word "book" with the disdain you might use for the word "flu" or "intestinal distress." After a few seconds, he added, "Actually, I'm having a ball doing the book . . . Are you familiar with the Arents Collection? It's a blast." He sounded like one of his students describing his new video game.

Both Harry and Ambler panicked at the same moment, fearing the exuberant young scholar would go on in great detail about his research project, or worse his social media innovations, and bore them to tears. Fortunately, one of his cell phones began buzzing—he'd arrived carrying two cell phones, an iPad, and a laptop computer—which knocked him off stride long enough for Ambler to change the subject.

C.R., as he liked to be called, had little interaction with Dr. Cartwright, he said. He was sorry when he learned she had died. She was nice but quite a bit older than him, and super traditional (his euphemism for "old fashioned") in her thinking, so they didn't have much to talk about. He got along with her, with Blake Beasley, with everyone in the visiting professor program, for that matter. But in truth, engrossed in his own work, he paid little attention to any of his colleagues. Nope. He didn't notice that Dr. Cartwright was worried or afraid of anything. Had no idea where Blake Beasley was at the time of her death, or at any other time. Heard no rumors about Beasley or her.

After C.R. left, Harry watched the doorway for a moment before saying wistfully, "I think we're out of touch with the new generation of readers. He told us he was writing a book like he might have been describing how he got a chance to drive a stagecoach."

Ambler didn't think things had gone that far.

Lynn Morris, a women's studies professor from an exclusive liberal arts college in the Midwest, was probably as young as C.R., but didn't come across as having been created by artificial intelligence. She was engaging and eager to help; her reserved manner bespoke a lack of interest in frivolity.

"I agree 100 percent that Cartwright's death was not what it seemed. Something was amiss."

Ambler was intrigued on a couple of accounts. First, that the professor thought something might be wrong about "Cartwright's death." Second, that she referred to her deceased colleague by her surname.

"Why not?" she asked. "Men do it all the time: 'Jones' over there or 'Spaulding' wearing his earpiece. Did you never wonder why men don't call women by their surnames?" She awaited a response.

Ambler hadn't, but didn't say so. Harry studied his hands folded in front of him on the desk. Professor Morris—or "Morris" if she preferred—obviously wanted to continue the surname discussion. Ambler much preferred talking about why she agreed with him that "something was amiss" about how

"Cartwright" died. He tried asking this using Robin's surname but couldn't quite get his tongue around it. Calling her "Cartwright" made him uncomfortable.

"What was it about Dr. Cartwright's death that didn't seem right to you?"

Morris considered her answer for a moment. "It's an impression, not something I can put my finger on. Cartwright was a serious scholar. I grant that we all have frivolous moments, need to let off steam, let our hair down." She glanced sternly from Ambler to Harry and back to Ambler. "I'm not a prude. I'm not scandalized by someone's dalliance."

Morris's seriousness came through as sincerity. "But Cartwright was focused on her research so intensely, I can't imagine her being distracted at such an important point.

"Men, even men in the academy, or perhaps especially men in the academy, expect young women . . ." She paused to consider her phrasing. ". . . make that *attractive young women* would be flattered by attention paid to them by 'accomplished' scholars, accomplished *male* scholars, that is, and be distracted by such attention."

Her glance at Ambler—was she glowering at him?—suggested he might be such a man. "I myself am not." This with enough emphasis to dissuade Ambler if had any such plans . . . which to his knowledge, he didn't. "And I know for a fact that Cartwright's head wasn't turned by such attention either, because I saw it with my own eyes."

Ambler's own eyes at this moment opened wider, as he silently asked who.

She appeared to hear him anyway. "Thomas Jones, if you don't know, is a star in his field. He could go to just about any university in the country with an appointment as a full professor and a substantial research budget if he had a mind to. He and Cartwright had a past, and he was quite interested to learn of her divorce when they arrived here together."

"A past together?" Another surprise, something else Jones neglected to mention. Their conversation later that afternoon might be quite interesting.

Morris didn't have much else to tell them about her dead

colleague, only a vague suspicion that "something wasn't right" about the circumstances of her death.

After she left, Ambler asked Harry what he thought about their afternoon of interrogations.

"Is that what we were doing?" Harry mopped his brow with his handkerchief, something he normally only did after a contentious staff meeting. "I found it more of an ordeal than I expected. Scholars, it appears, are quite anxious to discuss their scholarship." He raised his gaze to the ceiling. "I suppose I knew that. But I hadn't experienced so much of it at one time. Is this what you do when you're 'cracking a case'? I don't see how you accomplish anything."

"Often I don't. Yet every now and again when you think over later what was said, something strikes you that you didn't think important at the time. It also happens that you find contradictions in what people say. For instance, Dr. Morris observed a connection to Robin that Dr. Jones neglected to mention."

"Well, I don't expect I'll be getting any revelations." Harry paused, his expression thoughtful. "Do you think one of them might have been concealing something?"

"I wouldn't be surprised if all of them were."

# SIX

When Ambler arrived at the Library Tavern late that afternoon, he looked for Thomas Jones at the crowded bar and didn't see him. A quick glance at McNulty, who gestured with a flick of his head toward the tables, told him where to find Jones. That McNulty knew Jones was the man he was looking for didn't surprise Ambler, who believed when it came to what took place in his bar his friend had superpowers.

Jones stood and shook hands, the standing not something Ambler had expected. "I suppose you think it odd that I'd want to help with your investigation."

"Suspicious," Ambler said, hoping to press some buttons. "I'm suspicious."

"Suspicious?" Jones's eyebrows spiked.

"I asked myself why. The answers I came up with raised suspicions."

"As in I'm a suspect?" He sounded incredulous, exaggeratedly so, to emphasize the absurdity of the suggestion.

"Suspicious behavior raises questions. You might be trying to hide something. You might want to keep close to me so you can mislead me. You might do this to protect yourself. You might do it to protect someone else—"

Jones didn't raise his voice, but his expression grew hard and his tone harsh as he interrupted. "Your insinuation borders on insulting."

"Not insinuation. I'm letting you know I don't trust you. You might say I'm more forthcoming than you are . . . Suppose we start over and you tell me how well you knew Robin Cartwright."

Jones, who'd been self-assured, a kind of fortress unto himself, lost his footing for a moment. "I told you she'd been a mentor."

Ambler leaned back with a kind of bewildered expression that was more put on than genuine. "The first thing you told me was that you didn't know her well."

"I don't know why I said that. At the time, I guess I didn't want to get involved. I've changed my mind. As I said, she was a mentor."

"How does this work? You're a major figure in your field, I'm told. As I understand it, she wasn't a nationally recognized figure . . . In addition, you're not in the same field. She's a sociologist. How would she be a mentor?"

The server came by. Ambler ordered a beer. Jones asked for a glass of white wine and an order of French fries. He fidgeted in his seat, asked to keep the menu, and concentrated on that rather than looking at Ambler.

After a moment studying the menu with only quick glances at Ambler, he said quietly, "I wasn't always nationally recognized. I went to college on a basketball scholarship. I was a good enough college basketball player. But I wasn't going to the NBA. The expectation was I might get tightened up with a chance to run a local car dealership or some other glad-handing position by a booster. Kids who went to the kinds of schools I did growing up don't go on to grad school. Robin helped me do that.

"You don't have to be a star professor to have the respect of colleagues across the disciplines. You get respect if you're a bona fide scholar and a conscientious teacher. She had that respect. For God knows what reason, she took an interest in me. After the first course, I took all of her sociology and criminology classes as an undergrad. She taught me how to study, how to research, how to write an academic paper.

"She was a great teacher and a mentor—even after I graduated and got into grad school. Because of her help, my dissertation became a book and was published by a well-regarded university press, which meant a tenure-line position at a decent university. None of that would have happened without her."

His story made sense. It wasn't unusual for a professor

to take a student under their wing and put them on a path to success they would not have attained otherwise. Almost all successful people with a rough row to hoe, who might not have made it otherwise, have a teacher like her in their lives.

So what Jones told him rang true. But Ambler knew there was more. Not only had Dr. Morris said so, Jones's mannerisms, his nervousness, his tone of voice, his evasiveness, told Ambler there was more. He wanted Jones to come clean, partly because he wanted to trust him.

Yet Jones had a reason to want to be close to the investigation. And Ambler didn't know what it was. To know what Ambler found out and where the investigation was headed so he might head it off? The thing was, it might be a good idea to keep Jones part of the investigation, so Ambler could keep an eye on *him*.

"Anything else I should know about?" Ambler still hoped.

Jones slowly shook his head.

"You didn't tell me any of this when we first talked."

Jones turned his melancholy gaze toward Ambler. He sounded defeated. "I didn't think it was important. Knowing about my past wasn't going to help you solve her murder."

For the next few minutes, they talked amidst awkward silences about the library, about Jones's research, about the crime fiction collection. Jones suggested they split the check. Ambler said he'd get it. So Jones pulled himself out of the booth, taking a moment to stretch out his body and each leg before he headed off.

Ambler didn't stop to visit with McNulty on his way out as he might normally do. He was anxious to get home. The bartender shrugged and watched him leave.

When he got to his apartment, he went to the internet to do a search. He didn't like checking up on what Jones had told him. But the fact was Jones had misled him before—had lied to him—so verifying what Jones told him was in order.

A lot of what he discovered after an hour on Google bore out. Jones did grow up in Compton, that was true, the third of four boys raised by a single mother. He'd gone to college on an athletic scholarship, as he'd said; had played Division I basketball for one of the two hundred or so universities not part of a power conference and not a launching place for a pro career.

But then Jones's story began to go astray. He did graduate from the college where he played basketball, and he did begin graduate studies there as well, earning a Masters degree. The discrepancy: Robin Cartwright wasn't on the faculty of Cal State Oakland. Only later, when he entered a Ph.D. program, did he attend the university where Robin taught, so she was hardly his undergraduate mentor. What a strange thing to lie about. It wasn't something you'd expect a person would want to hide. But then something else popped up, a part of his life Jones might well be reluctant to talk about. Ambler called David Levinson.

"I need you to tell me how to find something," he told the lawyer, who never failed to answer his cell phone unless he was in court or on the phone with someone else.

"You're the gumshoe; you do the finding out. I'm the mouthpiece, who says, 'If you're not going to book him, you gotta release him,'" David said blithely.

"You've watched too many old movies. I need the transcript of a trial." Ambler told the lawyer that Thomas Jones had been arrested, tried, and acquitted on a charge of involuntary manslaughter. Ambler knew when the trial took place and that it was in the Los Angeles County Superior Court.

"I suppose I could have my intern look for it . . . Time, you know, is money. I'm a top-notch criminal defense lawyer; I should be rich. But because of you and the other deadbeats—no offense—McNulty sends my way, I'm barely able to pay my rent."

"Tell that to McNulty," Ambler said. David and McNulty both had living, unreconstructed, Communist fathers, so McNulty took advantage of David's allegiance to the toiling masses and kept sending him pro bono cases, of which Ambler was one.

"Out of idle curiosity, would you tell me why I might be doing this?"

Ambler reminded him of the uncertain circumstances of Robin Cartwright's death and told him about her research project and about Thomas Jones. "It's possible Robin knew about the case. It might be similar to the ones she was working on, except this one went to trial."

"You think your resident scholar offed somebody and walked?"

Ambler shook his head to clear it. Levinson sounded like one of his clients.

"What I know so far is the charge was involuntary homicide. The victim was a drug dealer. Jones's older brother was involved, maybe a user, maybe a dealer."

"So you think it should have been Murder One and that's why the dead woman was interested?"

"I don't know."

"We'll see what we can find," Levinson said and, after a pause, "I'll send the bill to McNulty."

The next morning, while Ambler sipped his coffee on the terrace behind the library overlooking Bryant Park, he received a terse text message from Harry: Please come to my office when you receive this.

He did as he was told, and found a large, rumpled man who wore a dark suit in such a way as to suggest he usually wore a pair of overalls and carried a monkey wrench in his large calloused, grease-stained hands. None of which was true. The man's forehead was large, as was his nose; his eyes were small, and their expression somewhere between sad and despondent, his gloomy features chiseled into place rather than the result of a temporary setback.

When he met Ambler's gaze and reached to shake hands, an awkward moment for both of them, Ambler felt afraid that the man—who turned out to be Robin's ex-husband, the college professor who'd left her for one of his students—would start crying.

"I'm sorry for your loss," Ambler managed to get out, though this wasn't entirely accurate since the man's loss took place years before when they divorced. He didn't look like a college professor, and certainly not like a magnet for younger women, though there was no telling what it was in an older man that sparked the interest of young women.

"I loved her," the man, whose name was George Nagy, muttered. His expression grew darker, if this were possible. His saying this, without context, created another awkward silence.

"It was my fault," Nagy said as if to himself.

Maybe it was Harry's priestly aura despite his defrocked state that brought about an urge to confess in people. Ambler for his part found listening to this soul-baring disconcerting. He didn't know what Nagy was confessing to, but he doubted it was his ex-wife's murder. And it didn't seem proper to ask him what he was confessing to since the confession was unasked.

"She loved me. She was perfect. Why would I want anyone else? I begged her. But she wouldn't forgive me. I should be dead, not her." His doleful gaze met Ambler's again. "You knew her. You saw how brilliant she was . . . brilliant and beautiful and loving."

Suddenly, his face lit up, exploded might be more like it, with what Ambler took to be anger. No. Hate. "She wasn't like that. That wasn't her." Ambler didn't know what he was talking about. Then, he said, "Why would she be in a place like that? Who was she with?"

He didn't wait for an answer. His tone became cunning. "Did you date her? Tell me the truth." He waited a couple of heartbeats for an answer. Ambler stared at him, so after a moment, he switched tracks again. "She wasn't experienced with men. I was her first. I shouldn't have let her leave. She needed me."

Ambler doubted Nagy was Robin's first, and he was getting fed up with the self-pity, the self-flagellation. It was as if someone you didn't know very well had begun taking their clothes off when you didn't want them to. Still, Ambler's detecting instinct kicked in. "Did you stay in touch with her after your divorce?"

Nagy wasn't surprised nor offended by the question. "I tried to stay in touch. She wouldn't let me. She stopped answering my calls and blocked my emails."

"When did you see or speak to her last?"

Nagy hesitated. Not a pause to try to remember, but a get-your-story-straight pause. "A couple of months ago. I wanted a reconciliation. Her mother tried to facilitate it, so I saw Robin for one day in her hometown, Longmeadow . . . It didn't go well. I begged her to forgive me. She wouldn't listen to reason. She barely spoke to me and rushed off."

Ambler did find out from him that Robin's memorial service would take place on Friday in Longmeadow. Going to it might mean missing Friday evening with Adele and the baby. Somewhat jarringly, he realized he had responsibilities he couldn't ignore. With a pang of conscience, he remembered the responsibilities he'd shirked when his son John was a child. He called Adele as soon as he got back to his desk.

"I can still get there Friday night," he said, after telling her what he planned to do. "I might just be a little late."

Adele laughed and then spoke in a hushed, sultry tone. "It sure makes a girl feel desired to know you'd rather go to a funeral than spend an evening with her. I remember the night you walked across town in a blizzard to climb into bed with me."

Ambler felt a rush of desire that would have made a teenager proud. He and Adele hadn't been in bed together *like that* since before Jennifer was born. "I'll not go at all if you'd rather," he said.

"Do I detect a renewed eagerness to visit River City?" Adele's tone was teasing. "Don't you miss Jennifer?"

"I miss you both."

"I hope I can stay awake long enough."

"Me, too."

Adele laughed. "We only have a tiny window of opportunity, you know. If the baby wakes . . ."

"Adele, I miss you . . ."

"Exactly what is it you miss?"

Erotic visions of what exactly he missed danced through his mind. He felt his breath come heavily.

"I wouldn't say I met him."

This man also had a military presence: broad shoulders, erect posture, buzz-cut gray hair. "Doug is forever fighting a past, present, or future war. He's the only person I know who's agonizingly disappointed when peace prevails."

"Who does he want to go to war with?"

"China, Russia, Venezuela, Iran. You name it. He'd take on California if he could." The man held out his hand. "I'm Robin's uncle, her mother's brother, Walt Monroe, U.S. Army-retired."

"Your friend's a colonel?"

"A lieutenant colonel. I retired a major; he outranks me and doesn't let me forget it. And he's air force, a more exalted branch of the uniformed services than the army. We differ also in that I much prefer peace to war. Other than those differences, I plain don't like the man. I don't know what Robin saw in him."

"Saw in him?"

Uncle Walt had an easy-going disposition. Ambler guessed the men who'd served under him liked him, the kind of officer who didn't pull rank, chose to earn respect rather than demand it. He looked puzzled by the question.

"You said you didn't know what Robin saw in him. He was a friend . . . a boyfriend?"

He took out a cigarette and lit it. "I don't know the whole story. Years ago, Robin's mother worked at the air-force base—Westover Field; it's nearby, not what it once was but still active as a reserve unit. Robin and a college friend did a class project at the base; I don't know anything about that. What I know is something terrible happened. All of this is blurry. Always was blurry. Robin's friend died tragically. The police said she fell asleep—or passed out, as she'd been drinking—in her car with the motor running."

"Was the car in a garage?"

"No. In a motel parking lot near the Mass Pike in Chicopee. Some defect in the car let the carbon monoxide in."

"Had she been in the motel?"

"I don't know. I don't recall that it came up."



"Kissing me?"

"Stop," he said. "You're killing me. I'll be there as early as I can. I'll get up with the baby. You can rest afterward."

"After what?" She laughed when he stuttered trying to answer. ". . . It's fine, Raymond. I miss you, too."

# SEVEN

The funeral home was a stately red-brick colonial with white trimmed windows and doors and round white pillars holding up the porch roof. A plaque near the door boasted that the house had been built in 1894. Thomas Jones was at Ambler's side as they read the plaque. He'd learned from Harry that Ambler would attend the Friday-night viewing, so he had tagged along on the flight to Hartford, Connecticut, and the short drive in the car Ambler rented from Bradley Field to Longmeadow. Ambler would drop Jones at a local hotel after the viewing and drive to River City.

A traveling companion wasn't something Ambler would wish for. And certainly not Jones, who had a lot of explaining to do that Ambler wasn't ready to tackle yet; he'd wait until he had his ducks lined up. At least, Jones wasn't a chatterbox. Like Ambler, he abided by Ghandi's dictum: "Speak only if it improves upon the silence." They exchanged pleasantries and spoke of essentials at the airport, and both read on the flight. Ambler didn't mention his recent discovery about Jones's past. Jones kept his own counsel.

There might not be much reason to attend the viewing. Honoring the deceased was of course a reason. This, he had to admit, was why Jones was there. And Jones assumed it was Ambler's reason as well. Ambler let him think this, though it wasn't the case. Mike Cosgrove had told him a long time ago that he often went to the funeral of the victim in a case he was working. More times than you'd think, he'd said, the killer showed up.

Considering this, Ambler took a photo of the sign-in book with his phone when he was alone in the foyer; the names might mean something later. He also scrutinized the faces of everyone he could, and introduced himself every chance he got as a friend of Robin's from the 42nd Street Library. He met



her mother this way. Her father had passed away years before. A youngish man, Robin's brother, sat beside the mother on one side and, on the other side, interestingly—you might say surprisingly—sat George Nagy. George remembered Ambler but had little to say this time around.

Jones spent a minute or two speaking with the mother and the brother, after which he shook hands with Nagy, with whom he spoke for a few moments, though Nagy showed little interest in the conversation, before he went and sat. Ambler stood in the lobby near the door to the viewing room, and once or twice followed someone who stepped outside for a moment for a breath of air.

One such person—stepping outside, oddly enough in this day and age, for a smoke—caught Ambler's attention because of how he carried himself. Ramrod straight, brisk, confident. You'd want to call it a military bearing.

Ambler followed him and watched him pull a cigarette out of a pack and light it. He thought about bumming one, but he'd stopped smoking twenty years ago and would probably choke on it if he tried to inhale. Instead, he sidled up beside the cigarette smoker and gazed out into the quiet darkness of the half-filled parking lot.

"I didn't know Robin well," he said in an appropriately subdued tone. "We met recently when she began a fellowship at the library where I work."

The man took a quick glance at Ambler before turning his gaze back to the parking lot, suggesting that whatever he saw among the parked cars was more interesting than anythin Ambler might tell him.

Undeterred, Ambler said, "Even in that short time, I coul tell she was a remarkable person. Did you know her profe sionally, or were you an old friend?"

The man turned to him again with a glare that wasn't ang but challenging. He flicked his half-finished cigarette into darkness beyond the porch and went back inside without a w

Another man whom Ambler hadn't noticed emerged fr shadows on the far side of the porch. "I see you've met Col James." He chuckled.

"No one asked?"

Uncle Walt shrugged.

"Did our pal the colonel have some involvement?"

"Rumor said he'd been with her that day. Rumor hinted they were having an affair."

"No rumor suggested they'd been at the motel together?"

"I suppose the thought was in the air, whether anyone said it or not." He gazed out into the dark parking lot for a moment. "There was another rumor. Not a rumor, really, an established fact after the autopsy. The girl was pregnant."

"And Robin?"

"That was murky also, what she knew or didn't know. She didn't say much. The girls spent a lot of time with Doug that summer. Much more than you'd expect for a college project. Doug had flown an F-15 in the first Gulf War. A decorated fighter pilot . . . He played the role of dashing airman to the hilt." Uncle Walt hesitated.

"And?"

"He was on track to make full-bird colonel, so he was careful. No scandal. No indiscretions. No blemishes. You might say something didn't look right with the two girls. They were in college; they were of age. Nonetheless, there was something unseemly about whatever went on between Doug and the two girls. But no one . . ." He paused. "Well, no one came forward to say, 'I saw' or 'I heard.' There were rumors. But they were dismissed as backbiting by those jealous of him."

"And Robin?"

"Ah Robin . . ." It was difficult to make out her uncle's expression in the shadows. When he took a long drag and the cigarette glowed for a couple of seconds, the creases in his face had deepened. "She knew . . . If anyone knew, she knew what happened. She went hysterical and was under a doctor's care, sedated. Yet she and Doug spent a lot of time with each other for a month or two after the girl's death until he was transferred.

"I supposed they comforted each other in their shared grief. They might have been lovers. If they were, it was a secret. Yet in a way, they were a portrait of a couple. And as close as they appeared to be, they battled. You could hear them fighting some nights when he dropped her off, like cats, hissing, screeching, unearthly, earth-shattering sounds from Robin.

"I talked to her after one of those fights. I'd been staying here for few months until my own house was ready when I came back from overseas. That night she was wild-eyed and enraged. I couldn't tell at what, but most of it was directed inward. So much so, I was afraid she'd harm herself . . . And she tried to tell me something. It's bothered me since that time. 'He did it,'" she said.

"I believed she was talking about Linda's death—her friend who died, Linda Porter—so later, the next day, I asked her. 'Was Doug responsible for Linda's death?'

"She denied it. 'I never said that. Why would you think such a thing?' Robin and I weren't especially close, even though she was my niece, not close enough so she'd confide in me. After that encounter, she didn't say anything about Linda to me again.

"One other time, she was distraught like that—crying uncontrollably, pulling at her hair, striking at herself—I held her arms to keep her from beating herself with her fists. She'd burst out of Doug's car and flung herself onto the lawn at the side of the house.

"After a long time of holding her, I said, 'Whatever Doug did to Linda—you don't have to tell me what it was—don't let him do it to you. You need to get away from him.' She leaned against me and cried and cried."

Ambler heard a hint of something in Uncle Walt's voice. "That was all?"

He gave a kind of "aw shucks" shrug. "I had a talk with Doug. I told him I was worried my niece might be headed toward a nervous breakdown. And if anything happened to her, I was coming after him. A month later, he transferred out, signed on for a Pentagon assignment."

"You never talked to Robin again about what happened to her friend?"

Uncle Walt lit another cigarette. In the light from the match, his expression was sad. "She wouldn't talk about it. Doug was gone. She'd gotten her life together, or it looked like she had—I thought it best to let the past stay in the past."

"It seldom does," Ambler said. He told him about the book Robin was working on.

Uncle Walt listened soberly. He held his cigarette in front of him and watched it, not looking at Ambler. "Robin said Doug murdered Linda?"

"No. She said she began the project because a friend of hers died in an accident that she suspected might have been murder. She regretted not saying or doing something at the time. She said she lacked the confidence to stand up against powerful people."

"Did she mention Doug?"

"No. Should she have?" They looked at each other for a moment in the faint glow from the houselights through the windows, an understanding of sorts passing between them.

When they went back inside the funeral parlor, they ran smack into a melee. George Nagy and Doug James were grappling with each other, both still on their feet but blundering around the room, knocking over chairs and bouncing off walls, while three or four other men, including Thomas Jones, tried without success to pull them apart.

James wasn't small and he was in good shape, athletic but no longer in the first bloom of youth. Nagy was a large man, not in such good shape, but bulky, much bigger than his opponent, so while James was quicker and more agile on his feet, Nagy lumbered after him, tying him up, wrapping his arms around him, so it looked as if someone had thrown a large bulky blanket over James and he was struggling to get out from under it.

The peacemakers were having a tough time getting Nagy—who was determined to either smother or squash James—off him. During the altercation, James had a lot to say, though Ambler couldn't make out any of it, and Nagy appeared to have nothing at all to say.

With a loud grunt and a kind of a twist and a shove, Nagy got James off his feet and heaved him to the floor, following him with a roar like a bear might make, landing on top of him like a tree toppling over. He might well have squashed him if Jones and another man hadn't pulled him off.

When Nagy was breathing more or less normally, he did speak, though only briefly. "You have no business here," he told James. "You're a disgrace to her memory." He spoke quietly, though his tone held a note of menace.

Thomas Jones stood beside him with his hand on his shoulder, ready to restrain him, but he didn't make any move to go after James again.

"I'll break your skull, you fat fuck!" James spat at Nagy. Two men were holding him back though it was no longer needed. "If Robin knew you were here, she'd throw *you* out, you pathetic pervert. I didn't leave her for a fourteen-year-old . . ."

Fourteen-year-old was a few years off. As Ambler remembered, Dr. Murphy had said the student was nineteen, an undergraduate; at least Robin was a graduate student when she married Nagy. But the point was well made. A couple of the men escorted James out, though he brushed their hands away and walked on his own, ramrod straight, glancing neither left nor right, his pace brisk but not hurrying.

"What was that about?" Jones asked a half-hour later as Ambler drove him to a hotel in Hartford on his way to River City and Adele.

Ambler had wondered that himself. Nagy was a college professor, not someone you'd expect to be brawling at funeral service. James didn't strike him as a brawler either, though it was easy to believe a lot of people had had the urge to take a swing at him over the years.

"I don't know," he said to Jones. "You were there. How did it start?"

Jones didn't know. He'd gotten involved when Nagy shoved James in his direction. "I'd met George a couple of times when he and Robin were married, so we'd exchanged a few words when I came in. I tried to stop him before it went any further. But he's like an ox.

"I said something like, 'Take it easy, George. This isn't the place for that kind of stuff.' I could smell liquor on his breath. He pushed past me like I wasn't there. You know how stubborn someone gets when a fight starts. I tried to restrain him. You saw how that went."

Ambler didn't tell Jones about his talk with Uncle Walt. This was something among quite a few things he wasn't telling Jones, who was perceptive enough to recognize this and to put two and two together regarding Robin Cartwright and James.

"So there was a tie between Robin and the air-force guy George tried to throttle." He leaned toward Ambler to make eye contact, but Ambler kept his eyes on the road. "I'm thinking this isn't news to you. What do you know about him?"

Ambler didn't answer for a minute or two until they pulled up to the front of the hotel. "Nothing that would tell me why he and Nagy were fighting. She knew him when she was in college . . ."

Jones wasn't dumb so Ambler wasn't going to try to put anything over on him. "There's more. I'm in kind of a hurry now. We can talk about it when I get back to the city. Perhaps you can tell me more about the Robin and George you once knew."

Before he got out of the car, Jones asked if Ambler minded if he looked over Robin's research journal. Ambler did mind—he still needed to go through it again himself—but couldn't think of any way to prevent it. So he told him where it was, which Jones knew anyway.

"I suppose I learned a lot by going to the funeral service," Ambler told Adele a little more than three hours later over pâté, cheese, and wine. "Unfortunately, I don't know what it is." He'd recounted the events of the evening along with a running commentary.

"This George Nagy," Adele said, "who marries a much younger woman and then runs off with an even younger woman, comes to the library for no apparent reason and gets maudlin about his ex-wife's death; later, he starts a fight at her funeral—what's with him? He's a college professor? What's he teach?"

"Criminology, I suppose."

"There you go," Adele said. "They teach people how crimes are committed. He's the perfect suspect."

"Perhaps . . ." Ambler caught a glint in her eyes, noticed a flush in her cheeks. From the wine?

He'd been sitting on the couch; she'd been sitting on a chair across from him but came now to sit beside him. She wore a short plaid skirt, no tights or stockings. The skin on her thigh was cool when he touched it.

"More wine?" he asked softly.

"For me? . . . I don't need it." She squirmed into his lap and mashed her mouth against his. Two seconds later a wail shattered the silence. Followed by another. And another.

Adele went for the baby. Ambler drank another glass of wine. She came back with Jennifer after she'd nursed her and handed the baby to Ambler, who awkwardly pressed her against his chest. She squirmed a bit and after a while settled down to sleep. Ambler felt himself nodding, too, as Adele dozed beside him.

The baby cried again a couple of hours after Adele had laid her in her crib and they had gone to bed, making love drowsily, and fallen asleep soon after. In the dimness of the small hours of the morning, Adele stumbled out of bed, got the baby and brought her back to sleep between them. They all woke before dawn, much earlier than Ambler was used to. Gray light filtered through the room's two windows.

Following two days focused on Jennifer and Adele, in the midst of bright sunlight, soft breezes, crisp air, and a kind of echoing quiet that brought him a peacefulness he hadn't experienced for longer than he could remember, with nary a thought about homicide, suspects, lies, or alibis, Ambler headed his rental car back to the city with much more regret than he would have expected.

Jennifer had only slept in short spurts, so Adele was busy all the time, feeding her, changing her, holding her; and when not doing those things, getting ready to do them, or washing dishes or clothes or cleaning up. Ambler tried to help but he wasn't much use, except to wash some dishes and hold Jennifer for a bit here and there while Adele did something else.

Except for the first evening, Adele had not the time, nor the energy, nor the interest to talk about Robin Cartwright's murder or who might have killed her. In a way, not talking about the case helped Ambler. He, too, was focused on the here and now and the unrelenting demands of the new entry into the world who required immediate gratification.

When he wasn't paying attention to Jennifer, he paid attention to Adele, realizing how overwhelming and exhausting and fraught caring for a newborn baby was, something he'd never noticed or thought about when his son John was a baby He was of the manly man generations, who had consigned all such work and worry to the mother. Without Adele asking, he told her he'd be back the next Friday.

On the drive south that morning, the Hudson peeking through the trees here and there, sometimes for miles at a time, he thought he might take inventory of where he was in regard to the death of Robin Cartwright, but found himself instead drifting off into thoughts of Adele and Jennifer, picturing himself back in River City, raising a child and checking out books in a small library, rather than investigating a murder case that pretty much no one beside him thought was an actual murder.

# EIGHT

This notion he was disabused of the next morning when his cell phone rang.

"Chris Lambert here. You got a minute?"

"I'm walking to work. I'll call you back when I get there."

The few minutes between Lambert's call and when Ambler got to the library gave him time to bring his mind around to Robin Cartwright's murder. He was properly perplexed again when he called the detective back.

"We picked up the deceased's laptop from the library. That notebook you mentioned wasn't there. I didn't take many notes the first time we talked, so I don't remember everything you wanted me to look at."

Ambler said he knew where the binder was and had no problem with turning it over.

"I'll pick it up from you this afternoon. I have an appointment at the library to talk with a Mr. Beasley."

"Good luck," Ambler said.

Lambert caught the sarcasm. "Is there something I should know?"

For a moment, Ambler thought he'd pass on the rumor Thomas Jones had told him about something going on between Robin and Beasley, and his suspicion that Beasley had stolen several of the pages from the binder, but decided against it. Instead, he asked, without expecting much in the way of answer, "Has your investigation turned up anything you can tell me about?"

After a short pause, Lambert said, "Everything's preliminary. We'd like to know who was with the deceased in the hotel room. That's the extent of the investigation at the moment. I'll talk to a few people at the library and see what that turns up." His tone changed, became harsher, perhaps angry, but not at him, Ambler realized; the anger was at what life deals out.

"I caught another case. A murder-suicide; it involves a child. You don't want to know about that one."

Not knowing what to say, Ambler didn't say anything.

"Sorry," Lambert said a moment later. "It's ugly. You try to think why. How could anybody? . . . I shouldn't take it out on you. You're entitled to ask questions. You won't get answers most of the time. But you're free to ask."

Then, as if making a peace offering, he said, "I'll tell you one thing. The computer guys downtown went over her laptop. The original blackmail email? The one she claimed to know nothing about? . . . It looks like the deceased might have sent it."

"*What?*"

"I don't know anything about this computer stuff. I'm telling you what they told me. She deleted all of her sent emails for the two or three weeks before her death, deleted them from her computer. The experts are supposed to be able to find deleted emails somehow—from the carrier or something—but they can't do that without a court order. The guy I talked to said they'd most likely be written over and permanently deleted by the time that happened.

"The point for me is why would she delete her emails unless she was trying to hide something. And how would whoever threatened her know to email her if she hadn't sent the blackmail note? . . . If I was blackmailing someone, I wouldn't leave the note I sent laying around either."

Ambler was flabbergasted. This turned everything upside down. Who the hell was the Robin Cartwright he thought he knew? A blackmailer? It felt like every day since her death he came across a new jaw-dropping revelation about her.

"You still there?" Lambert asked.

"Sorry. I'm in shock. Robin blackmailing someone doesn't make sense. She was writing a book exposing a murder. Why would she blackmail the murderer? If the murderer paid up, she wouldn't have a book. And if she had the evidence to prove he was a murderer, wouldn't it be in her notes, in the draft of her book?"

Lambert sighed, a sound like a valve letting off steam. "You wanna hear about things that don't make sense?"

From his weary, jaded tone, Ambler knew what he meant. Lambert was trying to get his head around why a person had killed a child and then themselves.

"I understand. It's tough." Ambler didn't want to say more. Trying to sympathize seemed useless. "I don't want to be a pest. Is there another possible explanation?"

"If there is, it'll be news to me. I'll be at the library this afternoon. I'll buy you a cup of coffee."

After the phone call, it didn't take Ambler long to come up with an alternate possibility for who did the blackmailing. The threatening message had been sent from Robin's email address, but that didn't mean she'd been the one to send it. He knew enough about hacking to know it was possible to send a fake email from someone else's account. It might be that the same person who sent the fake email stole the pages from her journal, and deleted any incriminating emails from her laptop.

For a moment, he thought he'd trot upstairs to the reference desk and run his dilemma by Adele. He'd made it as far as his office door when he remembered she wouldn't be there. She was gone, an hour and a half up the Hudson with a baby. The memory gave him a pang of loneliness.

He sat back down and tried to concentrate on his work. Book auction catalogs, call slips for collections, file folders with half-finished finding aids littered his desk. He had phone calls to return, requests to answer. On top of this, he was scheduled to do a lunchtime presentation on the library's crime fiction collection in less than a week. He'd done the presentations in the past. Still, the talk required preparation. He spoke from notes, and his notes were sloppy and speaking publicly made him nervous, so he over prepared to compensate.

After working for an hour, he realized that for some time—he wasn't sure how long—he'd been thinking about the blackmail message sent from Robin's email address and not about his work. He'd gotten stuck on the idea that someone else had gotten into her email somehow and sent the blackmail note, pretending to be her. So he took a break and walked down to the visiting professor reading room. One of the benefits of the designated reading room was that the room was secure—one needed a key card to open the door. This being so, the readers usually left their laptops and research materials at their desks or in their small storage spaces.

This had another benefit for Ambler. Since a limited number of people had access to the room, only a limited number of people could have sent a message from Robin's laptop and then erased them. The complication was that whoever did it—if in fact anyone did—would need to have known her password to get access to her email. Or they'd have to know how to jimmy the computer—or whatever one did—to get access. This thinking led him to C.R. Spaulding, the cyber genius of the group.

He found C.R., as cheerful as ever, working through an archive box in the Arents Tobacco Collection reading room down the hall. The young scholar was happy to talk about the basics of what he did with computers. But it wasn't any help.

"Most of the programs I use are intuitive," C.R. told him. "I turn the laptop on and follow the prompts. It's like turning on the radio. You don't have to know what makes it work in order to use it."

Ambler tried a couple more questions. C.R. was adamant that he had no idea how to access someone's email if he didn't have a password.

"I have two," he said. "A password to open my laptop, though I can use my fingerprint, and a different one to open my email. I don't know what Robin did. I imagine something like that. Still, if she logged into the library's Wi-Fi network, someone who knew what they were doing could hack into her email and send a message that seemed to come from her."

What did C.R. say? Someone could do *what?* Ambler didn't know that. He really didn't know how computers worked; he barely knew how to use them. Someone could send an email from his computer, pretending they were him? It was his own fault. He knew as much about computer technology as he did auto mechanics, which was nothing.

Deep in thought when he left C.R., he saw Benny Bevone wheeling a cart down the hallway, heading to one of the second-floor study rooms to deliver books from the stacks. He caught up with him.

"What do you know about Robin Cartwright's laptop?"

The question startled Benny. His eyes narrowed as he went into defensive mode. "Nothin'. Is it missing?" If you've had a Bensonhurst upbringing, when someone asks you about something that's missing, you assume it was stolen and they suspect you stole it—often, they'd be right.

"The police have her laptop. It looks like someone broke into it and sent an email from Robin's email address, pretending to be her." No one had actually said this except Ambler. He was taking a kind of poetic license.

"Hacked."

"Hacked?"

"That's what they call it when you access someone else's computer files. Hasn't that ever happened to you?"

"I don't know. I hope not. Do you know how to do it?"

Benny stopped his cart and turned on him. "Do what? Hack? No. Why would you think that?"

"I was thinking everyone but me knew how to do it. Does anyone in the library know how?"

"Probably a lot of people."

"The visiting professors?"

"Maybe Professor Spaulding. He knows more about computers than any of the rest of them."

"Who else?"

"The folks in IT . . ." Benny brightened. "Wait! You know what? Beasley's nephew is a computer geek. Not long ago, Beasley was bringing the kid in the reading room at night so he could do some school project. Mostly the kid played around on the computers. He's a . . . a nerd."

Benny glanced up and down the hallway, waited for a small herd of tourists to pass, lowered his voice and said, "He showed me how he could hack into the library's system and change phone numbers and room numbers and stuff like that." He glanced about him again. "He said he'd change them back again. He just wanted to show me he could do it. Showing off."

"Did you tell anyone?"

Benny's eyes, which had narrowed to slits while he spoke conspiratorially, popped open. "Who would I tell . . . Beasley?"

"You could have told Harry or you could have told security?"

Benny's Bensonhurst roots ran deep. "He was a kid. I'm not going to squeal on him. He's a nerd, joking around. It wasn't going to hurt someone even if they did get a wrong number."

Criticizing Benny for wanting to avoid *the mark of the squealer* would be a losing fight. Ambler had a better idea. "This kid. When was he here in the library last?"

Benny shook his head. "I couldn't say. Not so long ago. Not so recently."

"Since this cohort of visiting professors got here?" Ambler tried to keep the eagerness out of his voice.

"Yeh. It wasn't that long ago."

"Can you find him?"

"Find who? The kid? Why? . . . You gonna turn him in?"

"No."

Benny waited. "You wanna tell me where this is going?"

"Not yet."

Benny looked hurt. For him, hurt came out as anger. "I thought I was your partner."

"I don't want to jinx it."

Benny would understand that. After thinking this over, he nodded. His eyes had narrowed to slits again. "Suppose I could find him. What would I tell him?"

Ambler needed to be careful. Though Benny was as loyal as Gunga Din, he was frivolous. In a good way. He didn't keep secrets and would blurt out whatever he was thinking; anyone who talked to him for ten minutes would know his deepest secrets. So telling him what he wanted to know from Beasley's nephew would be risky. There was a chance he'd spill the beans to Beasley. Yet Benny might get the kid to talk. It was unlikely Ambler—older and decidedly unhip—would. Unhip wasn't right. People weren't unhip anymore; he didn't know the term for being out of step with the young computer hackers of the world.

"Would this nephew talk to you?"

"Jacob. The kid's name is Jacob."

"Beasley?"

"I don't know his last name. Just Jacob."

"How would you find him if you don't know his name?"

"Leave it to me."

Was he willing to do that, Ambler asked himself. After a few moments he realized he had no choice. He asked a few more questions to make sure.

The nights Jacob was in the library, he liked hanging out with Benny, who'd taken the boy with him on his appointed rounds into the back-of-the-house areas of the library and into offices and reading rooms the public usually didn't have access to.

That Benny might find the boy made sense, too. Jacob went to the math and science high school at City College, Benny said. His plan was to hang out on Convent Avenue on his day off at the time school let out and wait until he saw Jacob.

"There aren't that many kids in that school and it's not like they go home on school buses. They have to come out to the street for the subway or a bus. So I'll find him. Now, what do I tell him when I find him. 'Ray Ambler says, Hi?'"

"You have to swear by everything that's holy you won't say a word to anyone about this."

"They can pull my teeth out and my fingernails off, and I won't open my mouth." He glanced at Ambler sheepishly. "Except when they're pulling my teeth out, I guess I'll open my mouth."

"That's not what I'm worried about. I'm afraid you'll let something slip when you don't mean to. Or tell someone something, thinking they won't say anything. But if you tell them, they'll tell someone else, thinking that person won't say anything. That's how it works."

"This is about Beasley, right? Our chance to hang him by his balls."

Ambler moaned. Thomas Jones was walking past them in the hallway, close enough to have heard. "That's what I mean. We shouldn't talk here. Can you come to the crime fiction room when you drop that stuff off?"

A few minutes after Ambler got to his desk, Benny showed up.

"I'm going to put a sock in your mouth the entire time you're at work if you don't get serious about this. Robin Cartwright is dead. She or someone else blackmailed the person who killed her. If she was the blackmailer, this means we're looking for her killer. If she isn't the blackmailer, then the killing might not be over."

He told Benny what Lambert had told him. Benny caught on more quickly than he expected.

"So you think Beasley had his nephew hack her computer so he could open up her email account and send a message blackmailing someone so that someone would think the blackmailer was her and then erased all the sent messages?"

"I *suspect* that's possible." He leaned across his desk so his face was close to Benny's, whose eyes widened but who didn't flinch. "This is important. I don't know anything. If what I think is wrong and Beasley catches wind of what we're doing—or even if we're right and he finds out—there's no telling what will happen to us."

"What if Jacob tells him?"

"What the kid tells you will determine how we handle that. You'll need to figure out how much you need to tell him to find out what we need to know. You can run into him by chance at the college. Maybe you have a girlfriend there or went to see a former professor. Start reminiscing about when he was in the library."

Benny nodded enthusiastically. "One good thing is Jacob doesn't like his uncle. I don't think Beasley likes him either. I could say I want to play a trick on his uncle. Or I want to get Beasley in trouble. I might get by without bringing up anything about blackmail or murder."

Benny sat back and smiled broadly. "Listen to me! Who knew I'd be out on an assignment tracking down a murderer? Wait until I tell—" He froze, his eyes as large as manhole covers.

Ambler slouched back in his chair and buried his face in his hands.

"Did I say that?" Benny brushed his hands across his face. ". . . my grandchildren. Wait 'til I tell my grandkids what old grandpa did when he was young."

Ambler unburied his face. "Benny. Benny! You were doing so well. You have a great plan. If you can find out from the nephew without telling him why, it would be perfect. If you can keep from telling the person you're getting the information from what you're doing, why on earth would you tell anyone else?"

Benny stood, a stance from which he might begin a dance or throw a punch, but that suggested total confidence. "Relax, boss. We got this." Since he was off Wednesdays and Thursdays this month, Benny would have his first chance to track down Beasley's nephew in two days.

# NINE

A young woman whose name he didn't recognize called shortly after Benny had left. She spoke quickly and decisively, leaving little time for Ambler to say anything except acknowledge that he was indeed the person she'd asked to speak to. Her name was Samantha, and she wanted to meet him in front of the library. It took another moment of Ambler's befuddlement before she let on that she was David Levinson's intern and would be delivering the trial transcript he'd asked for.

When he met her an hour later on the library steps next to Fortitude, the uptown lion, she was as brusque and humorless as the nun who was the principal of his grammar school. No smile, a firm handshake once she established he was Ambler, cutting off his attempt at an exchange of pleasantries by shoving the envelope into his chest and walking away as he asked how she was faring under David's tutelage.

He pondered this, the second time in the last few days someone had walked away without acknowledging he was talking to them. Was it him, or was civility no longer part of the day's mores and manners?

For the next hour, he hid in the crime fiction reading room and read the transcript. The trial had been a bench trial, and it had been short, with three witnesses for the prosecution—the arresting officer, the medical examiner, and an eyewitness. The defense had four eyewitnesses and Thomas Jones himself, who matter-of-factly described what happened: A man had shot his brother at close range; Jones took the gun away from the man and shot him when he tried to take it back.

The prosecutor asked if he'd warned the assailant before he shot.

Jones said no.

The prosecutor asked why he didn't shoot the assailant in the leg or somewhere that wouldn't cause a fatal wound.

Jones said he just shot; he didn't aim. He was fighting for his life. "I didn't want to kill him. I wanted to stop him from killing me."

The judge's ruling of justifiable homicide came as soon as the trial ended.

From what Ambler read, it was pretty clear Thomas Jones's action wouldn't fit the criteria of an accidental death that was actually a murder. You had to believe Robin Cartwright believed this also, because she didn't include Jones's case in her database of potential deaths to investigate further. So why did Thomas try to cover it up? Why did he lie about how he first knew Robin? Time to find out.

He needed to track Jones down anyway to get the research journal to turn over to Detective Lambert. He found him in the visiting professor reading room.

"I have to take back Robin's research journal," he said. "The police want it."

Jones was distracted, and for a moment didn't remember what Ambler was talking about. When he did remember, he didn't show any concern and retrieved it from the storage nook where he kept his own research materials.

"By the way," Ambler said as he took the journal, "I came across something I wanted to ask you about when you have a moment."

Jones glanced at the file box he'd been working through, and then back at Ambler with dead eyes. "I suppose you want to ask about my arrest. I wondered how long it would take you to get to it."

It was a quicker acknowledgment than he'd expected. "That, and why you made up a story about how you met Robin Cartwright. You met her at your trial, I'd guess. She didn't teach at your undergraduate school."

Thomas was unfazed, his expression defiantly smug. "You've answered your own question. I foolishly thought you might not find out about the arrest if I kept quiet about it. You know I was acquitted? The trial was a formality. Everyone, including the cops and the prosecutor, knew I was justified."

For a moment, he was thoughtful, the smugness gone as quickly as it had come on, sadness in its place. "It's not something I like to talk about. I didn't want to kill him. I'm sorry it happened. You don't know what it's like to kill someone, even when it's justified."

Ambler actually did know how it felt; he'd had the experience. It wasn't something he wanted to talk about or think about either, although he did think about it often. So, it wasn't so surprising Jones wouldn't want to bring it up. Yet under the circumstances . . .

Jones waited for Ambler to say something. Not getting a response, he went on. "Most of what I told you was true. She did mentor me. It just didn't happen the way I said."

"I'm surprised George Nagy didn't go after you, too."

"Why would he?"

"Did you and she have an affair?"

Jones's reaction was surprising. It was as if Ambler had said something vulgar that he should be ashamed of. And Ambler did feel shame. He didn't know why he should, but he did, as if he'd demeaned Robin Cartwright in some way.

"We were friends . . . a truly important friendship for both of us. I'm embarrassed for you that your thinking is so reductionist that you can't accept a friendship between two people but need to sully it with innuendo, see it as sordid."

Was this what he'd done? Sullied their reputations by being simpleminded about how two people might conduct their friendship? He felt foolish and diminished and he didn't like it. Dr. Jones was intellectually running circles around him. Yet he didn't think Jones was trying to put him down, rather that he was sincere in demanding respect for his friendship with Robin Cartwright. Ambler felt as if—instead of asking if they'd had an affair—he'd actually said, "Were you fucking her?" And Jones had responded to that crassness.

Well, you learn something new every day, including manners. Jones had lied to him, withheld important information, but somehow Ambler had become the bad guy here.

"Sometimes I don't like myself," Ambler said. "You don't have to tell me anything you don't want to. I'm sorry my question offended you. I should have been more sensitive." He had nothing more to say. But he didn't leave. Perhaps he was waiting to be dismissed. It was a strange feeling.

"She was my mentor. She taught me how to do research, showed me how to write an academic paper—MLA style, as well as APA. I was finishing my undergraduate degree when we met at my trial. We stayed in touch. She helped me prepare for grad school. Her home life wasn't good. Nagy was arrogant but he also knew—like most bullies do—that he was a phony.

"He acted as though the three of us were great friends. He didn't mind Robin and me spending time together because he knew her . . . and he had his own interests—I think she was a sophomore, a student assistant of some kind. She followed him around like Mary's Little Lamb.

"Because of how he treated Robin, demeaning her, humiliating her in public, she'd lost her confidence. She was awkward and shy, apologetic about everything. Her effort to make a scholar out of me, who at the time was barely civilized, helped her regain her confidence."

He was quiet for a long moment, so deep in thought that Ambler thought he might not say anything else. It was difficult anyway to follow Jones's story, to figure out what happened when. But the timeline could come later. He wanted Jones to keep talking. The best way to do this was to stay quiet so as not to get in the way of his memories.

After another moment, Jones returned to the present. "I didn't want to tell you the truth about how close Robin and I were for another reason, which was why I wanted to keep tabs on your investigation. I had no reason to believe what I did, so I kept my thoughts to myself."

Ambler had caught on already. "You think George Nagy killed his former wife. You don't have any proof, so you didn't want to say so."

Jones didn't show any surprise at Ambler's surmise, nor did he confirm it.

"It's not a bad hypothesis," Ambler continued. "It makes

sense that she'd go to a hotel room with him. Most likely she'd go to talk. She'd be confident she could handle him. I don't know who else she'd go to a hotel with." He paused.

"Except me, you might say."

Ambler shook his head. "No one noticed the man she was with. That hotel lobby is like a subway station, and there are no cameras. Rooms turn over every couple of hours. No one notices anyone, except even in this enlightened era in liberal New York, a mixed-race couple, especially if the male of the party is six feet six or so, you'd think someone would notice."

"Where does that leave us?" As Jones waited for the answer, nothing in his expression suggested defensiveness. They might have been talking about where they'd go for dinner.

"You've told me different versions of the same story each time we talked. You may be trying to find the version that works best, so I don't know if any of them are true."

"You said you don't think I went to the hotel with Robin because I would have been noticed, so why would I lie?"

"I could be wrong about the first part, and I don't know the answer to the second part."

"What if I can establish my whereabouts at the time Robin was killed?"

"That would help."

"Only help?"

"We'll see. Let's talk about George Nagy."

"I don't have proof of anything. He left her because he was greedy and could get away with it. It's not difficult for a professor to dazzle an undergraduate. He'd have his pick of the prettiest girls, girls—not quite women, despite their demands to be considered such. As it was in the old days, if you went on to further education after high school, you found yourself a college *man*, no longer a boy. If you stayed home and went to work, you were still *a boy*. In reality, it should have been the other way around.

"Not long after he'd left her, George realized he'd made a mistake. Robin was better than he deserved, much better. I'd already told him he was making a mistake. He was arrogant enough to think he'd get her back when he wanted her back.

He'd bullied her for years. He thought he could do so again." Jones stopped; his elbow on his thigh and his fist under his chin; for a moment he struck the pose of *The Thinker*. Ambler wondered if he was aware of this.

"While they were separated, she'd found herself." Jones spoke softly. "I think I helped with that. Not by anything I did. She found herself helping me. She called it *Eros*, a love for each other developed out of our shared love of learning. She became admirable because she was admired—loved if you want, not for her beauty alone, not for her intelligence alone. For her whole self. For her soul, if you want.

"George was like a bull in a china shop—or, more properly, a buck in rutting season. Robin had become more attractive as she matured. He eventually saw that. Some women are prettiest when they're teenagers—peaches-and-cream, perky breasts, and all that. She was that, I guess, when she was young, but she became more. The woman—or girl—he wanted wasn't there anymore. A fully realized woman took her place and saw him for the empty suit that he was. Men as arrogant as George, as self-centered, as entitled as he believed himself to be, sometimes kill what they can't have."

Probably some of what Jones said was true; maybe most of it. But nothing he said made George Nagy a murderer. He had a couple of pieces to add but nothing that would change that. Nagy followed Robin to Longmeadow, Massachusetts a couple of months ago to try to win her back; he'd enlisted her mother's help. There was no reason to think he hadn't followed her to New York. His behavior at the funeral service could have come from guilt.

Jones expected Ambler to say something. But what would he say? It was a nice story with nice sentiments, making Robin's death feel like more of a tragedy than it already did, but it didn't change anything, didn't make Jones more or less of a suspect. He'd told so many different versions of how he knew Robin that Ambler was surprised he could keep them straight himself, much less expect Ambler to.

"George Nagy could have killed her. The ex-husband is always a good suspect. I would expect he'll go to the top of the list if the police determine Robin's death was a murder. As far as I know, they haven't decided.

"Someone we don't know about could have killed her. Or someone we do know, other than Nagy, could have. It might have been someone from the library, one of your colleagues, or someone she met in a bar. It might have been someone she was digging up dirt on for her book; any one of them could have killed her." He met Jones's gaze straight on. "Despite what I said, you might have killed her."

"I can put an end to that speculation. I said I could prove I was somewhere else when she died."

"That's not what you said. And alibis can be faked. I can name you a half-dozen mysteries off the top of my head in which seemingly iron-clad alibis turn out to be false."

"Mine won't." Jones spoke dismissively. "I take it you're no longer interest in my tagging along on your investigation."

This stopped Ambler for a moment. He wanted to say yes. But why not keep in touch with Jones? "I don't know how you can help. But if you come up with something interesting—you find evidence that George Nagy was in New York at the time of his wife's death, for example—let me know. If I find myself in a place where I think you can help, I'll give you a call."

As he said this, Ambler remembered the man McNulty had seen Robin Cartwright with in the Library Tavern, not long before her death. The man she'd called Preacher in her journal entry. He'd meant to ask the detective, Lambert, about cameras on Madison Avenue that might have picked up the man.

"You'll keep most things to yourself, though, I imagine," Jones said.

A library aide came into the reading room and told Ambler someone had asked for him at the information desk in the catalog room. He grabbed Robin Cartwright's research journal and headed out.

After a quick stop in the Xerox room, he found Detective Lambert in the Rose reading room, gawking at the ceiling where brass, flute-playing cherubs cavorted around murals of billowing clouds that might well be the gateway to heaven. The street-savvy big city cop looked for all the world like a country bumpkin visiting a traveling carnival that just hit town.

Ambler didn't interrupt him and took another look at the ceiling himself for the thousandth or so time, thinking for the same thousandth time or so how lucky he was to work in such amazing surroundings. When Lambert came back to earth, Ambler took him to the cafe in Astor Hall, the library's entrance lobby, where the detective did indeed buy him a cup of coffee.

"What are you looking for in the research journal?" Ambler asked when Lambert handed him the coffee. "If you don't mind my asking."

Lambert looked at the journal and then at Ambler. He shrugged. "To tell you the truth, I don't know. It's one of those, 'I'll know when I find it' things. Is there something in there you think I should look at?"

Ambler was quick to answer. "The men she was doing research on. Besides that, some of the entries are not what you'd expect. She wrote commentaries about what was going on around her, like in a diary, in addition to the research and bibliographic notes you'd expect. I already told you about the entry about the threatening email. She also has background information on the three subjects she decided to focus on in her book, including their real names. If it were up to me, I'd begin my search for the killer with them."

Lambert's reaction was mild. "If there is a killer. What we know is she had a lover—the man she went to the hotel with. I'll look for him first." His eyebrows went up. "Unless you think she'd be sleeping with one of the men she was writing about?"

"That's not as improbable as you might think." Ambler told him what Uncle Walt had said about Colonel James.

After a moment's thought and a couple of sips of his coffee, Lambert took out his notebook. "He's in the journal, Colonel James?"

"Yes. But she hadn't gotten to him yet; that is, she hadn't begun her research on her friend's death, as far as I could tell. I guess because a lot of it was in her memory. There's more information on the other two subjects she was concentrating on." Ambler met Lambert's gaze over his coffee cup. "She did a lot of your work for you."

"Is that a joke?"

"Yes and no."

"I'm hoping we're on the same side on this, Mr. Ambler." Lambert's expression wasn't playful. "I don't have conversations like this with a civilian. Why is it you think this woman was murdered when there's no convincing evidence of that? What's your interest? Do you get a charge out of proving cops wrong?"

The atmosphere had grown chilly. Ambler hadn't seen this coming; maybe he should have. Except for Mike Cosgrove, he'd never met a cop who appreciated his crime-solving efforts. If he were honest with himself, he might question his own motives. Yet he'd never done anything he didn't have a right to do as a citizen. Still, he'd much rather be dealing with Mike. They went back together a long time and knew what to expect from one another.

"I'm trying to be helpful," he said, though he doubted saying this would do much good. "I'd rather you be right than wrong. You asked me about the journal, so I'm telling you. Robin was a friend of mine. I care about what happened to her."

Lambert's expression didn't change much, except his face muscles tightened. He overflowed his chair and was really too big for the tiny section of the lobby set off for the cafe. "Most people care when a friend is murdered, but they let the police handle the investigation."

"If you didn't want to hear what I thought, you shouldn't have asked me."

"I was playing with you." He made a half-hearted attempt at a smile; he didn't look like he was playing. "Anything else?"

"I don't want to meddle." It was a childish, petulant remark. But he said it anyway.

Lambert made a face like he'd tasted something sour. "I'm asking about the journal, an area you know something about and I don't. I'll ask you about Miss Cartwright because you knew her; I didn't. Other people I might ask you about for the same reason. Otherwise, how the investigation is conducted we'll leave to me."

There was more he could have told the ornery detective, about Thomas Jones's complex relationship with Robin for example, but he didn't. He could have told him about Beasley and his computer nerd nephew, too, but he didn't. Why talk to someone who doesn't want to hear what you have to say? He did tell him what he knew about George Nagy because he'd just as soon the cop handled that investigation. And he asked about surveillance cameras on Madison Avenue. Lambert wasn't going to let him—or McNulty either—look at any of them. But *he* might take a look.

"Nagy was trying to win her back and she wasn't interested. He tried to catch up with her when she went to visit her mother in Massachusetts. He enlisted her mother to intercede. He started a fight at her funeral. I don't know that he came to the city. He knew she was here. She had dinner with a man from her past. I can tell you the approximate date. You can get a photo of Nagy, check any surveillance cameras on Madison Avenue. You might also get a photo of Colonel James. You never know."

"You don't give up, do you?"

There was a hint of something in the detective's eyes. Maybe he wasn't as sure of what he was saying as he sounded. So Ambler pushed his luck. "Why the hostility?"

Lambert thought for a moment before answering. He wasn't a shoot-from-the-hip cop; for him, it wasn't simply the good guys with the white hats and the bad guys with the black hats. Mike said Lambert would do the right thing. Maybe there was hope, but getting to him would be like going through armor.

The cop weighed his words. "You've rubbed some people on the job the wrong way. Mike Cosgrove says you're OK. But some guys aren't so sure about him either." He stood, the size, shape, and quick movement of a pulling guard. "I'm giving you the benefit of the doubt." His expression wasn't hard but it wasn't warm and fuzzy either. "Given what I've heard from you, you don't have a shred of evidence that this is a murder. So I keep wondering why you think so."

Ambler didn't have an answer. After the detective left, he sat for a few moments watching the flow of people—mostly tourists—pouring in and out of the Astor Hall lobby and wondered himself why he was so sure Robin Cartwright was murdered. He'd started out thinking her being in a short-stay hotel with a man was out of character. But now he wasn't so sure it was. It was as if now he was as interested in finding out what had made her tick as he was in finding out who murdered her . . . if she was murdered.

# TEN

Before handing the research journal over to Lambert, Ambler had photocopied a dozen or so pages, dealing with two of the cases Robin Cartwright was focusing on. For the first one, the drug overdose death of a young Puerto Rican woman, there were no newspaper articles. It might have been Robin hadn't found any or hadn't looked yet. More likely, though, would be that the death of the young woman in one of the poorest sections of the city was insignificant to the newspapers.

This lack of interest wasn't only from the insensitivity of the newshounds. The year the young woman, whose name was Sofia Torres, died, close to 200 people a day died in New York, probably five or six of them from drug overdoses. Fewer than one person a day was murdered in the city that year, down from the high-crime years in the '80s and '90s that Ambler remembered too well, though the count might be a bit higher if Robin Cartwright's theory of murders thought to be accidents proved correct.

She'd done a thorough investigation anyway, though nothing Ambler found in the research journal told him how she'd discovered Sofia Torres's death or why she thought it wasn't an accident but murder. She had notes on interviews with the young woman's father and mother, as well as with her brother and sister and some of her friends. Fortunately, she'd interviewed the homicide detective who'd investigated the death.

The police were called when Sofia's body was discovered in the lobby of a Grand Concourse apartment building. The young woman had been sitting in a chair in the lobby for a couple of hours before anyone checked on her. The police detective Robin had talked to tried to find out if the young woman had been a guest in an apartment in the building, but to no avail. He'd tried to find witnesses who might have seen her come in or seen her with someone. Again, he came up blank.

He'd spoken to the victim's mother and father, long-time residents of the Bronx, who spoke English. They swore she wasn't a drug user, and couldn't understand why she'd be in that apartment building. Her brother and sister, both younger and both carrying the grief of their loss, swore she used no drugs other than weed and was the best sister ever. None of her friends had any idea she was an IV drug user. The medical examiner ruled the death an accidental drug overdose, while finding no evidence she was a habitual user.

Though Robin's notes maintained the Torres girl was having an affair with a married man, who Robin believed murdered her, none of Sofia's friends or relatives knew about an affair. Nor did Robin come up with the name of said married man.

Ambler checked the draft of the book on Google Docs, only to find Robin referred to him there by an obvious pseudonym, as she did the other subjects. In the journal she called him Diaz, which wouldn't be much help finding him in the South Bronx. The most frustrating thing was the lack of sources in her notes.

The only way she could have gotten the information that informed her belief that Sofia Torres had been murdered was if someone had told her. Ambler was flummoxed. Robin had to have written the man's real name down somewhere, but where? Maybe she had another journal or notebook he didn't know about. That didn't make any sense . . . unless the pages with the man's name were among those someone had pulled from the binder after her death. But why?

He'd try to figure that out later. In the meanwhile, he thought he might try to talk to the detective who did the investigation. His interaction with Lambert was on his mind and he wasn't happy taking on another cop. He called Mike Cosgrove and asked about the detective on the Torres case. His name was Arturo Lopez. Mike checked and told him Lopez now worked out of the Bronx detective bureau. "That's the old forty-one,"

Mike told him. "The precinct they used to call Fort Apache back in the crack cocaine days."

Mike didn't know Lopez but knew a few of the Bronx detectives and said he'd ask around. An hour later, he called back. "He's a pussycat, I'm told. Less than a year from retirement and he isn't a hard-ass about anything. He survived the Wild West years in the Bronx and has the scars to prove it. When he retires, he tells them he's moving to Virginia to raise chickens and take care of retired racehorses. An old friend of mine put me on the phone with him. We had a couple of laughs and he said he'd talk to you."

This all sounded too good to be true, Ambler told himself after he called and made an appointment. And he was right. The phone call went OK and he met Lopez the next day at his desk in the squad room of the detective bureau. His desk and the room were well-worn and cluttered with tables and chairs and desks and people. The dozen or so men and women in the room were all busy, on the phone, on the computer, or talking to someone sitting alongside their desk, and paid him no mind.

"You think the girl was murdered. How come you think that? There's no reason." The detective got right to the point. "You want to make a complaint? I did a lousy job?" He didn't wait for an answer to any of his questions.

Ambler was taken aback for the moment, as if Lopez was throwing punches at him instead of questions. But he got his feet under him pretty quickly. Lopez, pussycat that he might be, was one of those folks—perhaps overrepresented on police forces—who talk rather than listen. They already know everything, so they don't need answers to their questions.

Lopez had been around for a long time, had made hundreds of arrests; some of them, the law of averages would say, the wrong guy. But you can't worry about that; everyone makes mistakes. Ambler thought to interrupt the soon-to-retire detective first-class. But that would make his trip to the Bronx a complete waste of time, so he was willing to listen to all the ways the detective was right about pretty much everything, until he might perhaps get a couple of questions in.

"Back then, no one said you could find the dealer and hang a murder rap on them. Now, sometimes—if the story's in the paper, if someone from 1PP gets a bug up his ass—we find the dealer and charge them."

Ambler, who had been standing next to Lopez's desk, sat down. The detective watched him pull up the chair and sit with an air of approval. He wasn't angry; you might say he was friendly and pleased Ambler had withstood his barrage.

"I looked up the case before you got here, so I remember now. She was young, long dark hair, big brown eyes; she was pretty. It was sad. Some creep tightened her up. Who knows why she did it? Kids do that to get along with the other kids. In the Bronx then, everybody and his brother was shooting up. I can't tell you how many ODs I handled. Kids younger than her. It was a shame. It was very sad."

Lopez had to run out of steam at some point, so Ambler nodded and waited. He more or less knew what he'd say to Lopez and what he'd ask him, but Detective Motor Mouth's long-winded monologue made him think twice.

"So your cop friend, Cosgrove . . ." He flickered his eyebrows at Ambler. "He's been around almost as long as me. He must know somethin'—says I should talk to you. Some questions about an old case—not a cold case." He glanced at Ambler from under his eyebrows. "This one we put to bed a long time ago. So I talk to you. What do you wanna know?"

He'd planned on telling Lopez about Cartwright's death, the book, and her theory that deaths deemed accidental might actually be murder, but decided Lopez wouldn't have a long enough attention span to follow all that—this was to say, Lopez's attention span wouldn't last long when he wasn't doing the talking—so he'd give him the Cliff Notes version.

"A woman friend of mine knew Sofia. She told me Sofia was having an affair at the time of her death with a wealthy man. My friend thought if we found out who the man was—if that was the man who gave Sofia the drugs, her family might be able to sue him and get some payback for him causing her death."

"Or blackmail him." Lopez's eyebrows spiked. He might be

a yacker but he was as sharp as most detectives at catching the criminal side of a scenario.

"I wasn't thinking that." In point of fact, Ambler was making up the story on the spot and hadn't thought that far. But funny how the possibility of blackmail lent itself to the situation. You find out about a criminal act someone wants to keep secret. And boom, the first thing that comes to mind is blackmail.

"My friend is a lawyer. She happened to learn about Sofia's death. She also learned the family was having a hard time financially, so this is how she thought she might help. Not to blackmail but to sue."

"An ambulance chaser, eh?" The guy had an answer for everything, saw the dark side of everything. The sooner he got to tending to old racehorses and raising chickens, the better for him and the criminal element in the Bronx.

"My question is, was there such a man?"

Lopez had the sordid facts of hundreds of cases rattling around in his memory. He took some time to sort them out. After a moment, he dug through a foot-high pile of binders and notebooks and file folders on his desk. The folder he pulled out had a photo of a pretty girl, barely a woman, with long black hair and deep dark soulful eyes, stapled to the front cover. He flipped through it, stopped for a moment and glanced at Ambler. "This is a murder book. You ever seen one?"

Ambler had, but he said no because he thought Lopez would like that better.

"You don't want to. This is the pretty girl. The rest of the pictures in here are from the ME. They ain't so pretty. They turn your stomach."

It took a few minutes for the detective to refresh his memory. Ambler waited and watched. When Lopez caught up with whatever memory he was chasing, he closed the file, and, his hands folded under his chin, thought about something for a few minutes.

"She'd been in a kind of high-class shooting gallery—high-class for the South Bronx, anyway—that's where she shot up. But we couldn't prove she'd been there. You know what junkies are like. No one knows nothin'. Remember what it was like back then?" He pointed to the stack of files on his desk. "I had three or four piles like this, all of them open cases. It was an accidental overdose, so we left it at that."

He met Ambler's gaze and held it for a long time. "I got a note in here." He slapped the file he'd been going through against the desk. "A phone tip. Sofia had been seeing a man she'd met dancing, salsa dancing at a local club. That was it. The tip was anonymous and probably meant something to the girl who called it in. She didn't tell us anything else and hoped we figured it out." This wasn't much, but it was something. Lopez gave him Sofia's mother's address.

After an agonizingly difficult and sad conversation with Sofia Torres's still-grieving mother—her father had passed away—which included being shown through a dozen or more photos of Sofia from childhood until her death, and a brief conversation with Sofia's sister, Ambler ended up with the names of two of Sofia's friends who'd stayed in touch with the Torres family and still lived in the neighborhood.

He caught up with the first, whose name was Emma, on the stoop of the five-story walk-up she lived in. She admitted—after a brief conversation—that she was the person who left the anonymous tip with the police about Sofia and an older man.

At first, she'd been reluctant to talk, looking over her shoulder for an escape route. But after she'd asked him, "Why now?" When he told her he was looking into Sofia's death because of another woman's death, she said, "He killed someone else?"

She was a short, stocky young woman, who wore glasses, but came across as pretty nonetheless. It might have been her smile, her large dark eyes, or her self-confidence. She looked Ambler in the eye and spoke as if she were the one in charge of the conversation. "That's what happens when you feel guilty," she said. "I've been waiting for ten years for me not saying anything about Sofia's dying to come back to haunt me. You might as well come in and talk inside. It's cold out here."

Ambler said fine.

"Don't be so sure," she said. "It's four flights up."

"It was a secret with the man," Emma said. "Me and Sofia and another girl used to go salsa dancing every Friday night at a club on 3rd Avenue." Her glance when she met Ambler's gaze was as if to scold him for his thoughts. "We were barely teenagers. We loved to dance; it was fun and maybe flirty. But it wasn't a pick-up place. We weren't that kind of girls. The men knew that. They might try but they knew we were good girls and there to have fun and not anything else."

She sighed and blinked a few times, her big eyes glistening. "But something bad happened. Sofia would dance with this same man every time for weeks and weeks, and then it was only him she danced with. They'd dance and then sneak outside. One night, I went out with a boy just to talk and I saw Sofia and the man kissing.

"The next day I asked her about it. She told me she loved him." Again, Emma met Ambler's gaze to make sure he wasn't getting the wrong idea. "I said, 'That's crazy, Sofia. You can't do that. He's old. You're too young. You'll get in bad trouble.'

"She said, 'I know. I can't help it. I can't stop thinking about him. I want to be with him all the time.'"

Speaking barely above a whisper, Emma continued, "She told me she'd been meeting him. He wasn't from the neighborhood. She met him near where he worked on Grand Concourse by the big courthouse. He had an apartment near there."

Emma paused, tried to look at Ambler but lost her nerve. "She was making love with him. Sofia was a virgin until she went with him. She was so pretty and so smart. She was smarter than me, smarter than all of us. She was the one who kept us from doing anything stupid. And then she did the stupidest thing of all.

"For a while it was a big secret that she didn't even tell me. But then she told me. He was rich, she told me. A lawyer. Finally she told me his name, Ricardo Diaz . . . and he was married." Emma's eyes went wide; her jaw dropped. She stared at Ambler, as shocked as if she were hearing this for the first time instead of saying it.

"So when Sofia died you called the police . . . because you thought Ricardo might have been with her when she overdosed, might have encouraged her to take the drugs, might have been complicit in her death?"

Emma's shocked expression froze on her face. She'd finally said what she'd kept secret for ten years and couldn't believe the sound of her own voice. Ambler prodded her gently lest he scare her away. He knew she had more to say. "This Ricardo, did you ever meet him?"

"I saw him plenty of times at the salsa club. He was handsome . . . and a good dancer. Any girl would want to dance with him. He'd smile at you and you'd blush because you'd want him to choose you. But he always chose Sofia."

At least she was talking again. He wanted to let her pour out all of what she'd been holding back. It would be better if she just talked rather than making her answer questions. But she stopped again, and glanced around her, as if someone might have overheard, though no one was in the apartment but them.

"And you think he got Sofia into using drugs?"

Emma jumped at him. "No way. Sofia would never use drugs, never shoot up. She saw what happened to her cousin." Emma looked at him as if he should know what happened to Sofia's cousin. He didn't but from her tone he could guess. She was going to say something else, so he didn't interrupt to ask.

"Sofia might smoke weed, but she didn't even like to do that, or even drink much. She was a Catholic. Her family was old-fashioned and very strict Catholics. So was Sofia, so it didn't make no sense for her to go with this man. Of all the girls, everyone would think she'd be the last to lose her virginity like that."

Emma leaned forward, her hands folded on her knees, as if she were beseeching Ambler. "Sofia was crazy in love with him. She couldn't live without him. When she thought he would leave her, she said she'd kill herself."

Ambler wasn't ready for that. Nothing in Robin's notes

pointed to suicide. Lopez would have told him if the police had considered that. But it was a possibility—a girl crazed by love killing herself. "Is that what happened?"

Emma's eyes bugged open. "Is *what* what happened?"

"Ricardo was going to leave her, so Sofia killed herself?"

Emma shrunk back from him. "Are you crazy? Sofia wouldn't kill herself. Killing yourself is a sin . . . It's a sin you can't ask forgiveness for. Sofia would never do that. Having sex, committing adultery is a sin. But you can confess and get forgiven. Suicide is the worst one. No confession. No forgiveness. You go to Hell."

Ambler shook his head. Not two minutes ago, she'd told him Sofia said she'd kill herself if Ricardo left her. Now Ambler was crazy for thinking Sofia might have killed herself? Emma might not be the most reliable of witnesses.

"He killed her. Ricardo killed her because he wanted her to go away so he wouldn't get in trouble with his wife. Sofia was sure he'd leave his wife and marry her. When he told her he wasn't going to, she told him if he didn't, she'd tell his wife that she was his lover.

"He didn't know Sofia. He didn't know what he'd got himself into. You couldn't pretend to love her, take her virginity, and then leave her. Sofia wouldn't stand for that. I knew something terrible would happen. If he didn't kill her, she'd kill him. I knew it."

She looked at Ambler beseechingly. "I was the only one, the only one in the world besides both of them who knew this, who knew about them and who knew something terrible would happen."

She collapsed back into her chair, lay her head back and stared at the ceiling. "And then it happened. She went to see him. I saw her go. 'It's going to be OK,' she told me. 'He loves me. He's going to leave his wife.' She went to meet him and he killed her. He stuck a needle in her arm with a heavy dose of drugs and killed her."

She continued to speak to the ceiling. "I called the police and told them. But the stupid police couldn't figure out what was plain as the nose on their face."

"What did you tell them?"

"I told them about how Sofia had been with Ricardo. I said they were lovers. I told them his name—Ricardo. You'd think they could figure it out from there. It wouldn't have been that hard."

What she'd told the police, despite her protests, wasn't much. Not anything they'd follow up on for an overdose. If the police had suspected Sofia was murdered, it might have been different. They might have interviewed people at the salsa club, gotten a name, tracked down Ricardo. They might even have found their way back to Emma.

He wasn't going to browbeat her about what she should have said. She was a scared kid alone with her guilty knowledge, and she did what she'd hoped would be enough.

"Now you know. Will you track down Ricardo? Are you going to tell the police?" Her tone was angry, challenging. "You can't tell them about me. I'll die if you do. My life will be over."

Ambler tried to calm her. She was shaking. "I won't tell the police about you. You think Ricardo killed Sofia. But you don't really know. You don't have any proof the police could use. I might tell them about Ricardo, but they don't need to know I talked to you. Your word against his wouldn't mean much. Though there's one thing I don't understand that you might help with . . ."

"You won't tell the police about me?" Her smile came back, and along with it her confidence. "I'm glad I told you . . . It's good I told someone finally. I've felt like a terrible liar all this time."

"The one thing is this." He went over Robin's research again. "She knew about Sofia's death and suspected she'd been murdered. How would she know? What led her to believe Sofia might have been murdered if no one knew about her and Ricardo except for you?"

Emma wrung her hands and her smile disappeared. "I think I know. . . I hope I didn't make a mistake. When I was at Hostos, I wrote about what happened to Sofia, a case study for a sociology class. I made up names and everything so no one would know it was her or had anything to do with me.

"I wrote about a girl and a married man and how that led to a terrible tragedy. The man murdered the girl by shooting her up with heroin, so she died and it looked like an accidental overdose. The teacher thought the essay was great and said she wanted to send the story to a friend of hers, another sociologist who studied accidental deaths that might have been cover-ups for a murder.

"At the time I thought maybe I shouldn't let her do it. But it would have been worse to tell her why I didn't want her to. And she didn't use my name, so I said OK. And I didn't think about it having to do with anything. I didn't think about it until you just asked me. Could your friend that died have traced the story I wrote back to Sofia?"

Ambler thought it probable that both Robin Cartwright and Emma's sociology teacher knew Emma's case study was based on an actual happening. He told her that even if that had happened, and no matter what would happen next, he wouldn't give her name to the police or anyone else.

# ELEVEN

The hell of it was that it would be easy to leave Emma's name out of it. She didn't have any proof Ricardo Diaz killed Sofia. And Ambler didn't know how to find any, ten years after her death. What was done was done. If he couldn't link Diaz to Robin's death, why try to prove he killed Sofia, which might be impossible?

He gave it a day's thought and decided that—even if he couldn't get Ricardo Diaz for Sofia's murder, if she was murdered—he should at least rattle his cage and see what that stirred up.

There were a lot of Ricardo Diazes in the Bronx but only a few lawyers. Ambler picked the one who seemed about the right age and whose office—a storefront law office—Ricardo Diaz Attorney at Law-Abogada—was around the corner from the Grand Concourse on 161st Street and not far from the Bronx Hall of Justice.

Diaz was in court when he got to the office, in a two-story block-long building set amongst drab gray and beige brick apartment buildings. The receptionist—a pretty, dark-haired and dark-eyed girl who reminded him of Sofia—said Mr. Diaz should be back any minute. He thought to ask her about Diaz—what kind of cases he handled or what kind of boss he was, or something like that—but decided not to since she was absorbed in the magazine she was thumbing through.

When the lawyer showed up, it took Ambler a few minutes to gather his wits. Diaz was in a wheelchair. For a brief moment, Ambler imagined this was a ruse the lawyer used to gain sympathy from a jury, and he'd step out if it and bound across the floor as soon as he was in the office. Such was not the case. Diaz rolled his way into the storefront and Ambler noticed a ramp on the front step that he hadn't noticed before. Once he was aware, he saw other accommodations made for the wheelchair to fit through the interior and exterior doors of the office.

Ambler, to his later regret, planned to try his own ruse—a dumb plan, he attributed to a too-close association with his bartender friend Brian McNulty—which was to pretend he intended to engage the lawyer to defend him on a murder charge. He described the circumstances—a girl he was having an affair with had committed suicide by purposely overdosing on heroin, but the police said he gave her the injection and planned to charge him with murder.

Ambler was barely halfway through his hastily concocted story when Diaz caught on. With jackhammer speed and surgical precision, the lawyer asked three or four questions—where and when did this death happen? Ambler hadn't thought that far ahead and stumbled for an answer before coming up with the Chelsea Hotel. Why the Chelsea Hotel, he had no idea.

Neither was he prepared for the second question: Who was the detective who told him he'd be charged? The only answer he could think of was Mike Cosgrove. And there'd be hell to pay if Mike found out he was using him to cover up a lie.

By the third question—why did he come to the South Bronx for an attorney when you couldn't turn a corner in Manhattan without tripping over at least one and more likely two or three?—he threw in the towel. Diaz was obviously disabled—as he hauled himself out of the wheelchair and across the room to sit behind his desk, it was obvious that his pants fit loosely around his legs, as if the muscles had atrophied—but his thinking skills were in good working order.

"I don' know wha' you want, man. I don' know wha' you doin here. You tryin' to pull some shit, you messin' wit da wrong guy . . . You ain't playin' me." He glared at Ambler as he spoke, using both the glare and the gangsta street accent to try to intimidate him. But an air of uneasiness hung over the lawyer beneath the glare. Ambler believed it to be the sinking feeling Diaz had that chickens were coming home to roost.

So he began his own barrage of questions. "Do you remember Sofia Torres?"

Diaz stared at him. His eyes were deeply dark, almost black, harboring anger or hate or fear or all three. No mirror to his soul.

Ambler didn't wait for an answer. "Do you know Robin Cartwright?"

Diaz was too smart to pretend he didn't know what Ambler was talking about. "What is this? Blackmail?"

"It's about murder, maybe two murders."

"Do you see what I look like? How do I murder anyone?"

Ambler was hard pressed to argue with him. "Tell me about Sofia Torres."

His response was swift and dismissive. "Why should I?"

"Someone thinks you murdered her. It might save you some trouble if you tell me how it was that you didn't."

An experienced criminal law attorney in the South Bronx, Diaz was not easily rattled. "Someone can think what they want. It doesn't mean anything to me." You'd think a person would be at least surprised when out of the blue he was accused of murder. With him, it was as if he'd been prepared for such a charge and had his answers lined up to challenge it. On the other hand, his response might be that of a trial lawyer, good on his feet, who's always ready to handle what's thrown at him.

Expecting a denial, Ambler wasn't sure what to make of his answer.

"You knew her?"

Diaz took a moment to think things over. Ambler waited to see what he'd come up with, wondering as he waited what a person might be thinking about if he'd committed a murder some years before, and had for all intents and purposes gotten away with it, and then—while perhaps thinking about where he'd go for lunch—the accusation he'd thought he'd put to rest came barreling back at him.

Diaz might ask himself if he should admit to having known Sofia. Even though his name hadn't come up at the time of her death, Sofia could have told one or more of her friends about him, despite her promise not to tell anyone. Her girlfriends saw him with her at the dance club many times. Girls tell each other their secrets.

On the other hand, Ambler told himself, it might be Emma Perez made up the story about Diaz and Sofia, though that was doubtful. It might also be that Sofia had lied to Emma about having an affair to show off for her friend, though this too was unlikely. You had to believe Diaz had known Sofia and had an affair with her. Why not admit it? The question of whether he killed her or not was easier for Diaz to deny. Somebody might well know he'd been with Sofia. No one, Diaz could be pretty sure, knew he killed her—if he did.

Robin's death was another matter. If she'd gone to the short-stay hotel with a man in a wheelchair, someone undoubtedly would have noticed. Unless his condition was an elaborate and convincing fake—which Ambler might look into—he was out of the running for her murder. And if he was, why waste time pursuing this? Having been as deeply lost in his thoughts as Diaz was in his, Ambler was startled when he spoke.

"Before I tell you anything, I want to know who you are and why you're coming to me with this bullshit about murders. I'd be out of my mind to talk to you when I don't know what you're up to." He'd dropped the gangsta lingo and his tone wasn't hostile. It was a direct question in a reasonable tone.

Ambler's response was equally reasonable. "Your name came up in connection with a criminology research project." He described Robin Cartwright's research. Part of what he told the lawyer he fabricated—attributing what Emma Perez told him to Robin's research rather than to Emma—but the outcome was the same; he told Diaz what he'd been told.

"The professor who came up with all this, she was murdered?"

"Let's leave that aside for the moment. The circumstances of her death are under investigation. We're talking about what happened to Sofia. It's pretty clear you knew her. It's known, if not common knowledge, you had an affair with her. It's alleged you killed her."

The lawyer became agitated, raising himself from his chair, shouting at Ambler. As he did, Ambler noticed how muscular his arms were. Despite the heated reaction, Ambler believed the reaction was an act; it was a bit too vehement. The lunge forward as he raised himself too theatrical.

"An allegation is nothing without proof. I don't have any problem calling the police on a shakedown artist." He lowered himself back into his chair. "You can't have any proof." He watched Ambler shrewdly like he might a hostile witness. "You don't have proof because it didn't happen." He sighed, the agitation gone, all at once gripped by a powerful sadness.

"I did the poor kid a terrible wrong. She was so full of life and so sweet." His tone became reverent. "A beautiful, passionate young woman. We met dancing; she was graceful, light as a feather, like dancing with a shadow, a smile like an angel, bubbling with life. I adored her. I was young and thoughtless, selfish. She was irresistible. When you're young and full of confidence and think everything in the world is yours for the taking, you don't think of consequences. Your heart is full; you can't help but desire her, and you know you can have her.

"I didn't mean to hurt her. I was careless. I only thought of how pretty she was, how passionate, how innocent—and how easily she could be mine. And then she was mine, and then came the consequences. I didn't kill her. But I caused her death. Not in a criminal way. I didn't stick the needle in her arm. I had no idea she'd do that." He half-smiled. "No charges. No conviction. No jail time." He gestured at the immobile part of his lower body. "Yet I paid a price. God has his ways."

They sat in silence for a moment, neither looking at the other. Ambler had gotten what he came for. He'd have a few things to check on—try to find some record of Diaz's injury. He'd like to have been able to tell Sofia's family and Emma that Sofia hadn't shot herself up with heroin either accidentally or on purpose, that someone had done this thing to her. He wouldn't be able to do that. Whether Diaz told the truth or lied, he'd be the only one who knew the truth.

# TWELVE

"I'm due a promotion," Benny Bevone told Ambler the following morning. He'd been perched on a corner of the reading table, with one leg crossed atop the other, waiting, when Ambler opened the door of the crime fiction reading room. "One day, it took me, and I got the goods." He uncrossed his legs and stood up. "Do you think it's too late for me to get a private eye license?"

"Never too late, Benny." Ambler took his place behind the table. Benny sat down across from him. "What did you find out?"

"You ain't gonna believe this." Benny let his gaze wander over the bookshelves of the reading room. "Maybe you will, since it's what you told me . . . Beasley had the kid hack into Professor Cartwright's email account."

The news that shouldn't have been a surprise unnerved Ambler nonetheless. Like the dog chasing the car until it stops, he had what he was after but didn't know what to do once he had it. Beasley was the blackmailer. Now what?

"One other thing Jacob told me," Benny said. "He also created a burner email account for his uncle."

"Why? What does that mean?"

"If Beasley sent messages from the account Jacob created for him, no one could trace them back to him. It's completely anonymous." Benny watched Ambler expectantly, but Ambler was deep in thought.

Beasley had, with the kid's help, hacked into Robin's laptop and sent a blackmail email from her account, pretending to be her. He'd then had the kid set up an anonymous email account, in preparation for something. For what, though?

Had the blackmail message and the threatening email both come from Beasley, using Robin's email for one and the dummy email account for the other? That didn't make any sense. Why would Beasley threaten her? The threatening email had to have come from the person being blackmailed. Beasley must have set up the dummy email account to give directions to whomever he blackmailed on what the ransom was and how to deliver it. He'd either pretend he was Robin or pretend to be the go-between. He couldn't very well continue that discussion on Robin's email account.

Would he have murdered Robin because she discovered his scheme? Or would the blackmail victim have killed her, mistaking her for the blackmailer? In either event, her death must have necessitated a change in plans.

Benny interrupted his ruminating, "So we go get him now, right? We got him dead to rights."

"It's not as easy as that." Ambler spoke slowly. "If we confront him, what's he going to say?"

Benny didn't take long. "He'll deny everything. And if we tell him his nephew told us, he'll get to the kid and make sure he changes his story. So what do we do?"

"I think we go to the police, but I want to talk to Mike first. I'm not sure we have enough for them to do anything."

He called Mike Cosgrove and met him at the Library Tavern for a late lunch. The detective wasn't in a good mood; down in the dumps as Ambler brought him up to date on what he'd learned about Beasley. Mike was pissed off at his captain for pulling him off a case he was working and giving him a different, high-profile one.

A croque monsieur and a beer didn't improve his mood. It wouldn't do any good to ask him about it. Mike would either say what was bothering him or he wouldn't. Usually when what bothered him was something internal to the job, he'd keep it to himself. This was one of the times when he wasn't talking.

"I want your advice," Ambler said. "Is what I told you enough to get a warrant and search Beasley's computer for a secret burner email account?"

Mike shrugged. "You never know. You got to get it authorized. You need an ADA to go along. And even if you get that, it depends on the judge, whether he got out of bed on the good side or the bad side that morning. No reason not to tell Lambert about it."

"He was a bit testy the last time we talked. I don't know how he'd take it."

Mike munched on his sandwich a moment before replying. "Does your friend Beasley hacking into Miss Cartwright's email prove she was murdered?"

Ambler was irritated. "It's Doctor or Professor Cartwright. Don't you guys ever investigate something to determine *if it is* a murder?"

Mike got irritated right along with him. "That's what Lambert's doing—investigating a death where the manner is undetermined; investigating a *suspicious* death."

He paused for a moment and softened his tone. "Look. I've got a lot going on, a bunch of flak from the brass. I can't help you on this one. I'm not going to piss off Lambert by butting in." He took a slug of beer and watched McNulty the bartender for a moment. "Give what you got to Lambert. If he doesn't do anything with it, you've done what you could."

"Would it make sense for me to confront Beasley?"

McNulty, who'd wandered over when he saw Cosgrove watching him, said, "What would make sense would be for you to leave crime to the criminals and move upstate with Adele and the rug rat."

"He's got a point there," Mike said as he stood to leave. "I get paid for dealing with this crap and it's gotten to where doing it doesn't make sense to me anymore." He started to pay but Ambler told him he'd pick up the check.

"What's with him?" McNulty asked after Mike left. "He looks like the bad guy got away."

"I don't know." Ambler ordered a second beer, something he rarely did. "Did you overhear what we were talking about?"

"What makes you think I overheard?"

"I'm sure if you did it was an accident. I don't want to have to repeat what I said if I don't have to."

When he was behind the bar, McNulty overheard everything

he thought worth hearing; he wouldn't admit it and he wouldn't tell anyone what he heard unless he had a good reason to. And of course, he would deny it if asked, so Ambler played along.

"In that case," McNulty said, "I heard something about blackmail and secret email addresses and whether or not you should go to the cops with what you know. My thinking on that is well established."

"And that is?"

"Going to the cops almost always creates more problems than it purports to solve."

One disregarded McNulty's advice at one's peril. Ambler knew this, but went to a quiet booth in the back and called Lambert nonetheless. The detective listened to what he had to say and asked for the names of the men Beasley might blackmail.

"The names are in the research journal." This wasn't strictly true, but if he could find out Ricardo Diaz's name, then so could Lambert.

"Right. I'll take a look." He sounded bored, uninterested.

"That's it?" Ambler felt his dander rising.

"I'm working on something. I'll get to it when I can." Lambert's tone was irritating, like a grown-up addressing a bothersome child.

He tried to fight back the temptation to argue. The last thing he needed was Lambert thinking he was trying to tell the cop how to do his job. But he couldn't resist. "What about Beasley? Couldn't you get a court order for his email account? He could be exchanging emails with the killer, even as we speak." As soon as he said it, Ambler knew he'd gone too far.

"Look Mr. Ambler, I already got a half-dozen bosses. I sure as hell don't need another one. Thanks for the information. You've been a big help."

That was it. That was all he was going to get. He almost asked if Lambert would get back to him. But that would be a mistake, too. Lambert wasn't Mike. He called the library and took the rest of the afternoon off.

"How'd that go?" McNulty asked when Ambler came back to the bar.

"Like you'd expect. I should've known better."

"How about a shot of Irish whiskey? That's what I do after I've been talking to a cop."

Ambler took the shot of Powers; McNulty joined him. They toasted Adele and Jennifer.

After a moment, Ambler asked, "What if I confront Beasley myself since no one else will?"

"Are you asking my opinion on the wisdom of that?"

Some of Ambler's worst plans came from consulting McNulty. But he went ahead anyway.

"Act like you know more than you know. Tell him he's been found out. You know all about what he did."

"And then what?"

McNulty rubbed his chin, always a bad sign. The more far-fetched his ideas, the more he rubbed. "You know he blackmailed someone, right? Tell him the guy he blackmailed is coming after him."

"I'm supposed to know who this person is?"

McNulty poured himself a beer from the tap into his coffee cup, his smug expression suggesting this plan was so simple a child could carry it out. "He knows who the killer is, right, and he's not telling you. For all he knows, you know who the killer is but you're not telling him."

"So we both know. But neither of us is saying?" Ambler thought this might make more sense if he said it out loud; it sure didn't make sense when he thought about it. Actually, in a way it sounded right, but it couldn't be right. "I say 'I know who the killer is that you're blackmailing.' Why would I say that?"

McNulty showed exaggerated patience. "You wouldn't say that. The fact that you're *not* saying it is why he'd believe you know."

Ambler shook his head, trying to clear it. "So I go up to Beasley and say, 'Hey Blake, you-know-who is coming after you?'"

"I wouldn't say that. It sounds stupid."

"This whole idea sounds stupid."

McNulty nodded sympathetically. This was the gesture Ambler remembered his algebra teacher used when he was correcting one of Ambler's tests. "That's because you're not approaching it right. You're trying to be logical. You need to be creative."

It took a while longer for Ambler to come around. But he began to get the glimmering of an idea. McNulty was—though his career pretty much died aborning—a trained and accomplished actor, with an Equity card and a scrapbook filled with good and sometimes rave reviews of off- and off-off-Broadway plays. He could easily pull off real actions and emotions in imaginary situations; he'd done this a few times in aid of one of Ambler's investigations. The idea, then, might not be as far-fetched as it first appeared *for McNulty.* For Ambler, it was a different story.

Nonetheless, McNulty persuaded him to give it a try. He would catch up with Beasley—who knew Ambler had been suspicious of the circumstances around Robin's death—and tell him he hadn't covered his tracks as well as he thought he had. Ambler knew what he'd done, and if he knew, it wouldn't be long before the police would know. Ambler would say, "I know you didn't kill Robin . . . but you know who did. I can't prove what I know. But you can. If you help me, we can take it to the police. If we do that—give them the killer—we can get them to look the other way and leave the blackmail thing by the wayside."

The next morning the plan still seemed workable. Who knew how Beasley would react? He set off to find him. What he found instead was Chris Lambert, two other detectives, and a fingerprint technician in Beasley's office.

"What's going on?" Ambler had a sinking feeling he knew. The three detectives turned toward him. The fingerprint guy kept working.

"I was thinking you might know." Lambert wasn't smiling; the expression in his eyes was what you'd expect from the hangman.

"I don't." Dread chilled his solar plexus. He wanted Lambert to stop beating around the bushes. The three cops watched him like vultures, hoping no doubt he'd have some guilty knowledge and give himself away. The way he felt—guilty, for reasons he didn't know—he might well do so. He stared at them in total confusion.

"Did you find Beasley's emails?" he asked after what seemed a very long silence.

"What we found was his body." Lambert continued to stare at him.

"Where?" He said the first thing that came into his head. It made no sense. Why did he care where the body was? Shouldn't he have asked how? Why? Are you sure?

Lambert ignored the question. "He's the guy you asked me about yesterday afternoon. When did *you* see him last?"

He shook his head. "I don't know. A week ago? A couple of days ago? I don't remember. What happened to him?"

Again Lambert ignored this question, too. "You're conducting a vigilante investigation. You tried to convince me he was a murderer. You wanted us to hack into his computer. And you don't remember when you saw him last?"

Lambert was good at the third degree. Ambler felt like he'd been backed into a corner. Any answer he gave would be wrong and get him deeper into trouble. As ridiculous as it felt, he was a suspect, so he needed to be careful. He didn't know what this outraged—probably it was an act—detective thought about him or knew about him. He wouldn't be the first innocent person to be brought up on murder charges because he said the wrong thing or was in the wrong place or couldn't account for his whereabouts at a certain time. And here it came.

"Where were you last night?"

"I'm not going to answer any more questions until you tell me what happened."

"I suppose you want a lawyer." Lambert's tone was nasty, sarcastic, and insulting. A good thing for Ambler that he'd caught on. The detective was trying to provoke him into doing something stupid, like feeling insulted and disrespected and saying, "I don't need a lawyer. Anyone but an idiot would know

I didn't murder anyone and of course I can prove I was somewhere else because I was."

After years of murder investigations, he knew better than to get involved in a back-and-forth with this cop who made his living asking questions and tying suspects in knots until they weren't even sure of their own name. He knew what he should do, but the temptation to straighten Lambert out, to tell him the simple truth, was overwhelming. He took a deep breath.

"I don't need a lawyer," he said. "Because I'm going to go back to work. You know where to find me." He turned and left, forcing himself not to look back over his shoulder, cringing internally while he waited for the long arm of the law to reach out, grab him around the neck, and drag him back.

Instead of going back to the crime fiction reading room, he went to Harry Larkin's office. Harry was on the phone when he knocked and then opened his door. Harry glanced up at him and hung up the phone.

"Good God, Ray! What's become of us?"

"So. Tell me what happened. I don't know anything."

"The police are here. Do you know that?" His eyes, unblinking, were open wider than Ambler had ever seen, magnified by his glasses. "The first thing the detective asked for after he told me Blake had been murdered was you."

"I saw them. I went to talk to Blake and they were in his office. Lambert gave me the third degree."

"They think you killed him?" Harry's eyes opened wider, if that were possible. They were like little lakes under his forehead.

"Lambert knows better. I spoke to him late yesterday. He's mad at me, probably because if he'd done what I asked, Blake might not have been murdered."

Harry moaned, put the palm of his hand against his forehead, and sat down behind his desk. "Why oh why do you get us into these situations? The story will be all over the papers. Another black eye for the library. The city is safer than ever and you're getting the library mixed up in another murder. President—"

"What about me? I'm the suspect. We can't worry about the president or the board right now. They're not about to go to jail. Tell me everything the police told you. They won't tell me anything."

"Someone shot Blake in his apartment. The detective asked me if I had any idea who might want to kill him. He was here quite a while and asked a lot of questions. I don't remember all of them."

"Did he ask about anyone by name?"

"Only you." Harry's expression was sympathetic, but sympathy tinged with a kind of I-told-you-so accusation.

"He didn't ask about the visiting professors, about—"

"Yes. He did . . . Wait. He asked about Dr. Cartwright and Blake. He wanted to know what kind of relationship they had. Then he wanted to know about the rest of the group. He asked what I knew about her research, the book she was writing; if I'd read her research journal."

Harry paused and Ambler knew he was holding something back. It wouldn't be like him to hide anything, Ambler was sure. But there was something. Harry, still a priest in his heart though he'd left the priesthood years before, was a terrible liar. He was honest to a fault and as compassionate as a saint. Getting the truth out of him was literally like taking candy from a baby.

"Is there something else, Harry?" Ambler asked innocently.

Harry squirmed for a moment, tried to busy himself with some papers on his desk, finally glanced at Ambler helplessly. "I mentioned Mr. Nagy's strange behavior when he was here after his wife's . . . or ex-wife's . . . death. His visit didn't have anything to do with Blake. I have no reason to think he even spoke with Blake. But he might have since Blake is . . . *was* in charge of the visiting professor program."

"Lambert was interested?"

"He wrote down Mr. Nagy's name, I think. He took notes as we spoke. He asked what Blake was like and who his friends were. I told him what I knew. Blake kept to himself. I didn't know that he had friends among the staff."

Harry began squirming again, busying himself with his papers again, searching in the desk drawer all of a sudden.

"And . . .?"

Harry's voice sounded like a bark. "He asked if Blake had any enemies. I said he wasn't especially well liked by some of the library aides." He glanced at Ambler helplessly. "I was thinking of what Benny had said and I gave him Benny's name and Victor's, the other aide who works with the study rooms. Then I remembered Victor and Benny heard you threaten Blake."

"Threaten him? I never threatened Blake."

"You said you hated his guts." Harry's expression was mournful. ". . . And then before he even talked to them, out of the blue, the detective said, 'Enemies? . . . How about Raymond Ambler?'"

An hour or so later, while Ambler was answering a handful of emails from readers with questions related to the crime fiction collection, Lambert knocked on the door. He was by himself.

Something in Ambler's expression must have told the detective he was ready for a fight because Lambert spoke placatingly . . . somewhat placatingly. "Take it easy, Mr. Librarian. I came to talk. For this visit at least, you're not a suspect." He smiled, or at least made an effort.

Pulling up a chair, he kept his eyes locked on Ambler. "Forget about what happened earlier; I didn't want anyone to get the wrong idea about where you and I stood." He shifted his gaze to take in the bookshelves surrounding them. "Nice place." His tone was borderline friendly. "You read all these?"

Ambler let down his guard a bit. "Not a chance. I don't get as much time as I'd like to read; I wish that were the job."

"Any Ed McBain?"

"The 87th Precinct books are in libraries all over the city. He wrote pretty much one a year for fifty years." Ambler looked away and softened his tone. "It's not a big deal, but I've been slowly building a collection over the years of McBain first editions. Surprisingly for the kind of books he wrote, most are in hard cover. You'd expect paperback originals. It's not a major collection. The major collection of his papers is at Boston University."

If Lambert was trying to soften him up, he'd taken the right approach. Getting Ambler talking about his collection was like asking to see pictures of a mother's baby. There was no funding for collecting McBain first editions. He'd picked up copies on his own over the years, finding them when he was nosing through used bookstores, or bookstalls on the street, or occasionally at book auctions, and donated them to the library.

"I can show you the books if you'd like. But since this isn't a social visit, I don't want to slow you down."

Lambert rubbed his chin—reminding Ambler of McNulty and what happens to best-laid plans—before he said, "Maybe later. I'll level with you. I didn't put a lot of stock in your idea that Robin Cartwright was murdered—I figured it was an unintentional death at most. Now I'm rethinking that. This guy's death and her death coming so close together, you gotta think is more than a coincidence. So now I want to listen more carefully to what you think happened."

This was good news, but cops being cops, Lambert had more up his sleeve than hearing Ambler's take on things. "Are you going to tell me what happened to Blake Beasley?"

Lambert didn't like the question. He kind of snarled at it. But his reply was civil, if terse. "As much as I can. I'm not going to tell you everything. I'd guess you know why."

Beasley was shot at close range in his own apartment. The building he lived in—part of a co-op built by the Ladies' Garment Workers' Union in the 1960s that he'd inherited from his garment worker parents—was on 27th Street between 8th and 9th Avenues. The building was not especially secure—no doorman or elevator operator; no security cameras—but the entry door was locked and required a visitor to be buzzed in.

No sign of forced entry to Beasley's apartment. No sign of a struggle. No one heard the shots; there were two. No one the police have spoken to so far reported any suspicious comings or goings. But the police are still interviewing tenants.

"That's about it." Lambert almost smiled again. "You're

our only suspect, and, to tell the truth, you're not much of one. You told me the victim had hacked into the other victim's email account and sent a message blackmailing one of the subjects of her book. How'd you come to know this?" The detective was no longer smiling.

This was a tough one. He couldn't answer without implicating both Benny and Beasley's nephew. And he couldn't *not* answer without becoming an uncooperative witness and ruining whatever rapport he might have developed with Lambert. So he tried to bypass the question. "Did your forensic I.T. department check Beasley's laptop and phone for his burner email account yet?"

Lambert rolled his eyes. "Do you have any evidence of emails from this supposed burner account? Do you know who he was sending emails to?"

"No . . . Actually, the only thing I know for sure is that there *is* a burner account."

"Right. That's what I asked you." He didn't try to hide his impatience. "How do you know Beasley had a secret account?"

Since he was such a big guy, it was hard not to cringe when he showed signs of agitation. "It's complicated . . . Isn't knowing he has a secret account enough?"

Lambert spoke with exaggerated patience. "You don't want to tell me because you don't want to get someone else in trouble. I understand that. You'd be surprised—or maybe you shouldn't be surprised, since you're an expert in criminal investigation—but that happens all the time. Sometimes I want to pick a witness up, turn them upside down, and shake the truth out of them."

He looked Ambler up and down in such a way that Ambler believed he might be about to do just that. But he calmed himself. "We don't want to get anyone in trouble with their boss, with their wife, with the neighbors, with anyone. We want to stop a murderer. You got that?" For a moment, the gigantic cop had the expression of a child whose ice-cream scoop had rolled off the top of his cone.

"I know you can answer the question. We can stay here for

an hour and I can badger you. I can drag you over to the precinct where me and a couple of the boys can play tag team with you . . . Or you can just man up and answer the fucking question."

Ambler sank into silence, embarrassed silence. He knew what he had to do; he knew all along. He'd got Benny to do something underhanded. Benny in turn tricked the kid. Of course, Beasley's nephew Jacob had done what he did, which was underhanded in its own right.

For all of them, they should have known there might be consequences. And now here they were: "If you can't do the time, don't do the crime."

He told the detective about his friend Benny Bevone, the apprentice private eye, and Jacob, the computer whiz.

"Some of these kids, I tell you." Lambert shook his head. "I interview them sometimes and I don't know what they're saying. They speak another language. I hear the words. But they're words I never heard of. They might be telling the truth. They might be lying. I don't know any more after I talk to them than I did before."

He took a moment to think things over. "I'll need to lean on the kid. I can't think of any other way. I said we try not to make trouble for people, but sometimes you can't help it. If this Jacob is a juvenile, we probably won't talk to him without his parents. I'll interview the other guy to see if he knows anything he didn't tell you."

He met Ambler's gaze, his own expression surprisingly sympathetic. "It might be easier on him—and it will save me some time—if you got him in here right now. Might not be comfortable for you."

"It's OK. Benny will hate my guts. And I don't think he'll have much to tell you." Ambler stood. "Sit tight for a minute. I'll see if I can track him down."

Ten minutes later, Benny appeared in the reading room doorway. Ambler had left a message for him with the librarian on the research information desk. When he saw Lambert, he froze, recognizing Lambert for a cop as sure as if he wore a uniform.

"Hold on Benny!" Ambler shouted. It was entirely possible Benny would take off running, an instinct bred into him over years of a misspent youth. "You're not in trouble. I swear you're not." Lambert took this in without raising an eyebrow, content to let Ambler settle things down.

"Chris Lambert is a detective investigating Blake Beasley's murder. We were talking about Blake's email account."

Benny was on full alert, as trusting as an alley cat, ready to deny anything and everything. "What's that got to do with me? I don't know anything about Beasley's computer or anything else."

Ambler realized he should have prepared Benny for a meeting with a cop and not just sprung it on him. Too late now. "Sorry Benny. I told the detective what we did. It's my responsibility. I told him so he could stop a murderer. I was wrong about Beasley . . . or mostly wrong. It looks like he was the blackmailer. I should have known if the murderer killed the wrong person, he'd come back for the right one. It's OK to talk."

"What about the kid?"

Ambler glanced at Lambert.

"I need to talk to him. Look, I'm interested in a homicide, potentially two homicides. I don't care about hacking or anything else that might be illegal. I'd like you to tell me what the boy told you, especially if he told you the name of the email service provider he used to set up the burner account."

"He didn't tell me or, if he did, I don't remember, because most of the time I didn't know what he was talking about." Benny went over what Jacob had told him. It was what he had told Ambler a day earlier.

"Can't you trace the emails by searching Blake's laptop?" Ambler asked.

Lambert smiled ruefully. "Our computers crime squad is really good at what they do. But they can't examine a computer they don't have."

Ambler stared at him uncomprehendingly. "You don't have Blake's laptop?"

"It wasn't in his apartment. I hoped we might find it here. No luck."

"What about his phone?"

"Protected with advanced encryption. We'll leave cracking it to the computer guys. For me, I'll be using the old tried-and-true method—wearing out my shoe leather."

# THIRTEEN

The following morning Ambler rented a car and drove for a little over five hours to Wolverton, a town of around 10,000 people nestled amidst the low, rolling hills of the Piedmont region of Virginia, fifty or sixty miles southwest of Washington, D.C., and fifty miles or so east of the Blue Ridge Mountains.

Wolverton was the home of the Conway County Circuit Court and the offices of the deputy commonwealth attorney who'd declined to prosecute a man named Clifton Kilgore. Kilgore had been charged some ten years before with negligent homicide in the death of a young woman, Anna Paxton, whom he'd run over with his pickup truck. The case never went to trial.

The death was the second of the three cases of accidents that might be murders that Robin Cartwright had been investigating for her book. Hearing Chris Lambert talk about the old-time investigation methods, Ambler decided he too should wear out some shoe leather since the plan to track down Beasley's killer through cyber forensics had fallen flat.

Following an infuriating slog through the D.C. area Beltway traffic, he arrived at the small town shortly after the lunch hour, parked in an empty space on the main street, and found his way to the courthouse less than a block off the main drag and the office of the associate commonwealth attorney he had called that morning.

He told the woman who introduced herself as Susan Johnson about Robin Cartwright's research, ascertained that she was the prosecutor who had handled the negligent homicide case against Clifton Kilgore and asked why she hadn't prosecuted.

"This is a strange request, indeed." Susan Johnson carried herself with authority, a no-nonsense style of haircut, a bun of some sort, severe business attire, a dark blue suit appropriate to a courtroom, little make-up, and a manner, if not forbidding, certainly standoffish. He wouldn't say she disliked him. On the other hand, he had no illusion they'd become pals.

"The case was ten years ago." She said this in the tone of a housewife who might say, "You've tracked mud onto the rug." "Strangely, I do remember it. Still, I've brought hundreds of felony cases to trial since then and dismissed hundreds more. I'd hardly remember why we didn't prosecute."

She thought about this for a moment. "It's not unusual to dismiss a case; that isn't why I remember it. If the driver wasn't under the influence, wasn't speeding, obeyed traffic laws, didn't leave the scene, the victim darted out into the street or somehow put themselves in harm's way, there'd be no reason to charge the driver because the driver wasn't negligent. Though if all that were true, he shouldn't have been charged in the first place."

"What if the driver knew the victim?"

The question gave her pause. "Is that true?" She didn't give him time to answer. "That's not unheard-of either. Sometimes the victim is a passenger, whom the driver would be likely to know. I remember one case where a man backed his car over his wife in their driveway."

It was starting to feel as though he'd be dismissed without getting anything, so Ambler said, "According to Dr. Cartwright's notes, neither the police nor prosecutors were aware at the time that Kilgore was acquainted with the victim."

The attorney went silent for a moment, scrutinizing Ambler's face. "You say this professor investigating these alleged crimes was murdered?"

"It's almost for certain."

"By one of the subjects of her investigation?"

"I don't know that. As the police would say, it makes sense to rule them out."

She folded her hands and, elbows on her desk, rested her chin on them. "Come back later this afternoon. I'll ask one of the paralegals to dig out the case so I can look it over. What you say made me think that something might have bothered me at the time." She shook her head. "Don't hold me to that. It may be nothing; I have only the vaguest of memories."

Ambler thought to wander around the town while he waited, but the old-town section he was in consisted of one main street a few blocks long, and a half-dozen side streets with only a couple of buildings or stores on them.

He went to the library after his brief walk and asked for a phone book. When he didn't find a listing for Clifton Kilgore, he asked at the desk if the man had a library card. The young woman at the desk, after consulting with the library director, told him they weren't allowed to provide that information. He should have known that. Libraries had a long history of protecting the privacy of their readers.

From there, he moved to the library's newspaper file and spent some time looking through back issues for any articles at the time of the accident. He hoped to find the name of the investigating officer. While the newspaper did cover the accident—the name of the road the victim was crossing when she was struck, the fact that it was night, that it was a country road with no streetlights—it didn't provide the names of any of the police who investigated.

The driver was arrested but not charged. A subsequent article reported the name of the driver and that he had been charged with negligent homicide. A sidebar recounted Anna Paxton's life in some detail, quoting an aunt and some high-school friends, like an obituary. She came across as a sweet young girl who loved horses and dogs and had won 4-H prizes for the chickens she raised.

Not finding any follow-up stories about the dropped charges or anything about a connection between Paxton and Kilgore, he gave up on the newspaper and asked for directions to the police station. The same library aide at the checkout desk who wouldn't answer his library card question asked if he wanted the Wolverton Police Department or the county sheriff's office.

In the city, you don't think about such distinctions, so for a moment he didn't know which one he wanted. The sheriff's office was closer to the library, and he reasoned that since the accident happened on a country road, the sheriff's department might be more likely to have covered it.

The sheriff's office was only a five-minute walk. This was an appealing aspect of the small town: everything was close, yet you were surrounded by space. The deputy who greeted him from behind a desk was young, earnest, and had a disarming smile. When he asked how he might help, Ambler recognized that both the greeting and the offer were genuine.

It wouldn't be that they didn't have criminal activity in Wolverton and its environs. Certainly, the deputies dealt with truculent drunks, deranged perpetrators of domestic violence, sullen drug dealers, wise-mouthed teenage troublemakers, rapists, arsonists, and murderers, so the deputy sheriffs had as much right as the city cops to be jaded, mistrustful, rude, and arrogant. Why wasn't this guy?

Remembering his walk through town and his more recent walk from the library to the sheriff's office, he wondered if it might not be the fresh air, the open spaces, the clear blue sky, and the leisurely pace at which the day unfolded—no jostling on the street, no blaring horns, no trucks or buses belching diesel exhaust.

Ambler told the deputy he was looking for the officer who had investigated a fatal accident nearly ten years ago. Clearly, the deputy was too young to have been on the force at the time. He might be too young to even remember it. "It involved a man named Clifton Kilgore."

The deputy surprised him. "That would be Sergeant Greenleaf. He was a deputy working patrol at the time and covered the accident."

"I wouldn't have thought you'd remember that far back."

"He's my father." The young deputy smiled. "It was a big deal at the time because of the prominent family."

Like father, like son, I hope, Ambler said to himself. "Is the sergeant available at the moment, by any chance? I'd like to ask him about the accident." The reasonable thing would be for the deputy to ask why he was so interested. But he didn't.

"He's at an accident scene. I'll let him know you want to talk to him. He'll probably come in pretty quick."

Why would he do that, Ambler wanted to ask but didn't.

The deputy told him anyway. "He'd be more than happy to talk to someone about Clifton Kilgore."

Once more, Ambler thought to ask a question but didn't. He'd wait for Sergeant Greenleaf to tell him why he'd be anxious to talk about Mr. Kilgore. The wait wasn't long. The deputy radioed his pop and twenty minutes later Ambler was sitting in a county sheriff's patrol car chatting with a man who was a broader and grayer version of his son, and just as amiable.

"I spoke to that young woman professor not so long ago," Sergeant Greenleaf said when Ambler told him about Robin Cartwright and why he'd come to Wolverton. "She came out here to talk with me, just like you're doing now." He nodded vigorously as a point of emphasis. "That young lady was as smart as a whip. She knew police procedure and how the criminal justice system worked as well as I did."

Ambler watched some movement in his eyes, a change of expression. Where at first his expression was guarded and maybe challenging. Now his face clouded with sadness. "She was murdered?" He folded his hands on his midsection and closed his eyes. "I'm sure sorry to hear that . . . 'Father of mercies and God of all comfort, have mercy on her soul.'"

When he opened his eyes again, he said, "No nonsense about her, she was determined. She was nice too, polite. You'd expect a lady college professor, from the city no less, to lord it over a small-town lawman out in the sticks. But she was respectful. She knew what she was doing, too. I thought for sure she'd come up with something. She said she'd let me know if she did.

"I've been waiting years to hang something on Clifton Kilgore that would stick." He adjusted himself in the seat, removing his hands from his belly and folding his arms across his chest, rattling his law enforcement accoutrements as he did. "I guess I'll need to wait some more." And after a moment, "You picking up where she left off?"

"Not exactly. I'm more interested in finding the person who killed her."

The sergeant nodded, and after a moment said, "You think Clifton?"

Ambler had no reason to think that, yet he said, "If he was guilty of murder and she was about to expose the crime, that would be a reason to silence her." He asked the big question. "Did Kilgore run down Anna Paxton on purpose?"

The sergeant answered as if he expected the question. "I can't say he did. At the time, I didn't think he did it on purpose. I thought he was careless, negligent. To me, it didn't look like he tried to avoid her. He said he didn't see her. My thinking was he should've. If he didn't, he wasn't looking. I charged him with negligent homicide. That didn't work out so well.

"When she was here, Miss Cartwright told me Cliff knew the girl he ran over. If I'd known that at the time, it might have been different. But even so, it wasn't up to me. I was pretty new. My job was to file the accident report and note what I saw and what the driver or any witnesses said. It was up to the crime detectives to investigate.

"Up to then, I'd seen one fatal accident. And I'd never seen a pedestrian accident like that. I was shaking like a leaf. Cliff was as calm as if he'd run over a squirrel. It bothered me he didn't care about the girl. What he cared about was making me believe the accident wasn't his fault. He wanted to get away with killing her, and he did."

The radio had been intermittently calling out streets and numbers and asking different cars for their locations. Ambler wasn't able to follow any of the back-and-forth. The sergeant did, and this time when the radio spoke he picked up his microphone and said, "10-4. I'm right outside."

He turned back to Ambler. "Ten years ago, Wolverton was a small town." He gestured toward the town around them. "I mean a small town in its way of thinking, too.

"When I was a boy, everyone knew everyone. Things were done with a handshake, off the record, you might say. A deputy caught a boy shoplifting, he might take him home to his folks. Guys were drunk and fighting, he'd throw 'em in the cooler to calm down and send them on their way in the morning.

"As new people moved out from the city, they brought their

attitudes with them. Change came slowly, but it came. Even ten years ago, we still had those small-town attitudes. I went out on patrol, I knew most everyone I saw. If I didn't know their name, I'd know where they lived or where they worked. Most things were still settled off the cuff, you might say, outside of the criminal justice system. We knew who the troublemakers were and we knew the big wheels.

"With Clifton, you got some of both. When I brought him in, his father was already there at the sheriff's office with a lawyer, a friend of his, sitting in the captain's office with the captain and the lieutenant. A fatal crash, one of them would have come in anyway. But I could see how this was going. They were chatting and laughing like good ol' boys having a beer.

"Luke Kilgore was a big wheel. Big wheels got special treatment. I didn't like it. But that's how it was, part of life, like heat in the summer. Luke and the lawyer made a big fuss over Cliff. No one spoke about the girl. I made my report. Nobody investigated anything.

"Later, I heard—I don't remember how I knew. Maybe I didn't for sure—Luke Kilgore made a donation to the girl's family. The family'd had some hard times—financial troubles. That was the end of it." He took time to take off his hat and scratch his head. "That was until the professor showed up.

"Like I said, I didn't know at the time of the accident that Cliff knew the girl . . . I don't know it right now. At least, I can't prove it. Miss Cartwright said she was going to get me the proof." He grimaced and turned away to look out the window. "I guess that won't happen now." He stared at whatever he was looking at. "You don't know what she had on him, do you?"

Ambler was going to ask him the same question. "Her notes were sketchy. You said you spoke with her, yet she didn't record anything about your conversation in her notes."

The sergeant turned back, his eyes were misty, not the hard-cop stare Ambler expected from lawmen. "That's because what I said was off the record. Luke Kilgore is still a big mucky-muck in the county, head of the Republican Party. He got rich brokering the buying and selling of land for most of the development that's happened around here." Greenleaf spoke gruffly. "This conversation, by the way, is off the record, too. You got me?"

It troubled Ambler, as it often did, how tentative so many Americans were about speaking up or getting involved in anything that might disturb the powers-that-be—people you'd think secure in their jobs and their lives who should have more spine. "Fine. I don't keep records. Robin . . . Professor Cartwright . . . got her information somewhere. Do you know who she spoke with besides you?"

"I know she talked to folks . . . I didn't want to know who." He lowered his voice. "I got the idea she might have met up with the girl's family, maybe some folks who know Clifton. He's pretty well known in the area. She spent a couple of days here, so I expect she found out some things. She didn't want to tell me what she found until she got everything nailed down."

"Any chance you'd start an investigation now?"

"Not without a helluva lot of new evidence." The radio crackled again. He gave it a dirty look and picked up the mic. "I'm right here, damn it. I said I'd be in."

"Before you go, can you tell me what Clifton Kilgore has been up to the last ten years?"

The sergeant stopped halfway out of the car and turned to face Ambler. "There's a bar and grill up on Main Street called the Happy Tavern. The bartender's name is Lorrie. She'll tell you all you need to know about Cliff. Tell her I sent you."

By then, it was well into the afternoon. Ambler had planned to spend the night and had made a reservation at a B&B which turned out to be a stately Victorian house, painted a subdued purple with more vibrant purple on the window and door frames, on the main street a couple of blocks outside the commercial section of town, a few minutes' walk from the Happy Tavern.

The slightly built white-haired man who checked him in and showed him to his room on the second floor appeared anxious to chat, reminding Ambler a couple of times not to miss the wine reception that evening at five. There's nothing wrong with being friendly and welcoming, Ambler told himself, though one gets weary of pleasantness. You'd want some gruffness now and again and perhaps a touch of rudeness.

When he found his way to the Happy Tavern and Lorrie the bartender, he thought he might have found the gruffness he missed. She was as close as you could get to a female version of his pal McNulty.

"What're you drinkin'?" She leaned toward him across the bar, not too close, looked him in the eye but didn't smile.

He ordered a draft beer from a local brewery and watched her for a moment. Clearly on the downhill side of forty, she was long and lanky with a faded prettiness and the weathered features and gravelly voice of a long-time steady drinker. She placed a coaster and the stein of beer in front of him but didn't stay around to chat. Still, when she met his gaze for a second, he noticed gentleness in her eyes that belied her gruffness.

After he'd finished half his beer and she'd finished her animated conversation with the waitress at the far end of the bar, she moseyed back close enough for him to tell her Sergeant Greenleaf had suggested he talk with her if he wanted to find out anything about Clifton Kilgore.

She stopped with a jolt and came back to lean on the bar in front of him, her eyes open wide, her tone that of a beat cop with thirty years on the job. "Why would you want to know about Cliff? Al should have told you—the less you know of him the better; I ought to know."

He didn't know how much to tell Lorrie about why he wanted to know about Kilgore. And he didn't want to lie. "A woman I knew back in New York told me I should look him up."

This was sort of true but not really. "I asked at the sheriff's office and the sergeant told me I should ask you. I don't know why." This was also true in its own way. He hadn't thought before about how two truths put together might make a lie . . . and he wasn't going to think about it for long now because he'd gotten Lorrie talking.

"Al told you to talk to me because I'll tell you the truth. Clifton Kilgore is a schemer and a liar, a 100 percent phony. A fraud." She spoke each word like she was hammering nails. "Either your friend doesn't know him well or she wanted to set you up for trouble." She stood up straight for a moment, glanced at the two other patrons a dozen barstools away at the far end of the bar. Her tone became thoughtful.

"The other possibility is she hasn't seen through him yet." Something like sadness floated in her eyes. "A lot of folks haven't. He gets near to a hundred or so people to that fake church of his, no matter how many lies he tells." She looked toward the ceiling, as if she were making a pronouncement to the assembled, though there was only him and the two other afternoon tipplers. "People are like sheep."

"Church?" he asked himself. "Church?" he asked out loud.

"The Wolverton Church of Jesus Christ. It's not a church. It's a scam." More nails hammered. Kilgore had opened the church—a non-denominational church— goin' on twenty years ago, she told him. He picked up believers because he told folks he'd talked with God. God told him to open the church and believers would come.

"Cliff's a charismatic guy. He could sell ice boxes to Eskimos. In fact, before he started the church, he owned a used car lot where he sold clunkers to poor people—on time and for twice what the junk heaps were worth. They'd come back and tell him he'd sold them a lemon and they wanted their money back. Virginia's a buyer-beware state so that wasn't going to happen.

"He'd sit down and commiserate with the guy. He'd have tears in his eyes just like the poor dumb fool he'd put in debt up to his eyeballs." She laughed, not mirthlessly as you might expect. Ambler liked her. She appreciated the irony in life.

"Then, to make amends, he'd sell the poor bastard another clunker and put him even deeper in debt. I wouldn't be surprised if folks are still making weekly payments to him all these years later. Ain't none of them folks goin' to his church, you can bet. You can believe *they* saw the light."

She looked at him and then at his empty stein. "You want another?"

He didn't. He should have nursed the one he ordered. But he wanted her to keep talking so he ordered one.

"Do you mind my asking how you know so much about Mr.

Kilgore?" Perhaps he should say Pastor Kilgore. It was amazing that someone could just start up a church—open up for business, give it a name, tell folks God told him to do it—and that would be legal. Even more astounding, people would come and worship, or whatever they did.

"I was married to him is how I know the scheming asshole." She scrutinized Ambler for a moment. "You want to know about Cliff and a woman from New York told you about him—"

"She didn't really tell me about him—" he began. Something was dawning on him.

Something dawned on her, too. "A woman was here a while back asking about him, too. But she wasn't from New York—"

"A professor?"

"You're working with her? I thought about that when you first asked, but it's not so unusual for someone to ask about Cliff—someone he swindled; a guy whose wife he's fooling around with. I shoulda thought you might be working with her when you said Al sent you."

"She's dead." Ambler didn't mean to be so blunt. He saw that he'd shocked the woman. "Someone killed her."

"My God! How awful. The poor woman . . . I told her she was treading on dangerous ground. Running afoul of Clifton is something folks around here are wary of. I am. I know what he can do when he's threatened . . . If he knew I was talking to you now, he'd be on me like a hawk on a chicken." She glared at Ambler. "He'd better not know."

"He won't know from me. I'm willing to believe he's a dangerous man." He again weighed how much he should tell her. He didn't know what Robin had asked her or told her. He didn't know how loyal Lorrie might still be to Kilgore or how afraid of him she might be. "Did Robin . . . Professor Cartwright . . . tell you why she was interested in your ex-husband?"

"She wanted to know about the accident. She wanted to know about Cliff and Anna Paxton. That professor was pretty smart. No one around here caught on to what he did with the girl. Anna was a minor and he was having sex with her."

"You know that?"

"I know what happened with him and young girls. I was fifteen when I married him." She sounded belligerent as she said this, but after a few seconds her expression changed to what might have been bewilderment and then sadness.

"That was legal?"

"Then, it was. Fifteen and pregnant, with parental consent. My mother was an alcoholic and stupid on top of that. She told me I was lucky Cliff would have me since I was a slut." Lorrie went to the service bar and poured some vodka into a rocks glass and drank it. "Well, that's enough about me." She smiled, which became a grimace. She put some ice cubes in the glass, poured more vodka and walked back to stand in front of Ambler.

"Cliff has been seducing—or raping—teenage girls since he was a teenager himself. He finds girls like me when I was young. Latchkey kids, they called us. Throwaway kids. No kind of home life. No one cared whether we came or went. Cliff would find one. He comforts her; he cares for her; she pours her heart out to him. I was sleeping on couches at my friends' houses or wherever I could. He found me sleeping in his church one night.

"He comforts you and sympathizes with you and then he fucks you. Fifteen, fourteen, thirteen, whatever. Little Anna was a child. I think she was thirteen when he met her. He'd bring her to the house, so it looked to the world like the pastor and his wife had taken her in. I didn't find out about the sex until after she was dead.

"Your friend the professor asked me if he killed her on purpose that night when he ran her over . . . I didn't think that was possible, that he could do such a thing. You'd think I'd have gotten over being so innocent like that, the kind of life I had. I knew he was scum; I didn't believe he was a killer. I don't know if I believe it now."

# FOURTEEN

Ambler went back to his B&B in time for the wine reception. He had a lot to think about, so wasn't so much interested in the reception; it was only him and his host. He planned to take a couple of sips of wine and head to his room, until his host, whose name was Charles Towner, told him his wife wouldn't be there that evening because she was at a church service.

Ambler thought for a moment and took a guess. "The Wolverton Church of Jesus Christ?"

"You know of it? And Pastor Kilgore?"

Ambler nodded. He was on a roll so he kept going. "I was told he's a fraud." He waited, knowing he took a chance saying this. But he'd sensed from his tone that Charles Towner might not be a fan of the preacher.

The innkeeper was about to take a sip from his wine glass but stopped so suddenly he sloshed a good bit over the rim. His eyes went wide. "A fraud, you say?"

"I'm really asking you. It's something I heard. You know him better than I do. I've never met the man."

"To tell you the truth . . ." Charles, who liked to be called Charlie, glanced about the room, lowered his voice, narrowed his eyes. "I stopped going to service myself. Sally—my wife Sally—says the man walks with God.

"Most of the congregation are women who are kind of taken with him. If you went there now, you might be the only man in the place. Not that you'd find many there at all. It's not a big congregation, maybe fifty people, a hundred on special Sundays. Pastor Kilgore is a slick talker. Silver tongued."

Charlie took a slug of his wine and refilled his glass, taking another slug before he got back to what he was saying, warming to the topic as he spoke.

"Sally and I took a good part of our life savings to open

this inn. We like serving people. We're convivial. This is work we love. Nonetheless, we need to make money to pay the bills. We need to be profitable to keep the inn going. We're not money hungry. I was lucky in life and made a good living. The inn is doing well. Even so, I don't want to give my hard-earned savings away for nothing.

"The pastor, if you look at him closely, you'll see he has dollar signs for eyes." Charles went on at length about the Wolverton Church of Jesus Christ and its myriad money-making operations. "There's the tithe—ten percent of your income off the top. Never mind you've got medical bills to pay. Never mind your roof needs fixin'. God forbid wanting to enjoy your old age and maybe take a vacation.

"Actually, if you ask the pastor, God does forbid it. The Lord gets paid first, right off the top, and Pastor Kilgore will take the contribution and pass it along to the Lord through his ministries—after taking his cut for expenses. Those include a fancy house a few miles out of town with ten or twelve acres, and a small herd of horses that he can use to ride to the hounds. That's in addition to a small cottage behind the church and a top-of-the-line Ford F-350.

"From the pulpit, he told us, 'Tithing is an act of worship and obedience to the Lord. Some people haven't had the opportunity to deepen their faith by tithing but they need to get on board if they want to be saved.'" Charlie turned an angry gaze on Ambler, "'Deepen their faith.' That's what he said."

The church had Pastor Kilgore's wife and his brother on the payroll. The wife was in charge of the Bible school and a nursery school. The brother was the sexton and ran the church store, as well as an online marketplace that sold all manner of religious articles, along with baseball caps, sweatshirts, umbrellas, and whatnot emblazoned with slogans from the Bible—"The Lord is my shepherd"; "The wages of sin are death", and such—along with the name of the church.

The innkeeper sipped his wine and continued a litany of indictments of the church and its pastor. Despite his anger and his vehemence, Ambler could see this was painful for the man, who more than once pronounced himself "a good Christian."

"In the church we belonged to back home, I was on the board of elders for a bit." His tone was modest as he said this, as if Ambler would understand the importance of such a position, and went on—in case Ambler didn't understand its importance—to tell him that elders, in addition to their spiritual role, kept an eye on the budget, might make a recommendation here and there, and more or less made everyone confident things were on the up-and-up.

He looked glumly at Ambler. "I asked Pastor Kilgore about that. Did his church have elders?

"'Didn't need 'em,' he told me. The congregation was small and every member of the church knew all there was to know about him and about the church and had as much say as anyone else in how things were done. His life was an open book . . . That's what he said, 'an open book'. . . But no one's ever gotten to open the church's books."

Ambler and the innkeeper talked for another hour or so and drank a couple more glasses of wine. Sally, the churchgoing wife, had left a casserole which they ate for dinner.

That Clifton Kilgore was a charlatan was well established, though it wasn't so clear that any of his money-making schemes were illegal. His congregation believed he was in touch with God and that by following his lead they were on the pathway to heaven, so whatever he did he must have a good reason.

Charlie had tried to talk his wife into finding another church, but she wouldn't hear of it. He did manage to protect most of the income from the inn from the tithing. He gave Sally half the income each month after deducting expenses, so she gave the church 10 percent of that. He thought she was crazy. But she did what she wanted.

The rumors about the minister's sexual dalliances were another matter. "Sally doesn't believe anything anyone says against him." From his tone, Ambler gathered he'd tried. "It's hard to argue with her because no one has come forward to make a complaint against him." Charlie looked at Ambler helplessly. "Who would they complain to? He's his own boss."

Ambler didn't put much faith in rumors. If you accuse someone of something you should have proof—catching the pastor coming out of Gertrude's house at five in the morning when her husband is on a business trip might mean something; a different husband finding the preacher in bed with his wife would carry a good deal of weight. Innuendo shouldn't count for much.

In this instance, though, he'd make an exception about the rumors. He wouldn't spread any but he wanted to know what they were. If he could find a woman hinted to have been led down the garden path by Kilgore, and who was willing to talk about it, even if she wasn't willing to come forward with an accusation, she might tell him something about the pastor others didn't know about. Charlie hadn't heard tell of such a person. But he said he'd try to find out.

First thing in the morning, after breakfast—sausage, eggs, and grits—in a small diner on Main Street, forgoing the B&B breakfast, Ambler made his way to the church, a Quonset hut-like building, with a large garage door at one end, set in a spacious paved parking area on the highway headed north out of town. It looked to Ambler like it might once have been an auto repair shop. A prominent billboard-sized sign read: The Wolverton Church of Jesus Christ. All Are Welcome, along with the times of various services, and the pastor's name.

He'd planned to speak with the wife or the brother. But as luck would have it, the pastor himself opened the door of the church when Ambler rang the bell next to a side door. Ambler hadn't thought through how he'd approach Clifton Kilgore. Actually, he'd thought about it quite a bit, but hadn't come up with a good plan. So he was as surprised as Kilgore when he said, "I was passing by, saw the church, and had a strange urge to stop in, sit for a few moments, and say a prayer. Something about the church attracted me."

"That was God talking to you." The pastor, who for some reason Ambler knew was the pastor and not the brother, wore a welcoming smile. He beamed when he smiled, as sunny a visage as anyone could wish for; fresh-faced, smooth-shaven, no blemishes, locks of curly auburn hair. You'd think of him as someone who really did want to befriend you; amiable, eager to please. The effect was disarming.

He put his arm protectively around Ambler's shoulder and walked him toward the pews. "Come right in, sit down, and talk to the Lord. I have a couple of things to take care of. If you're here when I come back in a few minutes, we can have a cup of coffee."

The pews consisted of one-by-eight boards stretched across stools. They looked a bit rickety, but the stools were close together so it didn't look like the boards would give way. At the front of the hall were a few substantial, red plush armchairs on a riser, and a fortress-like pulpit that you stepped up to from the riser and that loomed over the pews like the bridge of a ship over the deck.

It was probably not such a good thing to meet Pastor Kilgore under false pretenses. But here he was; the deed was done. The church—the physical layout of the place—wasn't the least bit inspiring, probably no more so than when it was an auto repair shop. The pastor was another story. Charlie Towner had called him "silver-tongued." Ambler hadn't heard him preach yet but could already feel his charisma.

One way to get to know him a bit would be by asking about the church—not the building, the religion—what they believed in; how it was different from another church. Kilgore had probably told the origin story dozens of times and had it polished as smoothly as stones in a river. What would happen, Ambler wondered, if he asked about Anna Paxton or Robin Cartwright?

The pastor was back in no time, with two containers of coffee and packets of cream and sugar.

"Black," Ambler said. "Do passersby often stop by your church? Is it a way station for weary travelers?"

"Not really." The pastor was relaxed, his manner congenial. Ambler sensed he was comfortable with strangers, liked engaging with others, not something Ambler himself was especially inclined toward. "We're a small congregation. God-fearing folks from town and some of the surrounding area come to our prayer meeting and Sunday services. Are you new to the town, or passing through?"

"Passing through. I had some business here. Do you know the Paxton family?"

Kilgore's expression changed dramatically, from the placid, friendly, perhaps innocent face of the guileless to the fierce, shrewd and angry face of a warrior. The pastor may have been a silver-tongued conman, handsome and charming as a prince, but he was no poker player. He couldn't control his features to hide his anger. And it might be he couldn't control the anger either.

After a long pause, he said dismissively, "I know of the family." He appeared uneasy as he waited to hear what Ambler would say next.

To keep him off balance, Ambler switched topics and asked about the church. Kilgore was still eager to talk but his manner had changed; the smile was there but behind it was wariness. He nonetheless spoke with the fervor of a man without doubts.

"We believe the Bible tells us the truth and we live by what it says. We believe to enter heaven one must be born again. We believe that any man or woman can be saved because Jesus Christ died on the Cross to redeem all who are willing to be saved."

Despite the authority in his tone, his answer didn't sound sincere. Ambler wanted to push him on that, too. "A lot of churches do those things. Why would anyone choose this particular church, as opposed to another? Why choose you as its pastor? Are you ordained?"

If Ambler expected an angry, defensive response, he was disappointed. Pastor Kilgore's expression became placid again, trancelike. "I never trained for the ministry. I received a calling . . . Who knows how the Lord works? He needed me to establish a church here. I was as surprised as anyone; I didn't ask for the calling. I resisted it. But God wanted me here to save souls who might not otherwise find their way to salvation."

Then, he turned quickly and, like a sudden storm, unleashed his fire and brimstone tone on Ambler, his eyes blazing. "Have you embraced Jesus? Have you been born again? Are you tending to your own salvation?"

Having done none of these things, and not expecting such vehemence, Ambler withered under the attack. He could see why folks might cave in under an onslaught from this man who'd turned on a dime and taken on the aspect of Moses charging down the mountain with the Ten Commandments.

"I'm looking into it," he said meekly.

Kilgore lowered his eyebrows, narrowed his eyes, and scrutinized Ambler. The preacher's manner, when he wasn't thundering hell and damnation or cajoling with charm and warmth, was at its heart condescending, Ambler realized. The shepherd watched over his flock, but held himself far superior to the sheep who followed him. Wasn't that what Lorrie, his ex-wife, had called his followers, sheep?

Maybe because he didn't like Kilgore's arrogance, or perhaps it was his hypocrisy or his narcissism, Ambler let his anger take over and went after Pastor Kilgore where he was weakest. It might have been a mistake to show his hand, but sometimes you throw a monkey wrench into the works and see what happens.

"I wonder," Ambler's tone was judicious, "if the accident that killed Anna Paxton had anything to do with your road-to-Damascus moment—the guilt, the remorse. I wonder if you felt a need to make amends for the tragedy. You might have needed to devote your life to serving others to atone for a terrible transgression."

Kilgore stared at him like he was watching Satan walk up into the church from the basement. His face drained of color. His mouth worked; no words came out but fire was building in his eyes. "Who are you?" He stood and his glance ricocheted around the empty church, as if looking for a weapon.

For Ambler, who followed the preacher's gaze, the Wolverton Church of Jesus Christ in the dim light looked old and worn; for all the world, it felt like the auto repair shop it once was, the scent of axle grease and old engine oil seeping into the air.

"Get out!" the pastor roared, as if to dispatch the devil.

Ambler kept his seat. Despite the pastor's booming voice and arrogant manner, the man was slight of build and didn't look like he'd be much of a bouncer.

Having made his demand and gotten no response, Kilgore lost his nerve. He had no audience other than Ambler to appeal to. It didn't look like the Lord would step in and help him out.

Ambler waited a moment for Kilgore's dilemma to sink in on him before he spoke.

"To answer your question, I'm a friend of Robin Cartwright's. If you don't remember, she's the woman who was on her way to proving you murdered Anna Paxton before she was murdered herself."

Kilgore sat down heavily, knocking over his half-empty container of coffee as he did so. He watched the coffee spill onto the plank-pew and then the floor with such grief that Ambler thought he might cry.

"It was an accident." Kilgore's tone was subdued. He was bent over, clutching his hands between his knees. "Everyone knew it was an accident. I didn't see her. No one ever said I saw her." He pleaded with his eyes, like a beggar might look at a passerby. Ambler almost felt sorry for him. And then he said, ". . . Until that crazy woman came with her cockeyed story."

Ambler felt fine leaning on him after that and bore down. "You didn't admit you knew the girl. Why? . . . Because if you did, someone might look into what your relationship was. If they did, they might have found you had something to hide. They might have found you had a reason to kill Anna, that you'd had a sexual relationship with her. She could ruin your life, put you in jail . . . You shut her up so she wouldn't tell the world you were having sex with an underage girl."

"You're crazy." The pastor pulled himself together. He wasn't dumb by any means; he possessed the shrewdness of the truly evil. He'd murdered a girl, lived with it on his conscience for years while he ran a sham religion, bilking people who didn't have much to begin with out of what little they had. This wasn't a man who'd fall apart at the seams being confronted with his past sins.

"None of that happened." His voice took on the tone of a censoring cleric. "Yes, I knew Anna. I knew her as a spiritual adviser. The poor girl had a troubled childhood, a very difficult home life. Her family—as you must know if you've been with them—was dysfunctional.

"She was a lost child and I helped her find grace. I taught

her to walk with the Lord. I didn't expect Him to take her home so soon. He must have seen no other way for her; her path on earth would be too hard. She would have strayed as she got older, so He took her to Him while she was still an innocent."

The pastor had regained his customary superciliousness that he wore like his clerical garb. "I don't know why He used me as His instrument. I was horrified. I couldn't understand. I struggled coming to grips with why He'd let that happen to her, why He'd let that happen to me. Sometimes Satan gets a hold on you. You need to battle to get free. I almost lost my faith over what happened to Anna. I cursed God for making me the instrument of her death. It took time for me to accept that it's not for me to know the Lord's ways."

"So you didn't want to admit to being spiritual adviser to a young girl. You didn't tell anyone you knew the child you killed. Why?"

Kilgore sat trancelike, as if he'd forgotten Ambler was with him. Either he didn't want to answer, or he couldn't form the words to do so. To Ambler, it looked like he'd been struck dumb.

"Because you were sleeping with her. I can't think of another reason."

Kilgore came out of his trance. "I was not. What you say is slanderous. If you state that to anyone else or make that slander public, I'll sue you." He gathered up steam. "I'm asking you to leave. Now! If you don't, I'm prepared to call the police."

As the preacher spoke, Ambler was half-listening because he'd realized something he should have thought of before. Robin's notes were sketchy. How did she know the truth about Kilgore? She'd created her database a few years before she started on the book. She went through newspapers from a half-dozen states whose newspapers she'd had access to. There had to be a suspicious death of a woman and a man who had some murky connection to the woman. She picked the three she was writing about because she came up with something more incriminating about them.

Everything doesn't get written down. Much of what

happened surrounding the death of her friend in her own life, she hadn't written down. Just as in the case of Sofia Torres's death in the Bronx, someone had told her about Anna Paxton's death. In Sofia's case, her friend Emma had written a paper for a college class that a professor sent to Robin.

Since Robin knew about Cliff Kilgore and Anna Paxton, someone had to have told her, which meant someone besides the pastor knew Cliff Kilgore murdered Anna Paxton. Whether he'd murdered Robin and Blake Beasley was a different question. The man from her past that Robin had dinner with whom she called "Preacher" might well have been Kilgore. Ambler was tempted to challenge him on it. Yet there was no other evidence to suggest they'd had any relationship in the past, so it would be better to wait.

There wasn't evidence that someone knew Kilgore had purposely run over Anna Paxton either. Yet that had to be the case. There was no question for Ambler that he needed to look for that someone. What was troubling was—now that Kilgore was threatened with exposure—he might be looking for that person, too. Kilgore might have killed Robin once he knew she was on to him. He might have killed Beasley for the same reason. And now he would need to kill the person who told Robin Cartwright he was a murderer, and perhaps kill Ambler as well.

# FIFTEEN

Anna Paxton's father, whose given name was Albert, lived in a trailer on a lot littered with scrub-brush, on a hillside off the main highway about nine miles west of Wolverton. Her mother had passed away a couple of years after Anna's death. Whether she'd died of grief wasn't known. Her death was from complications related to diabetes, and she'd been a heavy drinker for years even before Anna's death.

Ambler got this information, as well as directions, from Kilgore's ex-wife Lorrie, and had no trouble finding the rundown trailer. He did have quite a bit of trouble with a mean-tempered mongrel chained to a post in what there was of a front yard. The chain was long enough for the dog to reach the door to the trailer and anyone standing in front of it. The dog himself didn't act like he'd be susceptible to the "come-here-nice-doggie" approach, so Ambler sat in the car to see if the trailer's resident would take note of the barking and come out.

Noticing the curtain on the small window alongside the door move enough for someone to take a peek gave him some hope, but after a few moments when the door didn't open, the hope faded. He didn't have a phone number and, even if he did, it wouldn't do any good because, he noticed, he didn't have cell service that far out in the country. He'd have to go back to town to the Happy Tavern and get the phone number from Lorrie. Or . . .

He revved up the engine of the car, leaned on the horn, dropped the car into gear and drove directly at the dog, who—given a taste of his own medicine—turned tail and headed for the back of the trailer. Ambler got as close as he could to the trailer door and, remembering how proud country folks were about not locking their doors, bounded out of the car before Fang could get his feet under him again and barged through the trailer door. Mr. Paxton was seated in a Morris chair, drinking a can of Miller Light, watching what looked like an old Western on television.

There was, however, another trait of country folks that Ambler realized he'd failed to consider. Before his eyes had fully adjusted to his new surroundings, Mr. Paxton was out of his chair and standing across the room, pointing a double-barreled shotgun at him.

"Whoa!" said Ambler. "I was trying to get past the dog. I didn't have time to knock."

"If I'da wanted you to come in, I'da opened the door. I've a good mind to put the dog on you anyways. Fuckin' salesmen don't know how to take no for an answer." The man holding the gun was remarkably calm, not the least bit jittery, as easy with the gun as he might be if he were holding his pipe, which rested in an ashtray alongside his Morris chair.

"I'm not a salesman." Ambler chuckled awkwardly. "If you put down the gun, Mr. Paxton, I'll explain. I'm sorry to disturb you. I didn't want to create a ruckus. What I want to ask you about is personal and sensitive. I'm really sorry."

Paxton lowered the barrel of the gun. His expression didn't change much but something flickered in his eyes.

"It's about your daughter."

"Annie's dead. What's more to say about her?" Whatever had flickered went out.

"I'm concerned about how she died. Did a woman, Robin Cartwright, come here to talk with you about her a year or so ago?"

"That's what this is about?" He put the shotgun down, leaning it against the wall in the corner. "At the time when Annie got killed, I woulda killed him myself. Then Annie's mother got sick; time passed, and I didn't."

"Cliff Kilgore?"

"That's who the lady professor wanted to know about. He calls himself a man of God. Anyone what knows him knows he's a child of Lucifer. He brainwashed the girl, filled her with crazy ideas, made her think she was talking to God. She'd say she was getting saved and her mother and me weren't going to get saved." He teared up and his voice broke. "The things he did with her. They're not something any man . . . Even now, I can't stand to . . .

"I don't go into town anymore. I saw him on the street once with a young girl . . . I guess she was a woman . . . a young woman. She was laughing, looking up at him . . . and I mighta killed him right there."

"Would you tell me what you told Robin . . . what you told the lady professor? How did you know what went on with . . . between them?"

"Her diary. . . Annie always liked to write . . . since she learned to make letters in first grade, she wrote a diary."

"A diary? She left a diary?"

"Her mother found it hidden away, way back in her closet. It was weeks later, after the funeral, after everything . . . Martha never got over it. She never got over Annie dying. What was in the diary brought everything back, only worse." The pain was etched into Paxton's face, a grimace as bitter as death. "I couldn't read it. I only looked at a couple of pages. It made me sick. Martha tried to tell me about it. I wouldn't listen."

"You never showed it to anyone, to the police . . .?"

He shook his head slowly. "No reason. Everything had been done. Luke Kilgore had come by and gave us a big check . . . big for us. Nothin' to him. It wouldn't have made any difference to tell anyone about Annie's diary. Nothin' woulda changed."

The television droned on while they talked. Albert Paxton hadn't looked at it; nor had he picked up his pipe or taken a drink from his beer can. He remained standing, looking toward Ambler but not often meeting his gaze.

"Luke Kilgore is a big man in this town. His son is a snake in the grass, and he knows it. He as much as said so when he gave us the money. Martha wouldn't have done it anyway . . . let anyone see the diary. She said tellin' folks about it would besmirch . . . That's what she said 'besmirch' . . . would besmirch Annie's memory."

Ambler kept calm, forced himself not to push the poor man. Paxton spoke slowly, sorting through his memories, maddeningly slowly, stopping for long stretches to stare at the emptiness. He wanted badly to tell Anna's dad how important it might be to see the diary. But to prod him to go deeper into the memories he tried so hard to avoid would be cruel. So he waited while the father talked about his daughter in the years before she was damaged so severely she'd killed herself.

*Killed herself?* Was that what he'd said? Ambler was stunned. He didn't believe what he'd heard. The old man must have said it wrong, understood it wrong. Cliff Kilgore killed Anna, didn't he?

"I don't understand." Ambler's voice shook. "I don't think I heard what you said . . . I understood from Robin, from Professor Cartwright, that Clifton Kilgore intentionally killed your daughter."

"As sure as you're sitting there, he did. Same as if he took a gun to her head." Paxton's voice shook too, but from anger . . . and hatred, not the fear, the horror, that Ambler felt.

"Kilgore ran her over?" Ambler watched the man across from him, who looked back with unseeing eyes. "He ran her over . . . on purpose? He didn't try to avoid her?"

Paxton's face was a mask, frozen into the same look of horror that must have been there the night his daughter died. "She stood by the side of the road across the street from the house and watched his truck come toward her. She knew who it was. She saw him. She stepped right out in front of the truck. I saw it with my own eyes."

Ambler felt the never-ending pain of a father reliving the horror of watching his child die, as deeply as if Paxton had hit him in the heart with a hammer. Along with the pain, the realization that he'd been wrong about how Anna Paxton died also sank in.

He sat with the grieving father a while longer, with Paxton telling him more about his daughter as a child. Ambler had opened a spigot for emotions to pour out by asking about the girl, so he owed it to the man to listen for as long as he wanted to talk.

"Something happened when she became a teenager," he said. "She turned against us." His glances at Ambler as he spoke about this were furtive and apologetic. “Her mother and I took to drinking too much after I couldn’t work no more. I guess that’s what got to Annie. She’d always been the sweetest child.”

The trouble for the Paxtons started when Albert, a rough carpenter, a house framer, fell off a roof and broke his back. He’d been working off the books, so had no insurance or workmen’s compensation. The injury took a long time to heal and left him unable to do the type of physical work he’d been doing. He ended up working at a hardware store for minimum wage.

“We hadn’t been wealthy when I was working construction but we were getting by. After I got hurt, we were poor as church mice. Kids notice things like that and they’re ashamed, so Annie—even though she got good grades, and was cute as a speckled-bellied pup in a red wagon—she got looked down on. She didn’t have things other kids had. She dressed in clothes Martha bought from the thrift store.”

Ambler knew the story; not the poverty, but the troubled home life of a child. His own son had gone from being an angelic child to a mean-tempered, sullen teenager. His mother was an alcoholic who neglected him, and his father, to Ambler’s eternal shame, was absent.

John’s story ended up tragically, with the boy being sent to prison, where miraculously he did reform and become a loving father to his own son. Albert’s Anna never got a chance to recover and reform. The tragedy weighed heavily on Ambler as he drove away from Paxton’s weather-worn trailer, overwhelmed by the pain and suffering in the world. This valley of tears, his mother used to pray.

He was so sick at heart, so angry and depressed that he couldn’t keep his mind on what he’d started out to do. He’d come across evidence that Kilgore had a reason to play a role in Anna Paxton’s death. That role might be criminal and it might not. Ambler wasn’t satisfied Kilgore didn’t kill Anna intentionally. She stepped out in front of the truck. He didn’t try to stop. He could have run off the road to avoid her. Still, her father was right. The fact that Kilgore drove her to suicide and then killed her by accident or on purpose wouldn't make any difference to anyone anymore. Or would it?

It was late in the afternoon; the main street of the town was quiet. The quiet didn't extend to the Happy Tavern, where there was a full bar and folks waiting for tables when he got there. He ordered a beer and a pulled pork sandwich.

Lorrie remembered him but was too busy to spend time talking. Strangely, she had a worried expression when she looked at him, as if she wanted to warn him of something but couldn't. He didn't get a chance to ask her what it was before he felt someone beside him.

"You're the nosy fellow from New York," the man said. It wasn't a question. "I heard you were out here pestering my son."

Ambler didn't turn; he watched Lorrie drawing his beer. "Your son's old enough to speak for himself, Mr. Kilgore. I wouldn't think he'd need you to threaten me on his behalf."

The man didn't acknowledge he'd heard him. "I hope you're satisfied with what you've found out so far and you'll be leaving town this evening."

Ambler, who up to that point was planning to leave, decided on the spot that he wasn't. He was angry enough to do something stupid; a small voice told him to slow down, but he wasn't in the mood to heed it. "I've got unfinished business; I'll be here a while longer. Did you want something from me or just want to pay your respects?"

Luke Kilgore pushed in closer to the bar and in doing so crowded against Ambler. "There's an old saying in the South, sir, that you let sleeping dogs lie."

Ambler, in turn, pushed himself closer to the bar, and in the process crowded the senior Kilgore. They were like kids lining up in a schoolyard, elbowing each other out of the way.

"There's another saying, from a Southerner like yourself," Ambler said. "The past is never dead. It's not even past."

Kilgore pushed himself away from the bar, shoved an elbow into Ambler's ribs as he did, and walked away.

Lorrie the bartender, who'd been watching as she washed glasses, leaned over to Ambler. "That won't be the end of it . . ."

She glanced at Luke Kilgore's back going out the door. "Or for me neither if he finds out I talked to you."

He understood now why she'd ignored him this time when he came in. He finished his beer and headed along Main Street back to the B&B. He'd crossed one side street and was in the middle of the next block when he saw two burly men coming toward him. One was Luke Kilgore. The other was younger and larger, a barrel-chested, long-haired, scruffy-bearded redneck wearing overalls, who lumbered rather than walked along the sidewalk.

As soon as he saw them, Ambler knew this was trouble coming toward him. A jolt of adrenaline hit him, his heartbeat got stronger, his breath came quicker, his body trembled, but he wasn't scared. He slowed his pace and sank into a bow posture. He doubted either of the men would notice the posture or, if they did notice his steps become cat-like, know what he was doing.

His tai chi was rusty; even though he kept up the practice of the form, he hadn't done push hands competitions in a long time. Still, if he focused entirely on the moment, his muscles should remember how to react to an attack.

Pretty much that was what happened. The young man stepped into his path and nudged him hard with his shoulder to knock Ambler aside. Ambler didn't resist but relaxed, rolled with the shove, and kept his balance.

When they turned on each other, Ambler waited, most of his weight on his front leg. As the younger man charged at him, like a defensive tackle lunging toward the quarterback for a sack, Ambler, as soon as he sensed the man touch him, sank his weight into his back leg, turning from the waist as he did so, letting the charging oaf slide past him, providing a slight shove to help him on his way, propelling him stumbling into the brick facade of the building alongside them.

The young man, more like a boy, took a moment to clear his head and charged again. Ambler sank, and again turned with the charge rather than resisting it, not unlike a bullfighter, shoving the boy a little harder this time, propelling him into the street and against the side of a passing car. This encounter spun his antagonist around like a top and he went down. The car he'd run into stopped, as did the car following it and a couple of cars on the opposite side of the street.

Ambler glared at Luke Kilgore and, just for fun, snarled. Kilgore threw his arms up in front of him and stepped back. Ambler went on his way.

When he got back to the B&B, he called the sheriff's office and made an appointment to see Sergeant Greenleaf in the morning. So after breakfast, this time at the B&B, and before he left for New York, he stopped by the sheriff's office.

The sergeant was waiting for him and led him to a bare bones interview room. Ambler, glancing about, noticed the one-way mirror and wondered if anyone was in the observation room watching them. No reason anyone should be, and he didn't care if anyone did.

Sergeant Greenleaf, wearing something between a half-smile and a smirk, looked him over before saying anything. After a disconcerting moment or two, Ambler thought to start the conversation but then decided to wait.

Finally, now with a full-blown smile, Greenleaf said, "Did you by any chance run into Luke Kilgore yesterday evening?"

"As a matter of fact, I did. Or more precisely, he and his young friend ran into me."

"He's due in here later this morning to file a complaint against you. Aggravated assault and battery."

"Against him?"

"Against his nephew."

"The kid who's as big as an ox?"

"That's young Hank Grayson. A pretty good high-school football player a few years ago. Luke arranged a scholarship from a Division Three college down in southwest Virginia with an understanding he'd play football. You know they don't give athletic scholarships at D3, only academic ones. Academics not being young Grayson's strong suit, he flunked out. So he came home and went to work for Uncle Luke as a kind of swamper and gofer."

Ambler nodded "The fact is Kilgore sicced the kid on me. I gave him a shove when he came at me."

Greenleaf rubbed his chin and spoke quietly. "I ain't a lawyer, and I'm not supposed to give you advice." He stood and walked over to the one-way mirror, put his face close to the glass and peered at it. "If you get up close enough, you can see through from this side, too."

He came back to sit across from Ambler. "If it were me, I'd file a counter-complaint against Grayson. That way, it makes sense for both sides to drop their complaints. No one's gonna extradite you from New York anyway."

Ambler filed the complaint and then told Greenleaf about his talk with Anna Paxton's father. "He'd probably let you read the diary. I don't think you'd need a warrant. After all this time, I guess you couldn't charge Kilgore no matter what was in the diary. But I thought you should know."

"Don't be so sure about that. In Virginia we don't have statutes of limitations on most felonies."

Ambler nodded again. "Well, in addition to that, just on a hunch of mine"—Ambler didn't want to mention his hunch being the man named Preacher in another murder victim's diary—"can you check into Clifton Kilgore's whereabouts around the time of Robin Cartwright's death?"

Greenleaf nodded. "We'll be looking into a lot of things about the pastor."

# SIXTEEN

The realization that by attempting to track down Robin's killer he had put himself in danger—but worse than that, much, much worse, that he might have put his loved ones in danger—came to Ambler two days later when Adele called him at the library. Her voice shook with fear and anger.

"Raymond, something has happened."

His heart stopped. His first thought was the baby. But Jennifer was fine. Adele's voice wavered. "A man's been following me. I'm sure of it."

Ambler's knees went weak. Stupidly, he asked, "Are you sure?"

"Of course, I'm sure." Her tone was like stomping her foot. "That's why I said, 'I'm sure of it.' But I wouldn't be thinking this unless something strange had happened."

She'd seen the man twice. "He's hard to describe because he doesn't let me see his face. Each time I see him, it's from the back or the side; he's wearing a baseball cap pulled down over his eyes, or he's wearing sunglasses. Or he's in the shadows, or in a car too far away.

"I probably saw his face the first time, but I wasn't paying attention because I wasn't thinking someone might be following me . . ." She screeched, "Why would someone be following me? I wouldn't think someone was following me—I wouldn't imagine someone was following me—if it wasn't for you!" The rebuke in her tone made him cringe. "Is someone out to get you—or me—because of whatever you're mixed up in this time?"

Words failed him. How would anyone even know about her? But he didn't want to say this because it was dismissive. "I can rent a car right now and drive to River City. I'd be there in a couple of hours."

"Don't do that! . . . It wouldn't do any good. What would you do?"

"I'm coming. In the meantime, call the police and tell them someone is harassing you."

"No. I'm not going to call the police. I don't know who it is, what he looks like, or why he might be following me. Why would they believe me?"

Before he could say anything, she said, "My neighbor is really nice. She has a toddler and stopped by with some baby clothes the other day. She and her husband are both cops, so I could go over and tell her about it." She paused dramatically. "They'd be a lot more help than you'd be anyway."

She was right, of course. He might—if he was lucky—defend himself from a physical attack, like from the young tough the other night. But tai chi wasn't going to stop a bullet. He asked her to call him back after she'd talked to her neighbor.

After pacing his small apartment for a half-hour, he watched his dinner cooking in a frying pan with a dizzying sense that he'd done something terribly wrong. As inept as his investigation might be (he had no idea who he was after), clearly the killer took it seriously.

Anyone with half a brain would know, poking your nose in the wrong place when you're investigating a murder might easily force a killer out of hiding into action. Robin Cartwright opened the Pandora's Box with her book project. Blake Beasley upped the ante when, for whatever stupid reason, he tried to blackmail a killer Robin had uncovered. Both ended up dead in furtherance of their pursuits.

Was Ambler next on the list or—God forbid—Adele and Jennifer? He'd been careless. Why would a killer—covering up a past murder, who'd already murdered two pursuers—not come after the idiot who'd taken up the gauntlet?

He had three suspects left if he ruled out Ricardo Diaz: Robin's ex-husband, George Nagy, who wanted her back; Pastor Kilgore, who could be the mysterious 'Preacher' from her journal entry, and Colonel Doug James, who she believed had a hand in her friend Linda's untimely death.

He'd rattled the cages of two of them. And while they both might have killed in the past, he hadn't found anything to link either of them to the murders of Robin Cartwright or Blake Beasley. That left Colonel Doug James to investigate.

Of course, he could be wrong about all of them. Someone else might have killed Robin. But no one besides the three men she was writing about—not her ex-husband nor one of her colleagues in the visiting professor cohort, nor the man she had dinner with right before her murder, whoever he was—had a reason that he knew of to kill Blake Beasley.

Unless . . . unless the email threatening Robin wasn't sent by one of the subjects of her book but by one of her colleagues. Could she have found out something about one of them and that was who Blake was trying to blackmail? Ambler told himself to stop. He was thinking too much, chasing his own tail.

He recalled the shocking entry in Robin's journal: *I know what you're doing. I won't give in to extortion. I'll die first OR YOU WILL.*

The message was cryptic. It could be referring to something else Robin might have been doing—demanding alimony from her ex-husband, for example. Ambler had understood the threat in the context he knew about. He had every reason to think the threat came from one of the three men she was focusing her investigations on, any of whom she might expose as a murderer. Still, even Robin herself hadn't been sure what the message meant and even thought it might have been from her ex-husband.

He calmed himself down and thought everything through a couple more times. After Adele called to tell him her neighbors took her seriously and would keep an eye out for anything suspicious, he did calm down and decide to keep doing what he was doing.

There also might be another explanation for someone following Adele that had nothing to do with his investigation. And he didn't need to worry so much about her at the moment if her neighbors would watch out for her. What he'd concentrate on now until he hit a dead end was the killer who'd turned the tables on him.

He had only one suspect from Robin's research left to

confront, so he'd trust his instinct and see what he might find out about Colonel Doug James. What happened with that would determine what he'd do next.

The sensible thing would be to do some research on the man. Unfortunately for Ambler, despite his years working at the 42nd Street Library, he wasn't a librarian. He was a curator; his work revolved around subject area expertise—in his case crime fiction—and not librarian expertise. He didn't know any more about using the library's indexes and databases than a man off the street.

At the information desk in the Rose reading room, he'd hoped to find someone he knew. No such luck. The research librarian on duty had no idea who Ambler was. The databases the librarian sent him to—the Defense Manpower Data Center and the Servicemembers Civil Relief Act Centralized Verification Service—appeared to have been set up for bill collectors wishing to dun someone in the military. They were cumbersome to work through, required registration, and asked for information he didn't have.

All in all, they were too much work, the information in them was boring, and it wouldn't tell him what he wanted to know anyway. He wanted the librarian to do the research, like Adele used to do, point him to all the information the library had on Colonel Doug James. Tell him which buttons to push, which indexes to search.

He gave up after a few minutes and went back to the reference desk and asked about newspapers that would cover Chicopee, Massachusetts. This the librarian did help with. He looked something up and wrote down for Ambler, the *Springfield Republican*, the *Hampshire Gazette*, and some Boston papers.

He asked the librarian to show him how to use the microfiche reader.

The librarian looked at him curiously "You said you work at a library?" His tone suggested he was dealing with a moron.

"I work in *this* library. Would you please show me how to use the machine?" His tone was irate but he felt like an idiot. He searched through the newspapers for another hour, finding little about Linda Porter or her death, only an obituary, and not much more about Colonel James, although he did find where he worked. Back to the shoe leather.

The next morning, he once more booked a flight to Bradley Field in Hartford, rented a car, and this time drove to the offices of High Alert Security Professionals in Springfield, a few miles north of Robin Cartwright's hometown Longmeadow. The city, a one-time prosperous manufacturing center, was still trying to recover from deindustrialization—and not doing a great job at it.

Ambler had discovered—in his otherwise fruitless library research—that Colonel Douglas James, USAF-retired, was a vice-president at the security company. He'd also discovered that the retired military man's place of employment provided—among the company's many services: security guards, mobile patrol, loss prevention, event security, executive protection—cyber security, which, if Ambler understood the concept correctly, meant the company knew how to protect people from things like receiving anonymous threatening emails. Which in turn meant that folks at the company would know how to track down the sender of such emails.

Directly confronting Colonel James probably wasn't the best approach—especially after their initial encounter at Robin's funeral—but it was the only approach he could think of. He would simply say he was following up on Robin Cartwright's research and wanted to ask him a few questions.

The decorated fighter pilot and veteran of the Iraq War and the mission in Afghanistan—according to his bio on the company's website—might throw him out on his ear as soon as he opened his mouth. Or he might not. Both of Robin's suspects he'd talked to so far had told him a lot—maybe to justify themselves, maybe to mislead him; he'd figure that out later. It would be interesting to see how Colonel Doug James handled a couple of probing questions.

It did take a bit of doing to get past the security guard in the lobby. But after he repeated three or four times, "It's a personal matter I can only discuss with Colonel James," curiosity got the best of someone and he was let through.

James didn't get up from the desk he sat behind. He raised his eyebrows and might have opened his eyes a little wider and waited. When Ambler hadn't said anything after a few seconds, his spoke curtly. "A personal matter. You can only speak to me. Here I am."

Ambler took note of the colonel's buzz-cut gray hair, his smooth-shaven face, the wrinkles at the corners of his eyes, and the hardness in them. Nothing in his gaze or his manner showed anything resembling sociability, curiosity, warmth. It was like trying to make a connection with a rock. What was clear from his expression was his belief he was in charge.

Taking all this in, Ambler engaged James's gaze for a moment, searching for something. A soul perhaps? "You have an intimidating manner," he said, before sitting down in a leather armchair off to the side of the desk. He'd fought back the feeling he had that he should wait until the colonel gave him permission to sit. "It makes me uneasy."

James's response was silence, not so much as a blink.

Sounding calmer than he felt, Ambler said, "Your friend and likely former lover, Robin Cartwright, was writing a book at the time of her death, examining several deaths that were found to be accidental or self-inflicted that she believed might in fact have been murders."

James's expression didn't change, not a twitch, not a flicker.

"Linda Porter's death was one of the deaths she was examining."

Still nothing.

"You're not surprised?"

This brought a wrinkle of irritation to the colonel's forehead, a twitch to a corner of his mouth. Ambler had hoped for more of a response. Rattling the guy's cage might not be enough. He might need to poke him a couple of times. He took a deep breath and went on.

"Because I'd helped Robin with some of the research, I felt I should try to tie up some loose ends. You might be surprised—or you might not be—to learn you figured prominently in her investigation of Linda Porter's death."

Finally, a reaction. Something flashed in his eyes. His face muscles tightened. He spoke in a piercing clipped tone. "You're getting on my nerves. You talk a lot but don't say anything. What do you want?"

"I'd like you to tell me what you know about Ms. Porter's death?"

James made a movement now, leaning back in his chair, raising his gaze to ceiling as if he were trying to remember something, twisting his body slightly, reaching to rub the back of his neck, grimacing as if he couldn't catch up with the thought he was after. Ambler waited.

"Robin was murdered." James pushed himself forward forcefully until he was leaning on his arms on the desk, much closer to Ambler than before, glaring at him. "What do you know about that?"

Taken aback, Ambler stared at him while he thought quickly. How did he know that? "Last I heard, the manner of her death was still undetermined."

"The police consider her death a murder."

"How do you know that?"

"I have connections in the department. The police in New York told me about you, that you're a meddler. I knew who you were and what you were after as soon as you walked in my door. I'd told the guard to send you up because your insistence on seeing me led me to think it was you. Since you went to the trouble of tracking me down, I'll answer your question, as you're taking forever to get around to asking it. I didn't kill Linda and I didn't kill Robin." He sat back, arms folded across his chest. "Now, get the fuck out!"

Ambler stayed put, despite the menace in James's tone. He remembered something he'd learned from Mike Cosgrove a long time ago. Suspects or witnesses who aren't used to being interrogated—no matter that they're smart or that they're tough—will almost always give up information they don't want to give up. If you accuse them of something, they'll defend themselves, even though they know they should keep quiet.

"That's not the reaction I expected," Ambler said. He crossed one leg over the other and tried to sound avuncular. "I expected you to be helpful. Folks with nothing to hide don't mind letting the light shine."

He wanted to come across as deferential when he actually felt kind of smug. If he kept the conversation going, even though James wanted it to stop, he was in control not James, despite the colonel's obvious belief in his own superiority. Any change in James's expression was barely perceptible. But the change was there if you were attentive, and Ambler was. The colonel was itching to say something while his wiser self was telling him to keep quiet.

It was the librarian against the fighter pilot. The military man versus the man of peace. The librarian tried a diversion. "I suppose the military and the security business have a lot in common. But I don't see how your particular expertise transfers. You don't fly a jet here."

James watched him curiously, clearly not sure how to react to the question. He wouldn't think he'd give anything away by answering. But he would. Yet Ambler believed he'd answer because it would provide an opportunity to brag.

"I transferred to cyber system operations before I retired. After a couple of hundred combat flight hours in Iraq and Afghanistan, I'd had enough. I wanted to keep my feet on the ground until retirement." He tensed a bit, looking Ambler in the eye. "Did you serve?"

Ambler hadn't served and he suspected James knew he hadn't. The question was to put Ambler in his place. Men who spent time in the military were proud of their service and often felt this service put them one up on the man who hadn't. That they were proud was OK with Ambler.

His problem with the military wasn't with the soldiers. He just didn't like wars. Fighters on both sides—however brave and proud—thought they were the good guys and the guys on the other side were the bad guys. Most of the folks fighting on either side would rather be doing something else. James, as Uncle Walt had told him, wasn't one of them.

He wouldn't say this to James. James would see his unwillingness to fight as a weakness. Thinking Ambler weak, inferior, he might underestimate his questioner, get cocky, and make a mistake. Ambler said, "No." And didn't give him a chance to respond. "You said Robin was murdered. Did you speak with a detective named Lambert?"

"Lambert. That's right. I was put in touch with him by a friend of mine, an inspector in the department."

James let this sink in. Once more, he was blowing his own horn without actually boasting, reminding Ambler of his superiority. Ambler might know a detective to talk to; the colonel was friends with a high-ranking officer.

"An inspector?" Ambler nodded approvingly. The point was to act impressed. If James thought Ambler was impressed, it would be easier to keep the conversation going. "In the beginning, the police thought her death might have been accidental . . . until Blake Beasley was murdered. You suspected she'd been murdered before that happened? Is that why you asked your friend—the inspector—about her death?"

James's face muscles tightened. Ambler had pushed too hard. The colonel caught on that he was being pumped; his protective shield went up. His expression was scornful and mocking.

"You knew Robin for what? A month? A couple of months? You helped her with her research. Maybe you got close to her. Perhaps a bit of romance. Robin was like that. She fell in love easily.

"You think you knew her?" He raised his voice. "You didn't." He let that sink in and went on more quietly "Not like I knew her. I doubt you ever spoke about me with her—even if, as you say, I was prominent in her research. If you had, you'd never have begun your asinine investigation. If you could talk to her right now, she'd tell you that you were an idiot to think I killed her. She'd say you were nuts to think I'd ever hurt her.

"I asked you to leave once." He gestured at his surroundings. "This is a security company. It would be ironic to call security to have you thrown out."

Ambler stood. "You're right that Robin and I never spoke about you. You're wrong that I'm accusing you of murdering anyone, although I suppose I am investigating, if you want to call it that. I did hope you'd help me. I could show you what she wrote about you and about Linda Porter's death. Something might strike you—something I wouldn't have noticed—that would help us find the person who did kill Robin."

This caught the colonel's attention. He'd stood when Ambler stood and now sat back down. His facade slipped for a moment, revealing a troubled man deep in thought. James wanted to see what Robin had written about him. He'd been ready to jump at the chance until he realized he shouldn't appear over-eager. He took a minute to compose himself. When he spoke, he tried to sound casually interested in Ambler's proposal. He tried but couldn't fully hide his eagerness. "You think I might see something you missed that might lead to the killer?"

"You might. You were clearly an important person in her life. I wonder now why she didn't tell me more about you. She told me about Linda Porter's death. She didn't believe it was accidental; she believed her friend was murdered. But that's about all she told me.

"If she'd thought you were the murderer, you'd think she'd have told me that, too." He held up his hands. "You were a suspect because you'd spent time with Linda and Robin; you were a major figure in their lives at that time."

James watched him curiously. You'd guess he didn't know whether to believe Ambler or not. At that moment, Ambler didn't know himself if he believed what he was saying. Still, James's interest in what she might have written about him and Linda Porter's death gave Ambler an opening. He just didn't know what it was an opening to.

James helped him out. "I contacted the police in New York when I learned of the circumstances of Robin's death. I didn't believe it was an accident and I knew who killed her."

"So you told Lambert who killed her . . . I'm going to guess you told him it was her ex-husband." He caught a hint of uncertainty in James's manner when the colonel reflexively averted his glance for a split second before he regained his piercing glare.

"I'm also going to guess you told him this without proof."

Again a wavering in James's gaze, again for only a split second. "Why should I tell you what I told the police?" He said this but went right on and told Ambler anyway. "I told the detective Robin was afraid of George. He was a tyrant, a control freak. When she broke the hold he had over her, he went nuts—the type of man who—if he couldn't control a woman—was likely to kill her."

"She didn't tell me that." The truth was Robin had never even told him she had an ex-husband.

"It's on the record. She took out a restraining order. You think you knew Robin and you didn't. I've forgotten more than you ever knew about her." His glare intensified. "Did you know she was mentally disturbed when she was young? Borderline personality disorder they called it. She was irrationally jealous of Linda. She stalked her and at one point physically attacked her."

Whatever advantage Ambler thought he'd gained over his adversary was gone. He felt like a schoolboy being lectured to. James was good at dressing a man down, shaking the man's confidence in himself. Ambler's insides were churning. A moment ago he was on solid ground. Now he was sinking into the mire. James went on, lording it over him, telling him how little he knew about Robin Cartwright—how little he knew about her death or anything else.

# SEVENTEEN

"So there you are, stuck on the corner of left, right, and straight ahead." McNulty set Ambler's mug of beer in front of him. "Take heart! My pop used to say, 'Keep plugging away; let the world take a couple of turns. Something'll turn up.'"

"Maybe," said Ambler. "The problem is what that something might be. After all the work I've done, I'm less sure about what happened than I was when I began."

McNulty pondered this. "Far be it from me to offer advice . . ." This was a bold-faced lie. McNulty lived to give advice, asked for or not.

"Give it a try." Ambler took a swig of beer.

"In all probability you missed something."

"I already knew that."

Undeterred by the sarcasm, McNulty continued. "My point is you need to go back over everything you've found out and look for what you missed. It might have happened on a bad day when you weren't as sharp as you usually are."

He raised an eyebrow and tilted his head. You might say he looked at Ambler with sympathy. "You're getting along in years, Ray. The old brain cells are drying up. It's easier for someone to put something over on you, easier for you to miss something when you're looking right at it . . .

"Don't take it so hard." He met the disgruntled Ambler's gaze. "Happens to me. The other night I misplaced a Beefeater bottle—didn't put it back in the slot I took it out of. I hadn't done something like that since I was a rookie working my first service bar."

Ambler conceded. "I'm sure I missed something, probably a lot of things. But—"

Noticing the waitress at the service station at the far end of the bar, whom he must have seen through the back of his head,

McNulty went and made a few drinks for her. When he returned, he asked Ambler to tell him about everyone he'd talked to since the first murder.

"You have suspects, right? Let's talk about them. Telling me what you know out loud, you'll recognize what you missed better than thinking about it. You got that professor's ex-husband, what's-his-name. What's strange about him?"

"Colonel James said he was a control freak, that he dominated Robin, told her how to dress, kept her away from her friends. That kind of control. When she broke free of him, he went nuts. He couldn't accept not being able to control her anymore."

"So he killed her?"

"Right."

After a moment of thought, McNulty asked, "You believe this guy?"

"The colonel? I don't know. I'm still sorting through what he said."

"Here's a couple of things to think about. I don't know this colonel guy. For one thing, he might be wrong. For another, he might be lying. I know you think well of your fellow man. But most of us lie when it's in our interest. The guy's a military man, so he won't let on that he lies—bravery and honor, and all that—but he lies."

Ambler knew this. Many people in many ways had lied to him. He was about to say this, but McNulty wasn't finished.

"Another thing about the military . . . *it's* a collection of control freaks. He's a colonel, so the general bosses him around, and then he bosses the captain around, the captain bosses the major, the major the lieutenant, and on down the line. It's the promised land for control freaks."

This wasn't exactly true. When the illustrious bartender got going on one of his theories, he didn't use the scientific method. Nonetheless, he'd made a good point. Colonel James saying something didn't make it true. This was one thing he missed. While he was in Springfield, he should have checked James's story with Robin's Uncle Walt. This was another thing he missed.

The same went for the other stories he'd been told. He hadn't followed up on Ricardo Diaz. The lawyer wouldn't be the first to have faked an injury. He told McNulty about the disabled lawyer.

The bartender nodded. "You see a guy on the street wearing a blanket looks like he's missing a leg, you don't wanna say, 'Hey, lemme look under the blanket.' Even if you think he's got his leg folded up under there, you give him a couple of bucks; you don't take a chance on making an ass out of yourself if you're wrong."

Ambler grimaced. "Something like that . . . Not exactly like that. Of all the suspects—and there are a lot of them—he's the least likely. You have to wonder why Robin picked him, though; why he was one of the cases she went after."

"That's a good way to look at it."

"What's a good way to look at what?"

"Instead of trying to figure out who did the killing—something you're not getting anywhere with—think about who didn't do it. See who's left when you're finished doing that."

Ambler was exasperated and worn out. "I'm ready to try anything. It's not like this killer is sitting around waiting for me to find him. He's . . ." He waited before going on because talking about the threat to Adele might make it more real. He trusted that her neighbors—the local cop couple—would watch out for her. She'd told him they worked different shifts and had take-home police cars, which they'd begun parking in front of her bungalow at night.

"Adele said someone was following her, keeping tabs on her and not hiding he was doing it. I think it's a warning to me to stop looking for Robin's killer." He told McNulty about her police neighbors.

"They'll do a better job than you would." McNulty thought about what he'd said. "If the stalker is the killer you're looking for, and not your everyday deranged pervert, that means you've found something. You just don't know what it is. All the more reason to do what I said."

The bartender had convinced Ambler that something about the murders was wandering around in the back of his mind; he just couldn't put his finger on it. "Let's go back to the most unlikely suspects," he said. "One I didn't mention is her colleague, Thomas Jones. He lied about how well he knew her. He'd been acquitted on a murder charge some years back, and Robin knew about it. She never told me she and Jones had known each other in the past either.

"But since he was acquitted, even if the verdict was wrong, he can't be tried again. So he had no real fear of exposure from her. Yet he was nosey about my investigation. That made me suspicious. But again, he had no reason to kill her, so I should probably eliminate him, especially if he accounts for where he was at the time of the murders.

"Then there's C.R. Spaulding, another of her visiting professor colleagues. I have no reason to suspect him at all, except he knows a lot about computers. Also, he's too cheerful."

McNulty scrunched up his face. "Anyone with half a brain can send an anonymous email these days."

"How?"

Sheepishly, McNulty said, "I don't know; I'd have to ask my son. But I know you can do it. Look it up."

"Colonel James is a cyber expert, too."

"Forget about who did what with emails. Go on to something else." The bartender had the bit between his teeth. "That cheerful thing is a bad sign. Invite the guy for a drink and bring him over here. We'll give him the third degree and find out what he's so fucking happy about, the smug bastard."

Ambler chuckled. "You don't even know him. There's no reason to think he had anything to do with either murder. I'm inclined to scratch him off the list, even if he is unwarrantedly cheerful. I'm also willing to drop Ricardo Diaz. I'll ask Mike Cosgrove to check on the injury. But for now, all three are on the back burner."

"Who's that leave you with?" McNulty poured himself a cup of coffee. It was the doldrums time of the afternoon, the lull between the end of lunch and the beginning of cocktail hour. Two tables were occupied. No one sat at the bar but Ambler.

"Nagy, the ex-husband. The colonel. And a silver-tongued preacher in Virginia. Of course, I might be totally wrong. The killer might be someone I don't know about or never thought of as a killer. Maybe the police will figure it out, since it doesn't look like I will."

"You can't think like that. You're not the cops who gotta arrest someone or get heat from their boss. So you don't have to frame someone or hold back evidence or produce fake evidence and convict someone. Then there's the other side. The cops, they look at the evidence. They question a few people. After a couple of weeks, they run out of leads so they put the case in a file and go on to something else. They got stacks of other murders to investigate.

"You gotta find the killer. You can't take a chance that whoever is following Adele isn't the murderer you're looking for. If there's one chance in a million this guy will harm her, you gotta find him."

McNulty slammed the flat of his hand onto the bar. "Bring that cheerful guy in for a drink. It won't take long. A couple of slow curves, a fastball under the chin, a slider outside, and we'll know what he's got to be cheerful about and what he's hiding."

Despite his misgivings, Ambler took McNulty up on his suggestion and invited C.R. Spaulding for an after-work drink at the Library Tavern the following day. The bartender acknowledged the scholar's cheerful greeting with a scowl, plopped Spaulding's and Ambler's mugs in front of them and walked to the other end of the bar.

C.R. gazed after the retreating bartender, his face wrinkled with disappointment like a child watching his balloon float away. "What's the matter with him?"

"Nothing," Ambler said. "He says his job is to deliver your drink properly made or poured. He doesn't get paid enough to entertain."

"Oh." Spaulding sipped his beer and thought about that.

After a moment, he said, "I don't often go to bars. I can't remember the last time."

Ambler wondered if this was a rebuke. "I probably go too often." He was thinking about how he was going to get C.R. to open up . . . or if he had anything to open up about.

C.R. kept glancing about him with an expression of wonderment, a stranger in a strange land. "You come here a lot? What do you do while you're here?" He seemed entirely at a loss.

It sounded like a genuine question, rather than a rebuke. "I drink a beer or two, sometimes eat a hamburger. I talk to the bartender, occasionally to the person alongside me." It sounded foolish as he said it, boring. There had to be more to it than that. After a few seconds, he realized that it was easier to sit and watch the bartender, or stare into space, once you finished your first beer, and even easier after the second.

"Do you like the beer?"

C.R. looked at his mug and then took a big gulp. "It's very good." He stared at his glass for a moment and was about to say something, but Ambler beat him to it.

"Take another swallow; it grows on you."

C.R. did as he was told. "I do like it better." He smacked his lips, and after a moment took another sip.

Well, he'd gotten the ball rolling. "Have you remembered anything about Robin Cartwright you forgot to mention the last time we talked?"

For a moment, C.R.'s expression was blank. Then he brightened. "To tell you the truth, I haven't thought about her since we talked." He looked at Ambler curiously. "I had no idea what was going on when Harry called me into his office that time. It wasn't until days later someone told me you were conducting an investigation, a murder investigation. I didn't know anyone thought Professor Cartwright was . . . I didn't know the circumstances then. I thought she just died."

"Would your answers have been different?"

He thought this over. "I don't know. As I said, I haven't thought about it."

C.R.'s reaction to his questions was a surprise. Perhaps because Robin's death was so much on Ambler's mind, he assumed everyone else was thinking about her, too.

"What about Blake Beasley? Were you surprised when he was murdered? Did you think about who might have killed him?"

This brought a more animated reaction. "That was a real shocker." C.R's cheeks had reddened and his eyes glittered. "I was surprised when I found out Dr. Cartwright was killed. I didn't know her well, so it was like a stranger being murdered at a place you're familiar with. You're kind of shocked but it's not really personal. I couldn't believe Blake had been murdered, though. I was really shocked. It was like I talked to him the day before and . . ." C.R. froze, as if a thought out of nowhere had hit him.

Ambler kept silent and let the cheerful professor come to grips with his thought. C.R.'s beer as well as Ambler's was almost empty, so he signaled to McNulty for two more.

"Not the day before . . . I talked to him that day, the day he was murdered, right before he left for home." C.R.'s tone was hushed. He let his somber gaze burn into Ambler's. "I knew something was wrong. He was all in a dither. Distracted. Hardly aware he was speaking to me, he was so anxious to leave. I didn't think of it then . . ." He cocked his head like a confused pup. ". . . I didn't think of it until right this minute."

Wide-eyed, he met Ambler's gaze again. "He was afraid. It was as if he were running from something and didn't want to be bothered with me because I was hindering his escape."

This time it was Ambler who froze. "What was he running from?" He blurted this out. How would C.R. Spaulding know what Blake was afraid of? He calmed himself down. C.R. moved on to his second beer without seeming to notice that he had. Ambler watched his face, trying to read something in his expression.

"Where were you when you saw him?"

"In the library."

"Where in the library?" Ambler caught himself. C.R. was startled. He was badgering the poor guy.

"In the visiting professor reading room. Why? What are you getting at?"

"Would you please try to remember every time you saw Blake that day. And try to remember anyone you saw that day whom you didn't recognize, who for some reason seemed out of place? Someone who didn't seem like a regular reader."

C.R. squirmed as he waited for Ambler to finish formulating his questions, like a schoolboy wriggling in his seat and waving his hand to answer a question the teacher hadn't finished asking. He was nodding his head like he was bobbing for apples. Ambler expected him to start shouting "I know . . . I know!"

"One of the library aides came to the reading room in the middle of the afternoon to get Blake. A man had come to the information desk in the catalog room asking for him. Blake was in one of the back modules working on his laptop. He didn't want to go." C.R. bobbed some more. "I know this because Blake was irritated at the aide for disturbing him and told him in no uncertain terms to tell the visitor he couldn't see him. The aide went. But he came back—"

"Benny?" Ambler interrupted him. "Was the aide Benny Bevone?"

"The Italian guy who dresses like he's from *Saturday Night Fever*?"

"Yes."

C.R. nodded. "Yep. That was him."

"What else?"

"The second time, Blake went with him. It was not long after that I saw him leaving. *Fleeing* is a better word. He didn't want to stop and talk to me."

They finished their beers. Ambler offered him another, but C.R. said he thought he was drunk and should go. He laughed uproariously after he said this.

McNulty had dropped by their corner of the bar to eavesdrop on the last part of their conversation but didn't say anything until after C.R. left.

"You don't think our friend here was who he was afraid of?"

"No. I doubt C.R. is our suspect. But Benny might know who is. I'm going outside to call him." He stood on the corner and called Benny's phone twice, letting it go to voicemail both times but leaving a message the second time.

"He didn't answer," Ambler said when he got back. McNulty poured him half a mug of beer and himself a drop in his coffee cup.

"What now?"

"Wait till Benny calls me."

"You think it's going to be that easy. You'll sit here. Benny will call and tell you who the victim . . . what's his name?"

"Blake Beasley."

"Who Beasley met that afternoon, and that will be it? That guy will be the killer. They'll arrest him. It will be over. You think it'll be that easy?"

"It might," Ambler said defiantly. And then quietly, "It never has been." He thought about what could go wrong. Any number of things. He sipped his beer and thought about who it was Benny might have seen that day.

George Nagy came to mind first. He was unhinged enough to be capable of anything. He'd been an obsessively controlling husband, if Doug James was to be believed. But why should the colonel be believed? Ambler needed to make his own judgments about Nagy.

The main argument against the ex-husband being a suspect was that Robin wasn't trying to prove he was a murderer. He had other motives, of course. But she was murdered at a specific time, in a specific place. Why would he kill her right at that moment in that place?

On the other side of the scale, she might well have gone to a hotel room with Nagy. At one time, she slept with him regularly. Nothing strange about them being in a room together, even that hotel room. It was also reasonable to think she'd go to a hotel room with Doug James. At least—again his account—she was enamored of him at one time.

Cliff Kilgore, the pastor, was certainly still in the running, even if, as far as Ambler knew, Robin never had a romantic relationship with him. After all, Kilgore was a serial seducer of women. And there was the mysterious “Preacher” she’d had dinner with, a former lover. The simplest thing to do on that one was to ask Sergeant Greenleaf back in Virginia if he’d found out where Kilgore was at the times Robin and Blake were murdered.

# EIGHTEEN

Ambler got tired of waiting for Benny to call, and of his useless speculating, so he went home. He tried him a couple more times that night and still didn't reach him. In the morning, he called Sergeant Greenleaf, who told him Cliff Kilgore had refused to talk to the sheriff's deputies without his lawyer present. When his lawyer showed up, he didn't let Kilgore answer any questions.

"This means we have to piece together where he was and what he was doing at the times of three different deaths without any help from him . . . Well, on one of them we know where he was. He was driving the truck that ran down little Anna Paxton. We're moving along on that one, but I can't tell you anything about it yet.

"The ones you're asking about are too much of a stretch for our guys to spend time on. I'm already doing a lot of overtime . . ." He sounded apologetic. "I'll do what I can but don't expect much. On the other hand, Cliff's lawyer told old Luke to drop the charges against you. I expect he'll do that shortly."

After Greenleaf, he called Lambert. "What did you think of Colonel James?"

The detective didn't show any surprise that Ambler knew James had been in contact. "What was I supposed to think of him?" Lambert's tone was brusque bordering on surly.

"I don't presume to tell you what to think. He told me he'd wrapped the case up for you."

For some reason, this piqued Lambert's interest. "You've talked with him recently?"

Ambler said he had.

"What did he say? You thought *he* was a suspect."

"Do you?"

Lambert snorted. "Even if I thought you were on the

up-and-up, which I don't, I wouldn't discuss who's a suspect and who isn't. The fact is I never took you up on your suggestion. I didn't go looking for him. He came to me."

"He knew Robin years ago—at the time when a young woman died under suspicious circumstances, a friend of hers . . . and his."

"I came across that in that journal you gave me. The girl apparently committed suicide, or possibly died accidentally, and if I believe Professor Cartwright's own notes, she was the only one who thought the death suspicious."

Ambler was getting testy. "There are a couple of other cases where Robin was the only one who thought what appeared to be one thing turned out to be something else . . . and she was right."

Lambert barely kept his voice under control. "Is there a reason for this phone call, or was it just to tell me how to do my job?"

"Why did Colonel James get in touch with you? Why did he believe Robin—Professor Cartwright—was murdered when no one else did?"

"Except you."

"Weren't you curious? Did you consider his intention might have been to shift suspicion away from him and onto George Nagy?"

The pause this time was longer. "Maybe I should be curious as to why you want to throw suspicion on him. What makes you think he named George Nagy as a suspect?"

"He told me. Are you going to investigate Nagy?"

"I'm not going to tell you who or what I'm investigating." Another pause. "Let's go back to my earlier question. Why were you talking to Colonel James and what did he tell you?"

"Robin had written about him. I wanted to see what he had to say about that. He said you called me a meddler. Why did my name come up?"

Lambert cleared his throat before he said, "You *are* a meddler . . . You came up by accident. We were talking about Nagy. I told James I'd heard there was bad blood between them. I mentioned the altercation at the funeral. He wanted to know how I knew about it, so I told him from a nosy librarian who was at the funeral. He asked if it was you."

"How did he know my name?"

"I don't know. He asked a couple more questions and put together that you were—if you want to call it that—conducting your own investigation."

Ambler thought this over. Lambert was irritating. But, as much as it would feel great to put him in his place, he needed for them to stay on reasonably good terms. "You don't want to tell me about your investigation; I understand that. Mike never did either. He only told me what was public. But what's public isn't always in the papers, so how about if something is public but not widely known, you tip me off."

"Why would I do you a favor?"

"Because I'm trying to help you. I want you to bring in the killer, not me."

Lambert harrumphed. "I got too much going on to be worrying about whether you're up to date on things . . . Call once in a while, if you want. If I know something you should know, I'll tell you." His tone was not as antagonistic as it had been.

"By the way, I wouldn't take Colonel James off my list of suspects just yet, if I were you."

"There you go again . . . I don't know how Cosgrove puts up with this shit."

He'd barely hung up with Lambert when his cell phone rang. "Benny?" He hadn't looked at the screen before he answered.

It was Adele. "That man following me . . . I think it was the same man . . . He called me."

Ambler's heart stopped. This can't be, he told himself. He watched his hand holding the phone shake. He gripped the lip of his desk with his other hand, as if he needed to hold on even though he was sitting down.

"He wanted me to tell you he called. He said, 'Mr. Ambler's been looking for me, so here I am.' His tone scared me. I told him I didn't know what he was talking about. He said,

'Tell him he found me, so he should stop looking.' I said, 'I don't want to talk to you. I'm going to hang up and call the police.'

"He ignored me and repeated what he'd said. 'Tell him he found me. Now he needs to stop or it's curtains. You know what it means, curtains? . . . Of course you do. You have a new baby. You don't want curtains for him. You don't want curtains for you. Tell Raymond Ambler the hunt stops now. Or it's curtains.' Then he laughed . . . he laughed like a fiend in a horror movie, and hung up."

"Did you call the police?" Ambler's tone was rushed and he didn't wait for an answer. "They can get a warrant . . . They can find where the call came from."

"I think they're doing that." She spoke calmly but he could hear the tension, the fear, that she was holding back.

His first impulse was to go to her. But what would he do? Sit there and wait? The man who made the call wasn't a truth teller. If Ambler stopped looking for him, he wasn't going forget Ambler knew he was a murderer. He wouldn't let Adele and Ambler live in peace. He'd always be a threat to them because Ambler would forever be a threat to him.

Except Ambler wasn't a threat. He didn't know who this sadistic killer was. But he must be awfully close for the killer to think he did know. McNulty was right. He must have stumbled over something that would tell him who the killer was. Yet somehow he'd missed it. Like McNulty said, he needed to go back over what he already knew and find what he should have recognized but didn't.

Could it be George Nagy? James had set the police on him. Nagy might have thought it was Ambler. Nagy wouldn't know what Ambler knew, but his guilt might make him think Ambler had discovered what he'd done and that would be enough. Nagy had already shown he blundered into things half-cocked, shot from the hip, and asked questions later.

Having thought this, he immediately decided it didn't make sense. He hadn't hardly spoken to Nagy. One of the men he had confronted—Diaz or Clifton Kilgore, Doug James, or even Thomas Jones—was more likely to have panicked when he realized he was under suspicion. But who? Adele interrupted his frenzied pondering.

"It's all right, Raymond. Calm down." Despite his not having said anything for a long moment, she knew his state of mind, if not what he was thinking, how he was thinking. "It's not your fault, and I'm OK." There was a hint of insincerity in both parts of what she said. "Jennifer and I are staying with Lisa and Mike for the moment."

"Who?"

"The police couple next door . . . They didn't want me to be by myself with the baby under all this stress." Her tone was flat. No accusation. No reprimand. She didn't need to add emphasis. The words themselves carried the message.

"I'm sorry, Adele. It is my fault. This whole thing fell in my lap and then spiraled out of control. I don't know what to do." His voice was shaking. "I can come there. You shouldn't be alone."

"I just told you I'm not alone. And I don't want you to come here. I'm fine without you." Her tone was cold. Flat. Dead. The words hit his heart like a punch to the chest. He didn't know what to say. He had to say something; there were a million things he wanted to say, but he couldn't get any words out.

After another long moment, he heard Adele's voice coming from far away. "Finish what you're doing, Raymond. It will end one way or another. We can talk then . . . if there's anything to talk about. I'm safe. I'm busy all the time. And I'm exhausted. I'm not punishing you. I just really really don't want to talk to you now."

His heart sank. He felt a depth of sadness that seemed too much to bear. It was the level of sadness he felt when—years before—he had listened to the judge pronounce his son's prison sentence. Now this was his sentence and it had the finality of a cell door closing.

"Can I call tomorrow?" His voice sounded small like a child's; he already knew what the answer would be.

"No, Raymond. I don't want to talk to you tomorrow. For many many nights I've wanted to talk to you. Now, I don't. I can't say that more clearly. I know this makes you sad. And I'm sorry for that. I can't help it . . . I hope you get the man you're after. I do."

That was it. The conversation was over. As final as death, a good part of his life had gone down the drain.

He went through the motions at work for the rest of the day, thinking about Adele and little else, remembering the first moment he'd met her, years before, when she'd showed up at the library fresh from college in Iowa with her MLS degree; more recently, the moment she told him she was having a baby; and hundreds of moments in between. He replayed what she'd said over and over in his mind. He thought about the last time he'd seen her. He remembered the conversations they'd had since Robin Cartwright's murder. How little he'd talked to her this time compared to how much he'd talked to her during the many other murder investigations he'd been involved in.

Over and over, he heard the tone of her voice, a tone he'd never heard from her in all the time he'd known her. This was what turned his heart cold, the deadness in her voice as she told him she didn't want him to call. Never once in the time he'd known her—even when she was raging angry at him—had he not heard the caring she felt for him as an undertone in the sound of her voice, until now.

When he left the library at the end of the day, he had no recollection of what he'd done since the phone call with Adele. On his way to the Library Tavern—where else do you go when the world drops out from under you?—he realized he hadn't thought about the murders of Robin and Blake or any of the suspects since he'd gotten off the phone.

McNulty watched him for a full minute before he said anything. When he did, it was, "As my mother used to say long ago, 'Look what the cat dragged in.'"

Ambler nodded solemnly. He didn't have the words to tell his friend what was wrong. He ordered a beer. He knew McNulty wouldn't press him, would wait until he was ready to talk. So the bartender went about his business, leaving Ambler to his thoughts, though every now and then he'd catch the bartender watching him, his forehead wrinkled with concern.

When he was midway through his second beer, as the rush at the bar quieted, the bartender stopped by to wipe the bar in front of him. By then, Ambler was ready and told him about the phone call from Adele.

McNulty's response was to grab the bottle of Jameson and pour them both a shot. "Slainte!" He tapped Ambler's glass and threw down the shot. "Women often act strangely after they've had a baby," he said, "as well they should."

"I'm the one who acted strangely . . . strangely and stupidly." Ambler's tone was bitter.

McNulty shook his head. "Don't go maudlin on me. You wanna cry in your beer, go find another joint. It looks bad to your fellow imbibers. They came here to have a good time . . . a few drinks, a couple of laughs. You know the tune." He glanced at the few tipplers left at the bar, all of them engrossed in conversation, and drew himself a beer into his coffee cup. "As the lawyers say, 'We'll stipulate to your acting strange and being stupid.'"

He leaned closer to Ambler and lowered his voice. "You know this whole thing about telling the bartender your troubles? It's a myth. Bartenders don't give a shit about your troubles. Like everyone else, we got troubles of our own."

McNulty always approached anything really important obliquely. An outsider listening to him would believe he didn't have an empathetic bone in his body. Yet he was probably the kindest, most empathetic person Ambler had ever known . . . except for Adele.

"She said you'd talk when this—shall we say *problem*—you're working on is resolved. What you need to do is resolve it. Adele will take of herself while you do that. Then you can spend the rest of your life making up to her for being a heartless, inconsiderate jerk."

"I was hoping you'd talk to her . . ."

"And get my head bitten off? You're nuts."

After a second shot of Irish whiskey, Ambler found himself—under McNulty's prompting—trying to remember everyone he'd spoken to since Robin's death and what each one had said. Somewhere among those recollections was the key to her murder. Why did he keep coming back to Blake Beasley?

"I was almost certain Blake killed Robin. I thought I had it figured out."

McNulty nodded. "And then the guy went and got himself killed, spoiling your plan. Just like the bastard to gum up the works."

# NINETEEN

Ambler stayed at the bar long into the evening. Cocktail hour wound down, the dinner rush built and then slowed. He'd eaten a club sandwich McNulty forced on him and had been nursing a beer long enough for it to become warm and flat. He was ready to call it a night, though he expected it to be a sleepless one, when he heard the tavern door open and instinctively turned to look. It took him a moment to recognize the burly, rumpled bear of a man, with the large head and doleful expression.

It was one of those strange moments when someone you'd been thinking about, but had no reason to expect to see, suddenly appeared as if you'd conjured him up. He was looking at George Nagy.

Nagy took a quick glance around the bar, settled on Ambler, and made a beeline toward him. "They told me you'd be here."

Ambler was too astonished to say anything.

"I got in late this afternoon and came straight to the library. I thought it would be open. A guard told me I'd probably find you here."

"Funding. The library should be open until nine." Ambler didn't know why he said this to a man who'd recently been accused of murdering his ex-wife, the absence of any evidence for the accusation notwithstanding. Again he was struck by Nagy's woebegone demeanor and how misery seemed to be permanently etched into his face.

"Why did you want to find me? Did the police ask you to come in?"

Nagy ignored his first question and showed no surprise at the second one. "This detective called. He wanted to ask me some questions. I didn't want to talk over the phone, so I told him I'd come to the city and answer his questions."

"So what do you want with me?"

"I'm not a fool." Nagy acted like he expected to be challenged on his assertion, glaring at Ambler and scowling at McNulty (always unwise) while the bartender stood waiting for him to order a drink.

"A friend of yours?" McNulty asked Ambler.

"Not exactly. This is George Nagy. Robin Cartwright's ex-husband."

The bartender turned on Nagy. "You've been here with her."

"I've never seen you before." He said this dismissively, as if McNulty was an underling who spoke out of turn. He wouldn't dismiss McNulty so easily.

"You don't have to see me for me to see you. I remember faces . . . even one like yours." He gestured with his head at a booth toward the rear of the tavern. "You sat there, facing the door. She faced you. You looked like you were trying to sell her something but she wasn't buying."

Ambler watched the exchange, amazed. George Nagy was "Preacher," the mystery man Robin had dinner with? He'd been here in New York with her just a week before her murder? It was possible, yet . . . McNulty could be mistaken; even he wasn't infallible. But then . . .

Nagy was still blustering. But he didn't go to great lengths to deny he'd been there. "All right, you saw me. I didn't notice you. I had dinner with my ex-wife soon after she came to New York; what's it to you?" His tone was condescending. "I don't pay attention to the wait staff."

Ambler interrupted. He still didn't know why Nagy had come in search of him. But that could wait. "Your being with Robin not long before she was murdered might mean something to the police," Ambler said. "Funny you didn't mention it before."

Nagy was irritated but not defensive, and perhaps surprised. "It wasn't shortly before she was murdered. We had dinner here a month or so ago."

Ambler turned to McNulty and raised his eyebrows, but McNulty shrugged.

Nagy's face, when Ambler turned back, registered a kind of epiphany. "Am I a suspect now?" He sounded genuinely surprised. "Is that what the police detective wanted?"

How could he not think he was a suspect? Ambler watched him curiously.

"That's ridiculous." He glared at Ambler, even though he hadn't said anything. "No one thinks I killed Robin. I loved her." Not only did Nagy sound incredulous, he sounded angry. What he didn't sound was worried.

"Someone must think so."

Remembering the brawl in the funeral parlor, and taking note of Nagy's anger, Ambler got ready for him to do something stupid again. He stood up and moved a couple of steps from the bar, positioning himself so if Nagy did make a move toward him, he could redirect the larger man into a wall or the corner of the bar. "I don't know what they want with you. Why not ask them?"

"I will ask them." His tone was belligerent. "How do you know so much about it?"

Ambler hadn't made up his mind whether to tell Nagy that his nemesis, Doug James, had made the accusation. He told himself not to jump to conclusions. That Nagy lied about—or failed to mention—having dinner with his ex-wife in the city before her murder might be incriminating, but wasn't any kind of proof that he'd killed her, especially if he was telling the truth about when they had dinner.

In the meantime, Ambler wanted to know why Nagy came looking for him as soon as he arrived in the city.

"Robin's mother told me you'd been in Springfield to talk to Doug James. I want to know what you talked about."

"Why?"

Nagy's demeanor changed dramatically. The truculence was gone. His features softened, so that while his hangdog look remained, he appeared thoughtful, and, you had to admit, scholarly. You could see what his appeal as a professor might be now that he was both pensive and attentive, his tone reasonable, as if to encourage Ambler's confidence. "Because I believe he murdered Robin." He spoke quietly. "Robin was certain he murdered her friend Linda Porter years ago. She had proof. He had to get rid of her."

Ambler didn't react, although he was surprised—"astounded" would be a better word. Did Nagy know the significance of what he'd said? "That's quite an accusation. You have proof of a murder? Why didn't you tell the police?"

Nagy maintained his reasonable tone. "I don't have the proof. Robin had evidence; that is she said she could prove James killed Linda. I didn't know whether to believe her or not at the time. She didn't tell me what the evidence was. I guess I could have told the police what I knew . . . I will now. But it's an accusation without substance." He sounded perplexed. "How will it look when I tell them Doug was a murderer—with nothing to back up the charge—at the same moment they think I killed Robin?"

Things were either becoming clearer or they were becoming more muddled. First, Doug James accuses Nagy of murdering Robin and brings his accusation to the police. Now Nagy says James not only killed Robin but that Robin had proof he killed Linda Porter. One of them had to be wrong . . . or lying. Or both of them were wrong or lying.

Up until a few minutes ago, despite James's accusation, Nagy hadn't been in the running as a serious suspect, as far as Ambler was concerned. Now—because McNulty put him in the city with his ex-wife during her time at the library—he was a serious contender. Or he was, until he came up with his new revelation that his ex-wife had proof Doug James killed Linda Porter. What Ambler needed to do was separate Nagy's accusation from what he knew as fact.

"It's easy to throw accusations around. But they don't mean much. If you can sit down and stay calm, we can talk about what I know and don't know. I would expect you to do the same. Tell me what you know and don't know."

"I know Doug James murdered my wife."

"No you don't. You suspect. You don't know."

Nagy and Ambler both sat down. Nagy ordered a Scotch and water. McNulty brought Ambler another beer. What the hell, Ambler told himself. Might as well get this over with.

"You're a suspect because a distinguished colonel told the police you killed Robin."

Nagy's eyes bulged. Steam might have been blowing out of his nostrils. "He what? He's the one? . . . The bastard. I'll kill him."

So much for the calm, dispassionate scholar. "Slow down. Cops take it for granted that when a woman is murdered, if she has an ex-husband, he's a suspect. I don't know that the colonel has any evidence, nor how seriously the police take his accusation." Ambler wanted to sound reassuring, so he didn't mention that the fact Nagy was in the city during the time his wife was doing research at the library strengthened the accusation against him.

Nagy took a swallow of his drink and was thoughtful for a moment before he spoke. "You said you'd tell me what you know. How about you begin with why you suspected Doug?"

The truth was Ambler didn't know who he suspected. It meant something that Robin had accused Doug James of murdering Linda Porter, but it didn't prove he did. It also meant something that Nagy had been in town before his ex-wife's murder. Even if it was a month before her murder, it meant he knew where she was and how to get to her.

But this didn't make him a murderer. There were too many unanswered questions; too many things that didn't add up. Why would he murder Blake Beasley, for one? Number two, he wasn't susceptible to blackmail. Unless he rigged up the blackmail and the threatening email as a diversion?

Ambler looked at his phone—he'd been calling Benny every couple of hours. This time Benny Bevone popped up in the window; he'd missed the call.

"Excuse me a moment," he said to Nagy. "I need to make a call and McNulty doesn't let anyone use a cell phone at the bar." He went outside.

"Where are you?"

"I just got back from Philadelphia; I didn't call because I was staying at my aunt's house. It was a funeral and I didn't think it would be respectful to be doing library business when everyone was mourning my uncle." He hesitated. "Besides, I don't owe you any favors since you made me into a rat."

It would be some time before Benny forgave him for springing the surprise interview with a police detective on him. It would do no good to explain. He could only apologize and wait for forgiveness. Still, he needed help. He explained what was happening and why he needed Benny to come to the Library Tavern and tell him if George Nagy was the man who'd come to the library and asked to talk with Blake Beasley shortly before he was murdered.

"Not a chance . . . You know how long it takes to get in there from Bensonhurst with the trains this time of night?"

"I'll pay for a car service."

"Save your dough. I'm not coming."

"Benny . . . we're talking about a murder. You might be able to identify the killer."

This gave him a moment's pause.

Ambler pushed on. "You want to become a private eye. This would be a big step."

"I'm not so sure anymore. If part of the job's ratting on people, I don't want anything to do with it."

"Ratting on a killer doesn't count. It's OK to identify a killer; it's part of the job."

"What if I'm wrong?"

"You can't be wrong. You either recognize the guy who asked for Beasley that day or you don't." Benny was thinking it over, so Ambler kept at him. "Call a car service. I'll pay for the round trip . . . You can take a car service into work tomorrow morning, too, since I'm keeping you up late doing this. I'll pay for that, too."

"Where you getting all this money?"

Where was he getting all this money? . . . Never mind. He had Benny on the ropes. "Look, I was going to do this anyway; I didn't want to tell you in case it fell through. I'm asking Harry to make you the library information assistant in Manuscripts and Archives . . . for the crime fiction collection. You'll get to know the collection because you'll be doing the cataloging, writing finding aids, doing orientation for the readers. You'd be in charge of the collection when I'm not there."

"How do you know Harry'll do it?"

This was tricky ground. He didn't want to try to put something over on Benny. It wouldn't work for one thing; Benny was no dummy. For another, it wouldn't be right. "If we solve this murder, and you're a big part of the team that solves it, Harry will be really pleased we made the library look good. He owes me an aide position and has been putting it off, so now he'll feel like he has to do it."

There was some truth and a lot of speculation in what Ambler told his friend. It was true there was a vacant library information assistant position in Manuscripts and Archives. It had been vacant for more than a year. That it was about to be filled was the speculative part, as was the idea that Harry would be pleased Ambler got himself tangled up in another murder investigation.

The job itself—if it were filled—would include the work for the crime fiction collection Ambler described. But it would also include the same sort of work for a couple of other collections. All this could be arranged in due time, Ambler was confident. The important thing was for Benny to take a gander at George Nagy.

Benny finally said he'd come.

"All you have to do is look through the window or, if you need to, come inside, take a quick look around, and leave. I don't want to have to explain why you're there."

It took some effort to keep Nagy at the bar until Benny could take a look at him. McNulty helped by engaging the disgruntled professor in a discussion about Scotch. After their frosty beginning, they hit it off once they got talking about liquor. McNulty did this because Ambler had whispered, "We've got to keep him here," when Nagy went to the men's room. Loyal as ever, the bartender didn't ask why.

Ambler pretended interest in the Scotch discussion—even sipping a couple of different samples McNulty poured into pony glasses for comparison. They tasted pretty much the same to him but neither McNulty nor Nagy cared about his opinion.

When the Scotch debate ran its course, Nagy was beginning to get antsy, so Ambler asked about Colonel James, about whom he was sure Nagy would have something to say. "How did you come to know him? Whatever went on between Robin and him took place long before you met her."

Nagy took offense at the question. The chill that descended was palpable. His body stiffened and he hunched his shoulder, as if to put a barrier between him and Ambler. "She knew him when she was in college because he had an affair with her friend. Nothing went on between Robin and him." His tone was defensive and argumentative.

Should he tell Nagy the story Uncle Walt had told him, or what the colonel himself had said? It might drive the volatile professor off on another rampage. But so what?

"I was led to believe it wasn't only Linda Porter that James had an affair with." Ambler spoke softly; the revelation—if it was a revelation to Nagy—would be bombshell enough.

That this was in fact a bombshell Nagy confirmed by appearing to spontaneously combust on the stool beside him. He slammed both fists onto the bar, swung around toward Ambler, his face reddened, his eyes bulging. Ambler got ready to feel the lunatic's hands around his throat any second.

"You're a damned liar," he sputtered, spittle spraying as he spoke.

Ambler held up his hands placatingly. "It could be I'm wrong. I'm telling you what I heard from her uncle and from James himself."

"I don't know about her uncle." Nagy calmed himself and took a swallow of Scotch. "He was always OK with me, with both of us, but he didn't know much about her. James, she despised. I know that for a fact.

"For some reason, her mother—or maybe it was her Uncle Walt; he and James were friends—invited him to a family gathering. Christmas or Thanksgiving, I don't remember; it was years ago. I didn't know anything about James at the time, except to see that his presence cast a pall over the day. He was the war hero, so he thought he had to be the center of attention, the star of the show, that everyone came to see him, rather than what was actually the case, that he was a hanger-on, the uninvited guest . . . though I guess he was invited.

"Robin did pay attention to him. She was civil and polite because, I assumed, her mother invited him because she thought him to be her friend from the past, so she didn't want to embarrass her mother."

As Nagy spoke, something went on in his eyes. He paused in mid-thought, if not mid-sentence. When he began speaking again, the tenor of his voice grew harsh, as if in reliving the day he described, he'd just now discovered something about it that he hadn't remembered or remembered differently now in the retelling.

"If you'd seen the way James acted, you'd have thought the entire occasion was to honor him. At one point, I said something to him—something meaningless, the kind of mundane thing you say at a gathering like that—and it was as if I'd stepped out of bounds by addressing him at all—an enlisted man trying to get chummy with a superior officer. I wasn't important enough to talk to him.

"I almost smacked him then. He had that kind of attitude—he was the smartest man in the room, the toughest man in the room, the bravest, the most important man in the room. I guess you get away with that attitude when you're an officer and have men serving under you who can't speak up." Nagy was silent again for a moment, as if remembering something else about the encounter.

Ambler took advantage of the silence. "What was Robin like with him?"

The question troubled Nagy. But his reaction was different than when Ambler suggested an affair. This time, he wasn't reacting; he was remembering, perhaps seeing something for the first time.

While he rummaged through his memories, Ambler caught a glimpse of Benny peering through the window that faced the side of the bar. He couldn't see Nagy's face from there, so Ambler gestured with his head for him to come in and nodded toward Nagy. Benny opened the door, stuck his head in, took a gander at Nagy, and shook his head.

McNulty knew what was happening, so he distracted Nagy by asking if he wanted anything before the kitchen closed.

Nagy didn't hear him; he was clearly troubled by his memories. "Looking back on that day now after all that's happened, I'm not sure what her attitude was. If you'd asked me then, I would have said she treated him coldly, but just now I remembered something. They disappeared together for a time. I'm not sure how long . . . I'm not even sure if they were together. They were both gone at the same time for perhaps a half-hour. I never thought anything of it until this minute. I never asked Robin about it because it never seemed important."

The possible implication of what Nagy had said was clear to Ambler, and from Nagy's dismayed expression dawning on him also, so Ambler changed the subject before Nagy blew up again.

"This evidence, Robin said she had. Do you have any idea what it is?"

Nagy shook his head, but then Ambler had an idea.

"You still live in the house you and Robin lived in together, I think you said. Is it possible that she left some of her possessions in that house? I mean, things you'd store in the attic or some place, like diaries or notebooks."

Nagy said no and then his expression changed. "My God. You're right. She did leave a bunch of boxes in the attic, I think with her things from high school and college. I could look when I get home." He rubbed his chin for quite a while, reminding Ambler of McNulty and causing him a bit of worry.

"Are you thinking you might find something about Doug James among all that?"

"It's unlikely," Ambler said. "If she'd written anything about James, I think she'd have brought it with her to the library. But it's worth taking a look."

Nagy agreed. "I'm pretty sure what's there are notebooks and journals, photos, scrapbooks and such. Finding anything would be a needle in a haystack, though."

# TWENTY

George Nagy had his interview with Chris Lambert the next morning and left the city the same day. Later the following afternoon, he called Ambler to tell him he'd overnighted a box of Robin's diaries and letters he'd found in the attic. "Robin was orderly. She had the boxes dated. So I only sent a couple of small boxes, with stuff from the time she was in college up to a couple of years after that. Everything else she took with her. It's not a lot . . . and I didn't look through it." His tone changed and he sounded sad. "I guess I was afraid of what I might find."

He didn't say anything about his meeting with Lambert, which of course was his prerogative and none of Ambler's business, but he asked anyway.

"Quite uneventful. There were two detectives. They were polite. One asked hard questions, the other seemed to be trying to make things easier for me. Perhaps this was their idea of good cop/bad cop. They asked about my relationship with Robin, the divorce and all. One of them, the one asking most of the questions, wanted to know about my altercation with Doug James, so I told them Robin despised him and believed he'd killed her friend, or at least drove her to suicide. They didn't respond to that. They both nodded, looked intrigued, and asked where I was the day Robin was killed.

"When I told them, they began to lose interest in the questioning."

"Did they ask you about Blake Beasley?"

"I told them I never met the man. They asked where I was when he was killed, and I told them."

"They weren't at all interested in what you told them about Linda Porter's death?"

"If they were, they didn't tell me . . . I waited for them to ask who I thought killed Robin. But they never asked, so I didn't tell them. I wonder now if I should have."

"Probably wouldn't have made any difference since you don't have anything to back it up. For what it's worth, I've already put his name forward . . . though also without anything to back it up." Ambler had a thought he'd meant to bring up earlier but for some reason had hesitated. Now, he wished he had when he'd been with Nagy in person and could have gauged his reaction.

"Robin had a colleague here in the visiting professor program, Thomas Jones."

Nagy didn't hesitate. "I know Thomas. He was a personal project for Robin. She took him under her wing and became a mentor to him. He was a pretty good college basketball player—a kid from the slums in L.A., but not good enough to play professionally. She thought he could become a scholar. Why do you ask?"

"He knew Robin before the visiting professor program. I wanted to know if you knew anything about him or their, I guess, professional relationship that might have gone sour, any reason he'd be angry at her—"

"If he had a reason to kill her? Is that what you're asking?" Nagy's voice rose. He was winding up to bluster again.

"It's not an accusation. It's a question."

"You don't believe Doug killed her?"

"It doesn't make any difference what I believe. There isn't any proof."

"Why don't you look for proof instead of speculating and making charges against someone when you have no reason to?"

Ambler didn't understand what the hell was going on with Nagy, so he wanted to get off the phone. "I appreciate you sending me Robin's diaries and things. If I can find proof in those papers that James killed Linda Porter, that will make him a prime suspect in Robin's death."

Nagy seemed to have calmed down. He said he'd glanced through them but didn't read any. "I was surprised to see a few letters from Doug James. I hadn't known they corresponded."

He paused for a long moment, and through the phone Ambler could feel the pain that he felt.

"They may be what you're looking for . . . I didn't want to read them." Now he was almost apologetic. "I'm sorry I went off on you about Thomas. I get that you need to ask about everyone."

"Let me try my question another way." He debated with himself telling Nagy what Jones had said. Telling him could turn things ugly between the two men, yet it was curious that Nagy was protective of Jones when Jones was accusing his protector of murder.

"My impression talking to Jones was that he wasn't especially fond of you. He thought you were unkind to Robin."

There was a moment of silence before Nagy, sounding reasonable again, said, "I'm not surprised by that really . . . I *was* unkind to her. I was rotten to her. I kicked myself every day—even before this horrible tragedy—for how I treated her. Before the divorce, Thomas had recognized that I didn't appreciate her, and in his way tried to warn me while defending her. He knew what a remarkable woman she was and told me I'd regret throwing her over for a schoolgirl.

"I was surprised by how much respect he showed her; I dismissed it as a student/teacher crush. I thought he was in love with her and wanted to show he stood up for her. Later, I realized this wasn't the case. He knew she loved me and that I was cruel to her, so he said what he said because he wanted her happiness. Since she believed her happiness was with me, that's what he wanted for her. A kind of selflessness I admire.

"I got angry at you because I didn't think he deserved your disparaging accusation. Perhaps it was my way of thanking him for trying to help me."

George Nagy was a difficult man to figure out. On one day such-and-such a man appeared who was disheveled, maudlin, bitter, and despairing. Yet his reputation appeared to be that he was something of a Lothario, a heart-throb for young college women.

The next time an entirely different man showed up,

half-drunk and brawling in a funeral parlor. Before you'd adjusted to that, he became reasonable, rational, and scholarly, going out of his way to be helpful with the investigation into his wife's death. To top things off, he puts you in your place for throwing accusations around, while he praises the attributes of a selfless man.

Thomas Jones was also an enigma, lying when he had no reason to, telling the truth in such a way as to make it unbelievable—a denizen of the slums, a college basketball player, a killer, though justifiably in self-defense, a scholar of some renown, and a man who had acted selflessly, according to George Nagy. There was no evidence suggesting he'd murdered Robin Cartwright, but Ambler wasn't ready to cross him off the list just yet. Maybe if Jones came up with the alibi he was talking about . . .

The thing was, as McNulty had suggested, it was time to shorten the list of suspects. Perhaps he should cross off everyone he'd put on the list and begin an entirely new one. He'd ask Jones about his alibi. He'd call the detective Arturo Lopez in the South Bronx and ask him if there was a way of knowing if Ricardo Diaz was truly disabled.

Who was left? Clifton Kilgore. If Ambler could pick anyone to be the killer, it would be the con-artist pastor. Decent society would be better off with him locked up. But nothing had ever linked him to New York. That didn't mean he couldn't have gotten to the city, killed Robin, gone back to his flock, and then returned to the city once more to kill Blake Beasley. But it didn't seem likely he could be back and forth to River City to stalk Adele three or four or however many times without someone noticing his absence in Wolverton. That should probably be true for all of the suspects.

Ambler hadn't talked to Benny about Nagy yet, and he didn't have a photo of Pastor Kilgore, but it would be easy enough to have Benny check out Kilgore's church website. Kilgore's smiling puss was all over it. This left Colonel Doug James. Ambler had a feeling about him, not unlike his feeling about Kilgore. McNulty maintained that kids and dogs know when someone might be threatening to them. Could Ambler have developed a sixth sense that told him when he was in the presence of a murderer?

This would certainly make his crime solving easier . . . Unfortunately, his innate dislike of the colonel and the pastor had no bearing on who killed Robin Cartwright and Blake Beasley. He was coming to suspect there might be a dark horse, someone above suspicion, lurking in the background. Who might that be? A former student who got an F when he thought he should get an A in one of Professor Cartwright's courses? A criminologist writing a competing book? . . . This line of thinking would get him nowhere.

Having Benny take a look at photos of Clifton Kilgore—and maybe Colonel James—on their respective websites might eliminate both of them as suspects. On the other hand, the possibility remained, remote though it might be, that the person who spoke with Beasley shortly before his death wasn't the person who killed him.

Everything was a muddle. By this time in other investigations, he had some idea where he was going and whom he was after. Why not this time? It might be, as McNulty said, that the old brain cells were burning out. It also might be that he no longer saw Adele every day to bounce his ideas off her. She'd spoiled him.

For years, he'd been alone and more or less used to it. Then, he'd stumbled across a murder—in the library—which followed him around until, with a little help from him and counsel from Adele, it solved itself. After that, he'd looked into the reasons for other murders somehow connected to the library, and each one brought with it, after due diligence on his part and again Adele's counsel, its solution. Along the way, without any real intention on his part, an unknown driving force that had told him to go here and turn there and talk to this person had also thrust Adele into his life and soon after into his arms.

Now he was a father again without intending to be. And now somehow—absolutely without intending it—he was alone again. Adele had dispatched him. His son and grandson were in the North Bronx, even Lola the dog had taken a hike, moving in with the boys.

Perhaps what he needed was a cat to keep him company, some books to read, a few bottles of wine, some cheese and charcuterie, and to sit in his apartment, staying out of the way until the murders of Robin and Blake decided to solve themselves. Then again . . .

All thought of sitting by the side of the road letting the world pass him by disappeared that evening when Adele called. Ambler was thrilled when her name popped up on his cell phone. But his elation and delight were short-lived.

"Someone was in my house, waiting for me this afternoon. I'd gone to do some laundry and to pick up some things. They'd left by the time I got home. It's a good thing I've been staying with Lisa and Mike. The police are putting me under protective custody now. I'm going to a hotel—I can't tell you where—not that I'd be inclined to, anyway."

Dazed, he asked a few questions, getting mostly monosyllabic answers from taciturn Adele. He tried in a couple of different ways to tell her he was sorry, but his entreaties didn't move her, not a hint of forgiveness or even interest. She might as well have come out and told him nothing you say can change anything.

The lock had been broken on her back door. A chair that had been against a wall had been moved and placed near the front window so whoever sat in it could watch the front walk and the driveway. No calls this time. He tried to tell her he'd find whoever was threatening her. But he never even got the words out.

After the call, he stared at his wall. He'd never been so frustrated. Fighting an urge to run out of his apartment, to go he knew not where, to chase after he knew not whom, he took deep breaths to calm himself. At one point, he reached for the bottle of Irish whiskey that McNulty said he should always have on hand for use in case of emergency. This emergency he decided required a clear head, so he took a pass.

The one chance he had, he realized after a few minutes of frenzied thought, was to take McNulty's advice. He needed to go over everything he'd already done, everyone he'd spoken to, the journals he'd already read through. Another last hope were the boxes of letters and diaries from George Nagy that would arrive in the morning.

He put on a pot of coffee and took out the photocopies he'd made of Robin's journal. Then he called Benny Bevone, who was home, gave him the names of a couple of websites to look up and told him to examine the photos of the two men.

He poured a cup of coffee, then read over and over Robin's strange note about the man from her past she'd met on the library steps and then had dinner with shortly before her death—the man she'd referred to as Preacher. Each time he read it, he felt he kept missing something the note was trying to tell him, something just out of reach.

*After all these years (I wonder if he knows???), I ran into Preacher on the library steps. I almost died. I was shocked and felt so guilty that I was trying to hide something and got caught (like the time when I was in high school and my mother found a box of rubbers I was hiding). But why my reaction? He couldn't possibly know about the book. And even if he did, I don't have anything to be ashamed of. He does! Still, I had a ridiculous urge to confess.*

*He couldn't possibly know about the book . . . Even though I'm certain of that, a voice in my head kept telling me: He Knows!! Yet when he asked about my life since the last time I saw him, it was as if he didn't know anything about what I'd been doing. And he obviously has no idea what I was doing at the library. He didn't even ask.*

*As charming and tempting as I remembered him, he took me for a drink and dinner at the Library Tavern. Strangely . . . very strangely . . . we talked about everything, except that time. He's so convincing.*

*After a few glasses of wine, he began coming on to me—he can't help himself; he never could—and he's still very good at it. You look into his eyes and you're sure you're the only woman in the world for him. And still it was subtle, the same as back then. Subtly so we both could pretend the attraction hadn't happened. For a moment, it made me sick that he thought I'd want to be with him again after what happened.*

*Yet, I hate to admit it even to myself, he still turns me on. Then I got an idea. I might have batted my eyelashes. I might have blushed. Devious is my middle name. I told him I didn't know what was happening to me; I didn't know what I was feeling. It was so amazing to see him. The way I said it, my sultry tone—I put my hand on his thigh; I gazed into his eyes—would lead him to think I wanted to see him again. I gave him my cell phone number.*

After the third time through, he stopped and stared at it. The man from her past. Was it Nagy? Doug James? Thomas Jones? Had she known Clifton Kilgore in the past? Was it someone else entirely? Was she going to expose someone in her book he didn't know about? Who the hell was Preacher?

It had to be Clifton Kilgore. Everything pointed to it. Yet Greenleaf swore Kilgore's alibi was iron-clad, for both the day she was murdered and the night Blake was murdered. Alibis can be faked. Greenleaf swore this wasn't the case. If it wasn't Kilgore, then it had to be James. But the colonel had an alibi, too, or said he did . . .

He was rereading the note—the out-of-place diary entry—for the fourth time when Benny called.

"Neither of those guys looked like the guy who demanded I bring Blake to him."

Ambler's heart sank. Then a light went on. "Demanded you bring him?"

"Yeh. I went to get Blake. He told me he didn't have time to talk to this guy, whoever he was. I went back and told the guy Blake was busy. He shouted at me, the asshole. I told him to quiet down, he was in a library. He did one of those, 'Do-you-know-who-I-am' bits, told me he could put my ass in a sling if I didn't go back and tell Blake he'd better get out here or his ass would be in a sling too.

"The guy acted like he was the commanding general or

something. I almost told him to go fuck himself, but he was a tough-looking guy, and I figured getting into a tussle with a reader in the Rose reading room would probably not be real good for my career, so I went and got Blake. Let him deal with the asshole."

Ambler's heart was pounding. The man asking for Blake . . . "He didn't look like Colonel Douglas James on the High Alert Security Professionals website?"

"No. The guy looking for Blake had a mustache. The army guy on the website was clean-shaven."

Ambler looked at the phone, his heart pounding and his hands shaking. The man Benny described gave orders like he was used to being obeyed. He was arrogant and overbearing, showed disdain for his presumed underlings. Who did this sound like?

When he had his voice under control, he said, "Do me a favor. Go back to the High Alert Security photo. Look at the face carefully . . . Ignore the mustache. Look at his eyes, just his eyes. Then look at his haircut, at his ears. Look at him five or six times and keep picturing the man you spoke to in the library."

# TWENTY-ONE

Ambler went back to his reading, going once more through the outline and the couple of chapters Robin had already written, coming back again to the strange note about dinner with Preacher. Who the hell was Preacher if it wasn't Clifton Kilgore?

He called the sheriff's office in Wolverton, and whoever he talked to put him through to Sergeant Greenleaf, who was home eating dinner.

"When the first murder took place, he was conducting a prayer service in front of forty or fifty people. I didn't ask all of them, but he gave me names of a half-dozen people I knew. For the second murder, he'd taken the church's youth ministry group on an overnight camping trip." Greenleaf sighed and mumbled something Ambler didn't get.

"I wish I could tell you different, could poke a hole in his alibi. He's as slippery as a greased pig. All lawyered up now. His old man's putting pressure on everyone he can think of—I got calls from a couple of the county supervisors and so did the sheriff. Lucky for us, the sheriff doesn't like to be pushed around, so we're still working on the Anna Paxton case. The problem is Kilgore's lawyer's in pretty good with the commonwealth attorney's office . . . We'll see what happens."

Benny called back twenty minutes later. "I don't know, Ray. It could be the same guy. I wouldn't swear to it; I didn't spend a lot of time looking at him in the library."

"OK. You don't have to swear to it. Would you positively say it wasn't the same man?"

"Would I what? . . . No. I couldn't say I was sure he wasn't the guy. It might be him; I'm not sure."

"You've done good, Benny. You may make it as a private eye after all."

After the call, Ambler had had enough coffee. He went to the Library Tavern for a beer, a burger, and a consultation with the wise old bartender.

"Play 'em like you got 'em," McNulty said after they'd talked for a while. "This 'preacher' moniker could mean anything. Preacher Roe wasn't a preacher, yet they called him that his whole career. Maybe a Dodger announcer called him Elwin once in a while, but mostly it was Preacher Roe."

Easily-Sidetracked McNulty went on tell Ambler how Roe got his nickname. The story being that when asked his name as a three-year-old, he answered Preacher. No one knew why that was his answer, but it stuck.

Ambler wasn't to be sidetracked. "It could mean anything, but it actually means something. She had dinner with Preacher, a man from her past she ran into by accident—or she thought by accident; it might not have been—and was happy to have dinner with him, even though, if we believe her notes, she was trying to prove he was a murderer."

Having loaded the behind-the-bar glass-washer, McNulty returned to the conversation. "So the guy I saw her having dinner with—the ex-husband—is not the guy Benny saw right before your fellow worker in the library was murdered. According to your line of thinking, they should have been the same person. But the colonel guy—even though I didn't see him having dinner with her—might be the guy Benny saw."

"Nagy said he'd had dinner with his ex-wife shortly after she'd moved to New York. She could have had dinner here with another man more recently, and you missed it."

McNulty shrugged. "That's possible. I can't remember exactly when I saw her with Nagy. It's also possible Benny's wrong. Eyewitnesses—like your pal Benny—aren't all they're cracked up to be. They're mistaken a lot of the time."

"I'm not putting Benny on the witness stand. If the man he saw in the library was James, it's one more piece in a puzzle . . . You can't say for sure you never saw Robin Cartwright here with another man. Or they might have come in when you weren't here."

"I saw her with you. Maybe I saw her other times. Not having dinner, I don't think . . . You know, I've been wrong on occasion. I've missed things I should've seen. If you want, I can take a gander at that web page with this fly boy's mug on it."

Ambler pulled up the High Alert Security website on his cell phone and showed McNulty the photo. After examining it for longer than Ambler thought necessary, he said, "I might have seen him; I might not have. I don't remember every face. If I was looking through a bunch of photos—like a book of mug shots—I might stop and look at this one longer. His is the face—the expression—of a man I wouldn't like. If I want to be sure, I'd need to see him in person."

McNulty needed to see James in person. Could they do this? Invite him to come down from Massachusetts to New York to have a drink? That wasn't going to happen. And even if McNulty did recognize James, what would it mean? Just one more piece in the puzzle. So, if the mountain won't come to McNulty, McNulty should go to the mountain, this mountain being in Springfield, Massachusetts.

Ambler had sent McNulty on missions more than once in the past, either to get a good look at someone or to put something over on a suspect. He was good at subterfuge. For McNulty, bartending was a sideline; his real mission in life was the stage. He was an actor, trained in the Stanislavski Method. His lack of success, despite hundreds of casting calls and auditions, had yet to diminish his commitment to his art. Any part for McNulty was an important part. He could present himself to James in his office as almost anyone and put on a virtuoso performance even if he didn't have an audience except for the colonel.

"You could look him up in person then," Ambler said. "See if you recognize him."

McNulty—who was now unloading the glass-washing machine, which had run its cycle in an amazingly short time—stopped what he was doing and took a couple of steps closer to Ambler. "We're talking here about a guy who might be a killer. Maybe by looking at him I could not only recognize him, I could tell he was a murderer. Or maybe he'd take umbrage at my nosing around and kill me. Then we'd know for sure he was a murderer . . . or you would."

If there wasn't a serious chance that James or someone else would murder Adele, Ambler might have seen some humor in what McNulty said. But he didn't. It might be McNulty didn't see any humor in what he said either.

The focus now was on James, no doubt about it. Ambler was putting all his money on one horse. Everything Ambler knew about James didn't add up to enough to accuse him of murder . . . but it added up to something. If it turned out he was wrong—the colonel wasn't the murderer—he'd have to admit this was a good thing, an accomplishment, eliminating a suspect. But it would be a good thing with a bad side. Because if James hadn't murdered Robin Cartwright, he'd have run himself out of suspects.

When he got home, Ambler drew up a list of everything he knew about Colonel Douglas James, USAF retired, and how he knew it. What did he know: a hot-shot air-force pilot, a wooer of at least two much younger women—and a suspect in the murders of each of them, accused of the murder of one of them by the victim's ex-husband; accused of the murder of the other victim by Robin Cartwright herself. The accusations however didn't carry much weight because they lacked supporting evidence.

In the morning, a batch of letters and diaries and who-knew-what-else would arrive. With luck, they'd contain a revelation—the evidence. Colonel James might, in his ardent letters, have incriminated himself. It wouldn't be the first time such a thing happened. Was there anything else? Had Ambler exhausted his sources? He thought about this for a moment and remembered a source—his first source, Uncle Walt.

He hadn't spoken to Robin's uncle since her funeral. Now he was thinking—hoping?—Uncle Walt might know more about James than he'd said then. At the time, Ambler didn't know then what he knew now, so he might be able to ask more probing questions, though at the moment he didn't know what they were.

He found a listing for Walter Benjamin in Longmeadow in the white pages online and called, even though it was late. Luckily, the retired army major was happy to speak with him, despite the hour. They didn't exchange pleasantries. They had no background in common except for the circumstances surrounding Robin's murder, so Ambler didn't ask what kind of day he'd had or about his well-being since they last talked. Not so surprisingly, Uncle Walt knew why he called.

"I suppose you've come up with new questions about Doug. I understand you paid him a visit. You certainly put his nose out of joint."

"He told you about it?"

"My sister, Angela, Robin's mother, told me. For some reason Doug thought I had something to do with you finding him—which we both know I didn't—so he called to ask me about you.

"When Doug feels he's been attacked or threatened, his defense is to defame whoever attacked him. One thing I do know about him is he had a pretty awful childhood. His father was strict, mean, if not downright cruel. Doug's the only man I've ever known who hated his father.

"What he took from his miserable upbringing formed his approach to life—which he is quite proud of. If someone hits you, hit them back harder. If someone hurts you, though he won't admit to being hurt, hurt them more. If someone criticizes you, you malign and denigrate them, drag them through the mud. That's what he's doing with you.

"If you haven't yet, you'll realize you've been maligned. You'll hear calumny from your colleagues, your boss, your friends, people you know casually, or even strangers. My sister, for instance, believes you're out to destroy the colonel's reputation, as is George Nagy."

Still digesting the first part of what Walt had said, he only half heard. "Why would I do that? Why would he do that?"

"Because you, like George, are consumed by jealousy. You were both in love with Robin and you hate Doug because she loved *him*; he was the only man she ever loved."

"Jesus," Ambler said. "That's what he thinks?"

Uncle Walt chuckled. "He doesn't have to believe it. It's a way of harming you; that's what's important. What you'll hear is you're blaming the murder on Doug because you want to divert attention from you and Nagy. But most important, you're doing it to destroy Doug . . . There's more if you care to hear it . . ." Walt chuckled.

"Sure."

"Robin tried to destroy Doug, too. He refused her overtures. She offered herself to him and he rejected her. She hated him for that. He told her he was in love with Linda Porter. He planned to marry her. They were preparing to elope when she died. Probably, none of this was true. Robin came to hate him."

"My God." Ambler truly was astonished. "He must have stayed up nights making all of this up."

James knew Ambler would accuse him of Robin's murder and had prepared an elaborate counter-story. And he'd gotten out in front of Ambler with his story. If and when Ambler accused him, the accusation would be seen as based on falsehoods that everyone already knew were coming.

"He's good at it." Uncle Walt was no longer chuckling. "I can tell you of three or four men whose careers he ruined by innuendo, false accusations, and calumny because they crossed him. In two of the cases, I know for sure that what the men reported on Doug was true—a runway accident that damaged a fighter jet that was his fault, and an incident report that he made disappear. On each occasion, he skated, and the accusers ended up getting court-martialed and losing rank."

This time, Ambler chuckled. "Are you thinking if I don't go to Colonel James on bended knee, I'll end up charged with murder?"

No mirth from Uncle Walt. "If you're going to pin something on Doug, I'd make sure the case you make is iron-clad. If it isn't, you or George Nagy will be in irons and he'll go scot-free. It's not that he's smarter or more cunning than you. He's more ruthless than you could possibly be. You have a moral code of some sort; you have principles, some standard of decency that governs what you're willing to do or what you won't allow yourself to do. Doug has no such impediments. No rules of engagement for him."

After a moment to let this sink in, Ambler said, "It's interesting that he's gone to such measures to defend himself from an accusation that hasn't been made, at least not by me. Is he building this elaborate defense because he did murder Robin and this is how he plans to get away with it? Does his ruthlessness go as far as murder?"

Uncle Walt spoke slowly and deliberately. "I'm sure he'd kill someone if it was important enough for him. He'd do it in such a way as to get away with it without having to go to extremes after the fact to prove himself innocent."

"Make it look like an accident or a suicide, for example?"

Uncle Walt didn't get the reference. "Something foolproof. I'm not ruthless enough to know what that would be. Do you believe he killed Robin?"

"Everything points to him, except for anything that would count as evidence."

Uncle Walt let some time go by before he spoke again. When he did, he spoke softly. "Have you considered the possibility that someone else killed her? Even though most of what Doug said about her and about him and Linda are lies, in his own way I think he was really fond of her, perhaps in love with her."

"Someone else?" Ambler was grasping at straws. "Can you think of anyone else from her past who'd have reason to murder her?"

He took a moment to think it over. "No one at all. I knew some of her friends—there weren't many—some of the people in her circle when she was young didn't like her. She and Linda were frivolous. There were men she treated badly. She could be nasty if she didn't get her way, and dismissive of men she got tired of."

"Did you ever come across anyone she knew called Preacher or the Preacher?"

"Preacher?" Uncle Walt sounded surprised. "Preacher!? That was Doug's call sign."

# TWENTY-TWO

"A call sign," Ambler told McNulty the next evening, "is a kind of nickname pilots give one another. The call sign sticks with them; it's the name other pilots use on the radio; they put it on their uniforms, so it becomes kind of official."

"So that makes him your guy, right?"

"It means he was here in this restaurant with Robin shortly before she was killed, and he was one of her subjects."

"So I did miss him."

"It must have been your night off."

"If it was, Sid would have been working. I'll call and tell him to look up Colonel James's photo on that website."

"Does he know what Robin Cartwright looks like?"

McNulty shook his head. "He'll have to look for a photo of her, too . . . This is going to be a challenge for Sid. He doesn't like it when you ask him to do something."

McNulty called his fellow worker on the house phone and took a good amount of time to explain what he wanted him to do.

"Well?" Ambler asked when he'd finished the call.

"His son is going to help him do the looking up. It may take a while."

While they waited for Sid to call back, Ambler told the bartender what Robin's uncle had said about James's plan to flood the world with lies about him and George Nagy. "And it's working. Harry has already gotten a call from someone—he won't tell me who—who told him I'm a suspect in Robin Cartwright's murder.

"It's true. I am a suspect. I found out from Lambert. The police got a tip that I'd sexually assaulted her and killed her to keep her from reporting it . . . Her uncle said this was going to happen and a day later it happened as he said it would."

McNulty showed no surprise that Ambler was now a suspect in his own murder investigation. He nodded knowingly. "As Hurricane Carter said, 'A lie can circle the world twice before the truth even gets its boots on.' What are the odds of them hanging the murder on you?"

Hanging a rap for murder on him was not something Ambler had thought he'd be discussing. "I don't think they will. I was out of town when Robin was killed. Lambert said they'd check on the claim because the tip came to the precinct from One Police Plaza.

"James—who I'm sure is behind this—would have done better to try to pin Blake Beasley's murder on me. At least he was someone I'd considered murdering. Still, I don't like it that Lambert is going to investigate, even though I told him where I was."

McNulty appeared to be amused by Ambler's predicament. "With Adele? . . . What if she's still mad and tells him she hasn't seen you in months?"

This stopped Ambler in his tracks. "She wouldn't do that . . ." He looked pleadingly at McNulty. "Would she?"

The phone interrupted them and McNulty went to talk with Sid. When he finished, he told Ambler Sid was pretty sure he'd seen James and Robin having dinner together not so long ago. "So," the bartender said, "that's that. The question now is: What are you going to do about this guy you think is the murderer?"

Sid's recollection wasn't rock-solid evidence that Doug James was Preacher, but it was good enough. "I have a plan," Ambler said, with false enthusiasm covering his doubts. "I spent most of last night and all of today thinking about it. Having read extensively in crime fiction has made me what I am today, and it's now going to get us over this hump."

McNulty made a face. "I'm not sure I like the *us* part of your plan."

"Remember Jules Maigret, Chief Inspector Maigret, from a whole series of books I told you about, and you read some years ago?"

McNulty, for whatever reason, took on his judicial pose. "I remember. He had a bunch of assistants that I always got mixed up, smoked a pipe, and would often stop for a beer, a glass of wine, or a nip of Calvados in the middle of an investigation, pretty much at any time of the day—morning, noon, or night—and almost always, unless he was interrogating a suspect, went home for lunch, which his wife, who never seemed to go anywhere, would have ready for him."

The bartender had rattled off his description without acknowledging aspects of the Simenon novels Ambler knew McNulty was very much aware of and moved by—their compassion for victims and perpetrators alike. Ambler didn't push him on this because it was a different aspect of the Maigret novels he was interested in at the moment, The chief inspector's interrogations.

"Yeh. I remember those, too," McNulty said. "In most of the books he ended up practically talking the guy to death until he gave up and admitted he was the killer . . . I liked that when he sent out for beer and sandwiches from the Brasserie Dauphine, he included the culprit."

"That's the plan."

It took a lot to cause the bartender to do a double take. But he did this time. "We're gonna bring him in and ply him with beer and sandwiches?"

"Not precisely. We'll go to him."

"Why would he talk to us? And why is this an *us* proposition?"

"The two are connected."

Ambler had caught up with McNulty on his one-day shift, during the dead period in the middle of the afternoon between the end of lunch and the beginning of cocktail hour. No one besides Ambler was at the bar, and only one couple was at a table, speaking quietly and earnestly long after their lunch dishes had been cleared.

His plan was risky, one might say foolhardy, though not McNulty after Ambler had explained.

"We're not cops, so he can't demand a lawyer. And the

reason he'll talk to us is because me and Lumps will be there to keep him from leaving."

"Precisely." Ambler spoke with more confidence than he felt. He'd never done anything like this before, hadn't ever considered doing anything like this. Colonel Doug James would be a tough nut to crack. But through a night and a day of considering the situation from every possible angle, he could think of no other approach.

Lumps, whose given name was Dennis Gannon, was a friend of McNulty's—they'd grown up together and followed different paths into the entertainment world: McNulty into the theater, and Lumps, who was the size of a small delivery truck, into the world of professional wrestling. Since his retirement from the ring, he'd worked as a bouncer at a number of what McNulty called Bucket-of-Blood establishments, as well as doing some muscle work for a couple of loan sharks.

Ambler's plan was this. There was no chance James would talk to him voluntarily. He was a tough guy, in good shape, even at his age. Ambler wouldn't be able to physically intimidate him. But Lumps, who could fill in "intimidator" on an occupation blank if he wanted to, could. McNulty would be there to offer advice and to discourage James from trying Lumps one-on-one if he was foolish enough to think he could.

Nothing physical would take place unless James tried to leave. The only thing the ace pilot had to do was talk. They might talk for a long time—might have to send out for beer and sandwiches. Ambler would be the one to decide when the talking was done.

He couldn't explain if he wanted to why he thought this crazy scheme would work, why James, a decorated combat airman, would at some point throw in the towel and confess. But the very fact James was a decorated war veteran, an air-force lifer, was the reason he thought it might work.

Somewhere in his deranged psyche, James had to have a sense of honor. It might not be Ambler's sense of honor—and certainly not McNulty's. James prided himself as having always been the good guy fighting against the bad guys. His entire sense of self-worth was dependent on it, Ambler believed. Who knew what he might do when forced to come face-to-face with the reality that he was the bad guy?

# TWENTY-THREE

It took longer than Ambler expected—a night and most of the next day—to trap James alone in his not especially luxurious Tudor-style house in a tidy neighborhood in Enfield, Connecticut, a few miles across the state line from Springfield.

The delay gave Ambler—ensconced in a chain motel room just off Interstate 91 near the state line while Lumps and McNulty alternately shadowed James and staked out his house—a chance to skim through the letters and diaries of a young, mercurial, romantic, and depressive Robin Cartwright. The diaries were neither informative nor especially interesting. Either she didn't know herself very well, or she didn't care to reveal much about herself even in a diary. They could have been entitled *The Diary of a Generic Young Woman.*

The only letters he was interested in were those from Lieutenant Colonel Doug James. And those weren't any more revealing about him than the diaries were about her. If Ambler had hoped to find the epistolary equivalent of a smoking gun, he was, to quote McNulty, "Shit out of luck."

On the evening of the second day, McNulty called to tell him James was home alone. When Ambler rang the doorbell, and announced himself, James opened the door and Lumps grabbed him by the throat, pinned his arm behind his back, and pushed him down onto his own sofa, from where he listened, dumbfounded, while Ambler explained the rules of the game.

"You're insane!" James shouted, loudly enough to be heard over a jet engine. "This is kidnapping. It's a home invasion. It's a crime. You'll go to prison for years." He said all of this without lowering the volume a decibel.

What he said had a good deal of truth to it, Ambler had

to admit, except, he hoped, for the prison-for-years part. The problem was he hadn't counted on the shouting. The house next door wasn't that close, but it wasn't that far away either.

"We're going to need to talk calmly and quietly," he explained. "Nothing physical is going to happen—despite Mr. Gannon's significant expertise in that area—unless you try to leave . . . or you make too much noise with that shouting. All we plan to do is talk. No strong-arm to make you say anything you don't want to say. If you wait me out, so be it."

"I'll say it again. You're crazy." He didn't shout this time.

Ambler scrutinized him for a moment. "You've been telling lies about me."

James stared back but uneasily. He didn't have anyone to appeal to, nowhere to turn for support. He could deny Ambler's charge but both of them knew what Ambler said was true. He didn't speak but shifted his gaze to take in his own living room and the two other intruders.

Ambler spoke softly. "I haven't told lies about you; I haven't accused you of anything." He turned to McNulty. "You recognize him?"

"No. You should have brought Sid, except he'd have brains enough not to come. He said this was the guy. What else do you need?"

James had listened to Ambler and McNulty without seeming to understand what they were talking about. "I'm not going to say anything, so you're wasting your time." He spoke quietly, not quite assuredly. It was interesting that he'd lost his arrogance.

"How often do you come to New York?" Ambler's instinct told him to begin with ambiguous questions.

James smirked in response. "I grew up in New York—in Brooklyn. I go there a lot."

This interested McNulty. "Brooklyn? I did, too. Where?"

"Canarsie." Strangely, James found this topic interesting, also.

"Flatbush. Both of us." McNulty nodded toward Lumps,

who nodded toward James in acknowledgment in what might have been a friendly way. McNulty continued, "You went to Canarsie, right? We played you in basketball. Erasmus Hall."

"We weren't very good."

"You sucked."

"We beat you in football."

The talk—about high school football, basketball, baseball, girls, candy stores, egg creams, fifteen cent tokens, Thom McAn shoe stores, and other reminiscences of Brooklyn back in the day—was not the conversation Ambler had hoped for.

James had caught on that the only thing happening in that room would be talk, and must have told himself he could outduel Ambler and his henchmen in a battle of wits. This was OK with Ambler; he'd counted on the colonel's hubris to make him vulnerable.

McNulty had reminded Ambler the day before as they waited to corral James that because he never drank when he played poker, he'd made a lot of money off poker players who did. "Inspector Maigret knew what he was doing when he sent out for sandwiches and beer," McNulty said.

"In vino veritas?"

"Works with beer, too."

When Ambler had had enough of the old days in Brooklyn, he told McNulty it was time for sandwiches and beer.

"You drink beer?" McNulty addressed the colonel.

The colonel laughed, not nervously, a relaxed chortle. "Sure. Craft beer if I get a choice, an IPA." He turned to Ambler. "You guys have a method of some sort? You should have asked your cop friends how to do an interrogation."

"Let's say I believe you can tell me how Robin Cartwright died."

James stood up. "I need to use the bathroom."

"Mr. Gannon will go with you."

James looked at Lumps and then at Ambler. "I'll leave the door open." He started to walk away but stopped. "You're not going to get anything out of this idiotic stunt . . . and you're not going to get away with it. You said I told lies about you. Is that what this is about? What lies?"

"That I murdered Robin Cartwright because she resisted my advances."

"I might have said that. I might think that. But so might a lot of other people, including the police. Why pick on me?"

"Because you're the source and you pushed the idea on the police." James could have asked him why he thought this. But he didn't, which was an admission in itself.

Ambler liked that they were talking. If James talked, there was a chance he'd make a mistake, let something slip. Or he might even tell the truth, admit his crime. If he kept his mouth shut, didn't talk at all, there was no chance he'd slip up or say too much.

James moved a step closer to Ambler and took a combative stance. "You don't know how the police get their information. Why shouldn't I think you'd fallen for Robin? I know what she was like. You were obsessed with her. You still are, obviously, given this charade . . ." He waved an arm at his surroundings, including Lumps Gannon. "You're out to pin Robin's murder on me. Whether you killed her or George did. Either way, you want me to be blamed. I'd be crazy to let you get away with that."

The remarkable thing was that—even though James was lying through his teeth and everyone in the room including him knew it—he came across as believable; because of how he said what he said, with such assurance, such confidence, it was difficult not to believe him.

There was no telling where this exchange was going, but Ambler was sure it had life. "You and I know the truth. Why the pretense when we both know what's true?"

James was unfazed. "You accuse me. I accuse you. You say you tell the truth. I say I do. You think you have the upper hand because you have this lug here," he nodded toward Lumps. "He might not be as tough as you think he is." He straightened his shoulders and rolled his neck as if he were about to find out.

Ambler's plan wasn't foolproof, he knew. James could take a run at Lumps, could create a commotion, break a window, start a fire, do something to attract attention. He might do that. But Ambler didn't think he would. James wasn't dumb. He'd rather not have the local police refereeing an argument over which of them was a murderer.

If Ambler was right, James believed Ambler could make a case against him. He didn't know what Ambler knew, and in fact might have thought Ambler knew more about what he'd done than was the case. Because he was conscious of his guilt, James would tell himself he was better off playing mental gymnastics with Ambler and settling things without intervention from the police.

The intervention at that moment was McNulty returning with the sandwiches and beer—a case of a local craft brewery IPA. "I got a bunch of Italian heroes. The guy at the deli didn't know what I was talking about. They call them grinders. So I got Italian grinders." He looked at James. "You got room in the fridge for the beer? Or do you call it something else up here?" McNulty turned to Ambler. "Why's he standing up?"

Lumps answered. "He's either going to take a piss or make a run at me."

McNulty turned back to James. "If I were you, I'd take a piss. You may be tough. But Lumps does tugging and mauling for a living."

James began to walk toward the back of the house; he cocked his head toward Lumps. "I'll leave the door open." Lumps followed him.

In the ensuing conversation—after the sandwiches, the beer drinking continuing—James asked as many questions as Ambler did.

"If you intend to grill me," James asked when he'd finished his sandwich/hero/grinder, "can I ask for a lawyer?" He chuckled, enjoying his own humor by himself.

"How did you come to know George Nagy?" Ambler thought his tone was pleasant enough.

"I didn't know him. What makes you think I did?" James's tone was truculent.

"You knew him well enough for him to attack you at Robin's funeral." Ambler's tone was not so pleasant this time.

"I knew who he was. I didn't bother him; I didn't even talk

to him. I have no idea why he wanted to punch me. I told you he was insanely jealous and controlling."

"Did Robin tell you that? Had you stayed in contact with her while she was married?"

James froze for a second. His eyes went blank. He wasn't ready for the question, but it took him only a moment to switch gears. "Did Robin not tell you the same thing, that Nagy stalked her and threatened her once he realized she wouldn't take him back?"

She didn't. She hadn't even told him she'd once been married. He didn't see any reason he should tell James this. "So you were in contact with her?"

James was quick on his feet, keeping the conversation where he wanted it. "We weren't talking about her; we were talking about Nagy. I told you I'd never met him before that night."

"You met him at a family gathering at Robin's mother's house, some holiday gathering years ago."

James looked blank for a moment and then nodded slowly. "I guess I did meet him. He was there. I didn't remember."

"He said you and Robin disappeared for a period of time during the gathering. Do you remember that?"

James tried to fight back a smile and turned away from Ambler as if he were embarrassed. "I do."

"What was that about?"

The smile widened. "Do you really want to know?"

Ambler waited.

"Robin was a playgirl, a flirt if you like—she liked to get it on. I told you before she was attracted to me. We had sex—for old times' sake—in my car."

Ambler wanted to wipe the smirk off James's face. The problem with asking questions when you don't know the answer is you don't know when the person answering is lying or telling the truth. The best you could hope for was inconsistency, conflicting answers.

"The last time we talked, when I asked about Robin and Linda Porter, you said you were in love with Linda and Robin was jealous."

Ambler took note that James had opened his third beer. He

studied the can and then took a drink before he answered. "Robin was a tease, both of them were. I wasn't the only airman they slept with. It was a game to them. They joked about it, as if it were a major accomplishment to get a horny pilot to sleep with a promiscuous teenager. If you want the graphic details, I can give them to you." His smile was both smug and lewd.

"You were sleeping with both Robin and Linda Porter?"

"With both, yes . . . occasionally at the same time." Now you could add arrogant to smug and lewd.

This was close enough to prurient for Ambler to wonder how he'd gotten himself tangled up in this pornographic rendering that James was having so much fun with.

Perhaps Maigret's beer and sandwiches weren't such a good idea, after all. Ambler was still on his first beer and it appeared that James, despite his three beers, had taken charge of the conversation. He wished he knew more than he did—as much as James might think he knew—and could drop a piece of incriminating information on James that would knock him off his perch.

"You're not drinking, Mr. Ambler. Is your plan to ply me with alcohol so you can twist my words and pretend I've said something that I didn't say? I've drunk a lot of beer in my time—I'm a veteran airman—I can drink all three of you under the table."

Aha, said Ambler to himself. The hubris! To James, he said, "I don't care how much you drink." This, of course, wasn't true. The more the flyboy drank the better.

"It's good beer," McNulty said from a couch on the other side of the room.

"I don't know," said Lumps, who sat beside him. "I don't know about these fancy beers. An IPA used to be Ballantine."

"The poor man's whiskey," said McNulty.

"I like it," said James, who'd taken an interest in their discussion.

For the next few minutes, McNulty and Lumps Gannon talked about Ballantine Ale and Ballantine IPA and then Mel Allen and the Yankees and Vince Scully, the Dodgers, and

Schaefer Beer, while Ambler and James continued their back and forth, which might have appeared to the casual observer to be friendly. But beneath the banter each had his own serious, if not deadly, purpose.

Ambler, remembering what Robin's Uncle Walt had said, tried to get James to talk about his father. Something that had scarred him so deeply as a child would have a lot to do with what he was capable of doing as a man. Talking about his father, whom he hated, might trigger something in his psyche, causing him to say something he would otherwise keep to himself.

James had just compared piloting a fighter jet to handling a pompous librarian who thought he was a detective and a couple of clowns pretending to be hitmen. Ambler wanted to get him onto another subject before he talked himself into trying to take out Lumps Gannon—and finally he saw an opening. "Was your father an air-force pilot?"

The question had a remarkable effect on James. "Why would you ask that?" The response was thrown at Ambler like an angry wife might throw a bowl of spaghetti at her errant husband.

Ambler shrugged. "A lot of times men follow in their father's footsteps; in spite of themselves they become like their father."

"I'd sooner become a mangy dog than become like my father." He glared at Ambler. "My old man was a sick fuck. He treated me like I was the worst kid ever born—something God inflicted on him. He couldn't get enough of telling me or anyone who'd listen all the things that were wrong with me.

"Once I got to be eight or nine, he beat me with a belt once a week like clockwork for any tiny infraction at all—until I got big enough to stop him. I kicked the shit out of him the last time he tried to hit me. He was lucky I didn't kill him."

"Didn't your mother try to stop him?"

"My mother was a cowardly bitch. She was weak and scared to death of him and would do anything to please him. She cared about saving her own ass, and let me look out for myself. She'd tell the old fuck it wasn't her fault I was such a loser."

"That's awful." Ambler was serious. It was awful. "Didn't anyone try to help you? A teacher? The police?"

"The police, hah! My old man was a cop . . . A cop everybody thought was a hero. What were the cops going to do to him? The old man was straightening me out, making a man of me . . . What he was doing to me was criminal. Child abuse. The bastard should have been in jail. Instead, the other cops felt sorry for him with such a rotten kid. A juvenile cop. Can you believe that? He'd beat up kids on the street for nothing and then come home and beat me up. The bastard.

"He was a fucking coward on top it. When I was old enough to stand up to him, I slapped him around. I broke his nose and loosened his teeth. I told him if he touched me again, I'd kill him." The more James talked, the more agitated he got. His voice was a roar, his eyes blazed. "The old bastard whimpered like a baby and begged like a little girl, like I should feel sorry for the son of a bitch."

He stopped for a moment, as some thought caught up with him. "I didn't sympathize with anyone. I never did. Whatever it takes to care what happens to someone else, I didn't have. My old man knocked it out of me. He showed me how to hate, to not care, and to hit first. I'd kick the shit out of kids at school for no reason. I'd fight in the playground if another kid bumped into me or looked at me wrong. All the kids were scared of me. I got suspended. I got thrown off the basketball team."

He glanced at Lumps and then back at Ambler. "You think I'm afraid of that big oaf? I'd take him on; I'm not afraid of anyone." He glared at Lumps, whose expression was as placid as a cow chewing grass.

James's tone changed then. After a moment when he was quiet, deep in his thoughts, he spoke softly, as if he were asking Ambler to understand how he became like he was. "You don't believe me? I don't care. My father was a monster, so he created a monster. That's how it works. Most people don't catch on to how cruel I can be because they don't cross me. You caught on better than most people. I'll give you that."

His eyes were watery, the arrogance and the smugness replaced by a mournful sadness. "You know why I became a pilot? . . . I told you my old man was a cop. When I got arrested this one time near the end of high school, it was serious. Felonious assault."

This struck a chord with Ambler. "What for?"

James was bothered by the question; not, it appeared, because he was ashamed, but it interfered with the story he was telling and he didn't like being interrupted. "It doesn't make any difference. A girl I was going out with cheated on me with another guy. I found them together. I'd been drinking." He glanced over at McNulty and Lumps. "Schaefer actually . . . a lot of it. I got carried away and beat them both pretty bad with a baseball bat."

He was expressionless as he said this. If the memory brought him any regret, it didn't show. "Because dear old pop was a hero cop—a hero because of *his* felony assaults—instead of booking me, the cops told me to join the army. I joined the air force instead. Even though I got in trouble in school, I got good grades, so they gave me a diploma. I went to college in the air force and then flight school."

James had continued drinking beer, and once he got to talking about himself, his demeanor and manner changed, so that Ambler could see the bewilderment or suffering, or possibly even some remorse, in his face as he tried to understand himself. He caught himself feeling sorry for his antagonist. Equally surprising, he felt again that in a strange way James might be asking *him* for understanding.

"I don't know why I'm telling you this. You're trying to con me. But you won't get anything out of me. I don't give a shit what you think." James spoke in a rambling way, without any force, without feeling. After a long moment of thinking whatever he was thinking about, he started talking again.

"I loved flying. I loved combat. It was glorious. I didn't care who we were fighting; they were the enemy. They were out to get me, so I was going to get them first. In combat you're supposed to kill people so you don't have to feel remorse, which I never felt anyway. I got paid for hating the enemy, for killing them when the opportunity came up. It was a perfect job."

After saying this, he quieted, drinking his beer, lost again in his own thoughts. Ambler wondered, did he think about what it meant that he liked killing people. It was a strange thing to say, wasn't it? Ambler had run across people who'd killed another person. Some of them might have felt it was justified. None that he remembered would have said that they liked killing.

For some, like for Ambler the one time he killed a man, it was unavoidable once a certain set of circumstances unfolded—this happened; that happened; the gun went off. Unintended. Unavoidable. Nonetheless, killing the man shook him to his core. He wished it had never happened and he would never want something like it to happen again.

After a long silence, Ambler decided it might be his time to talk. He didn't know how he would bring James around to admitting what he'd done. If, as it appeared, he didn't have a conscience, guilt wasn't going to bring him around. What would?

"You became your father after all," Ambler said, "brutalizing people from the sky as he brutalized you and kids on the street. Did you also hurt those around you, as he did?"

He didn't know what the question might provoke—anger, violence, denial, stubborn silence? He had to be ready for anything. McNulty and his friend Lumps also sensed this might be a crisis point, as if the tension now had gotten into the air. They watched intently.

At first, James showed no reaction, as if he might not have heard the question. He finished the beer he was drinking—the third? fourth?—and stared at the can for a moment. After that he looked at a full can on the coffee table in front of him. McNulty had placed it there unobtrusively, as he had done with the others James had drunk. Maybe he was thinking he'd had enough.

When Ambler had given up on his answering the question, he began to talk, speaking quietly, as if, as had been the case earlier, talking to himself as much as to anyone else. "I don't let anyone get close to me; I never needed to be in love. I never wanted to have kids; I knew I'd be a father like my old man. Him, I never saw after I joined the air force. My mother wrote. I never answered. So after a while she stopped.

"The air force found out somehow when he died. I was in Afghanistan training Afghani pilots. These guys went from driving donkey carts to trying to fly hundred-million-dollar jets. But they did OK. I kinda liked them. The captain said I could take emergency leave to go to the old man's funeral—that's what happened when someone's father died, so he expected I would. I told him I'd send flowers; I didn't want to go. He thought I had such a great sense of duty, I wouldn't leave the mission. I let him think that." He looked at the beer can again and then opened it and took a drink.

"I don't know why you wanted to hear all this. You don't know me. I don't reveal anything about myself unless I want to, for my purposes. I can handle people like you." He took a slug of beer. His expression became defiant. "I know myself better than you think . . . and a lot better than you do.

"A long time ago, I figured out something wasn't right with me. I didn't have the same feelings other people had . . . I never felt sorry for anyone. People got frustrated with me or angry. I didn't care. Later, I read some things and thought I was probably a psychopath. No one else figured that out. In school, my teachers told my folks there was something wrong with me. My old man didn't believe in psychology. The school wanted me tested, but he wouldn't do it."

James laughed and guzzled some beer. "He knew if I was tested, they'd come after him. He was a psychopath, the bastard, and made me into one. Knowing what I was capable of—and not capable of—served me well.

"I never got into any real trouble in the air force—nothing I couldn't get myself out of. My buddies, such as they were, said I was crazy. But that wasn't a diagnosis. They called me crazy because I was reckless. I liked strafing. Strafing's dangerous. You're close to the ground and could get hit. I volunteered for every strafing mission that came up, even when I was in command and didn't have to. They meant crazy like Evel Knievel—daredevil crazy.

"I was ruthlessly ambitious, too. I cut down a couple of guys who got in my way. Word got around. A lot of my so-called buddies didn't like me. They thought I played dirty. But they didn't know how merciless I could be if pressed. I didn't care what they thought.

"I loved combat missions. I didn't give a shit what I hit. You got too fussy about what you were trying to hit, you were likely to get hit yourself. The air force told us we had to be careful about civilian casualties. Some pilots cared too much. They got overwhelmed by guilt. That never happened to me."

James stopped suddenly. "I said I knew myself. I knew what would happen if I had a family, so I didn't want one. I never loved anyone anyway. The air force was my family. I didn't have anyone close to me to hurt. I hurt the enemy, like I was supposed to do."

Ambler took a chance on interrupting his reverie. "And Linda Porter or Robin? Did you get close to either of them? Did you hurt them?"

James laughed, a disturbing laugh. "I knew this was where you were going. You think you fooled me?" He stopped laughing as abruptly as if he'd run into a wall. "I don't know what you think you know. But if you knew everything you needed to, we wouldn't be sitting here. Actually, Robin was the only one besides you who figured out what I was."

"She knew you killed Linda Porter."

He was taken aback. Stumbled but recovered. "It's more likely she murdered Linda, if anyone did."

"She had proof you did, and now I have it . . . You knew this. That's why you threatened my friend Adele."

That he had proof wasn't exactly the truth. Ambler had hoped he'd find the evidence he needed among the diaries and letters Nagy had sent him. But he'd taken a pretty good look through the diaries and batches of letters and hadn't found anything to implicate James.

Nagy said Robin had evidence that James had murdered Linda Porter. But he never saw it either. It was possible there was something in that packet he didn't recognize as being incriminating that James would recognize even if Ambler hadn't. Maybe someday someone would figure out what it was. Even though he hadn't found the evidence yet, James's actions implied there was evidence somewhere.

A flash of panic in James's eyes told Ambler the fighter pilot was rattled. His expression went through a number of contortions. He rubbed his face. He rubbed the back of his neck. He made to stand and then sat back down. He jerked around on the sofa, as if he were tied up trying to get loose. After a moment, he sat still; a calmness came over him.

"I don't know what you think you found. There were circumstances around Linda's death that only Robin and I knew. We might have been accessories to her death. But I didn't murder her.

"The point was . . . I could have saved her, but I didn't. Robin knew this. Linda wanted to die—Robin didn't believe this, or later she decided she didn't believe it. But I knew—so I let her die. Robin knew what I did. She could have stopped me. She didn't because she'd fallen in love with me and believed if Linda was out of the way I'd be in love with her . . . That's the truth." His expression dared Ambler to defy him.

"Linda was by far the more desirable woman. This was undeniable. So obvious, even Robin would have had to admit it. Truthfully, . . ." He spoke casually, perhaps trying to sound debonair but coming across instead as heartlessly callous. "I didn't desire either of them, not for anything serious. They were over-sexed playgirls, bimbos."

Listening to James, Ambler could now read between the lines of a couple of letters Robin had kept. The letters were from James in answer to letters she'd sent him. He was making fun of her concerns without mentioning what the concerns were—in a mocking way that bordered on cruelty. One of his remarks was something like, "You didn't make a mistake trusting me. You knew damn well you couldn't trust me. As I recall, you told me that more than once."

What Ambler needed to do was persuade James he knew something that he didn't know. What might work in his favor was that James already thought that he knew.

"Linda Porter believed you were in love with her. Robin believed you were in love with her. They believed this because that's what you told each of them. Robin believed that—with Linda out of the way—it would be you and her forever. She believed this because that's what you told her. Later, she came to understand you lied about everything, so she turned against you.

"Except women can't shut off their love that easily. She moved away, tried to forget about you. But when she saw you again a few years later at her mother's—she was married by then—she fell under your spell and snuck off and made love with you. She did this even though she regretted what happened with you in the past . . . and especially regretted what happened to Linda."

James watched him with a look of fascination, as if Ambler were telling him a story and he was on the edge of his seat waiting to hear how it turned out. Ambler, for his part, wished to the heavens he knew how it would turn out.

"Years later, she saw you on the steps of the 42nd Street Library. What a coincidence—*Of all the libraries, in all the towns, in all the world, he walks into mine*—and, despite knowing by then you had murdered Linda Porter, and being intent on proving it, that old magic was still there. She felt the old attraction and thought you did, too. But she was wrong about that, just as she was wrong in thinking that running into you on the library steps was an accidental meeting.

"You knew she was at the 42nd Street Library because you'd gotten an email from her attempting to blackmail you. When you met her 'accidentally' on the library steps and had dinner with her, you hadn't realized at that point it wasn't her who'd tried to blackmail you. You played along with her flirting game and didn't mention the blackmail or your threat because you'd already determined to kill her. She didn't say anything about the blackmail or the threat because she'd pretty much disregarded it and didn't connect it to you.

"The hardest thing to figure out initially was why she went to a hot-sheet hotel room and with whom. At the time she was murdered, I didn't know her as well as I thought I did. The walk-on-the-wild-side part of her character I didn't know about. So, you luring her into a hotel room, or she luring you, makes perfect sense. She was 'stuck on you' in the worst possible way, so she thought a tryst might be fun—*and* she might dig up some missing details on Linda Porter's murder for her book. All you wanted was a nice quiet place to smother her."

At that moment, James made a desperate, but half-hearted, lunge for the door, followed by an equally desperate and half-hearted attempt to resist the grasp of Lumps Gannon.

"You'll never prove any of this." He gurgled this because Lumps's tree limb of an arm was wrapped around his throat.

"Everybody says that," McNulty told him. "First, Ray doesn't have to prove it. Some assistant D.A. will. By the time the cops get through with you, that'll be easy."

Lumps had loosened his hold on James's throat and James seemed to have become resigned to his captivity. "You held me prisoner. You threatened me. You can't coerce a confession. Any court will throw it out."

"What coerced?" McNulty, for some reason, had taken over as master of ceremonies. "You didn't confess. No one coerced a confession. Ray told you what happened. You didn't contradict him. Did he get anything wrong?"

James glanced wildly around the room like a caged animal. "Everything's wrong. Nothing happened the way he said. You don't know what Robin was like. She lured me to that hotel."

Ambler spoke calmly. "Robin was naive and tried to trick you. A fateful mistake. You, Colonel, made an unforgivable mistake. You jumped to conclusions and killed the wrong person. You only realized your mistake when you got a second blackmail email from Blake Beasley's burner account, asking for money and arranging for a payoff . . .

"You committed a terrible crime and compounded it by committing another terrible crime. Could you not regret what you'd done even then?"

James looked at him uncomprehendingly.

Ambler watched him with what he recognized after a moment as sympathy. The poor wretch couldn't even feel sorrow for what he'd done.

"Regret? Why? What you did, you did to protect yourself. How could you regret that? The only thing to regret is getting caught. Once you realized your mistake, you knew enough computer forensics to find out who was really blackmailing you—Blake Beasley. You came to the library to 'negotiate' a payoff and arranged to meet him at his apartment that evening.

"Beasley was in over his head, scared to death that you'd found him, but greedy enough to meet you that evening in his apartment. And that was that for Blake."

James had almost regained his composure. "It's your word against mine." He laughed, a humorless, sickly sound. "When a lawyer gets you and these two bozos on a witness stand, he'll tear you apart."

"It's not our words the cops will be listening to." McNulty held up his cell phone.

James, open-mouthed, looked at McNulty for a moment. The dire truth of his situation was crashing down around him. "You can't take that recording to court either." He tried to sound confident and challenging but it came out more like a whimper.

# TWENTY-FOUR

James was right on one count of Ambler's criminal behavior. He and his two henchmen had committed a crime when they held James captive. On another count James was wrong: McNulty hadn't committed a crime when he recorded the conversation with James without his consent.

"Lucky for you, you were in Connecticut. In Massachusetts, it would have been illegal." David Levinson admonished the trio of miscreants standing in front of his desk. David, it turned out, did have an office, after all. It was a one-room affair above a noodle shop in Chinatown near the Manhattan Criminal Courthouse.

"It has to do with one-party versus two-party consent for recording a conversation. There's also a telephone versus in-person distinction. I could explain all this to you in detail—but it would cost you three hundred dollars an hour, so I suggest you take my word for it.

"As for the unlawful restraint, it depends somewhat on the circumstances—anywhere from one month to five-to-six months, depending on how they charge you. A good lawyer would probably get you probation . . .

"There's also the possibility Connecticut won't go to the trouble of extraditing you." He cleared his throat and paused. "Unfortunately for me, I'm licensed in Connecticut also, so if and when it comes up, we can talk about it then." He sounded a bit sorrowful.

"As for how you should handle yourselves, that's entirely up to you. As an officer of the court, it's unethical for me to advise a client to do anything illegal, to knowingly withhold knowledge of a crime, or to advise a client to testify falsely. Given all this, I feel it's unwise to continue this conversation. For anything illegal, I suggest you consult McNulty, who has a finely attuned criminal mind."

He handed each of them his business card. They'd all three been standing in front of his desk because he only had one chair in the office besides the one he was sitting in. "Call me if you're arrested or have any adverse contact with the police."

McNulty's son helped him make a copy of the voice recording of the conversation with Colonel James, which they sent to Chris Lambert. Ambler called to tell him what he was getting.

"I'm not going to ask how you got this," he said. "But I do need to know that it's not illegal before I listen to it. This guy James has connections at One PP and my ass is grass if I do anything out of line."

Ambler told him what Levinson had said. "I might be in some trouble. But the recording is arguably legal."

"I'll get back to you."

When Lambert called the next day, he said simply, "We'll take it from here. I need an affidavit from you and the two thugs—I mean your two associates. They can just affirm what you write. I'm not going to tell you what we have, but I'm pretty confident we can get a search warrant."

What Lambert didn't tell Ambler he had, Mike Cosgrove did: A partial fingerprint from the door to Beasley's apartment. Mike said it wasn't much good by itself, but matched against a full print it might be. With the print, Ambler's testimony, and the possibility of a DNA match from the bedding at the Mystique Hotel, they could extradite James and most likely convict him.

"Lambert said they also had flight records of James flying five times from Bradley Field in Hartford to a small commercial airport that used to be an air-force base outside River City. If Adele could identify a mug shot, they might get James for felony menacing also. They're dusting Adele's house for fingerprints."

In between the first and second call with Lambert, Ambler got an update from Sergeant Greenleaf. Pastor Clifton Kilgore, Greenleaf told him, had copped a plea to vehicular negligent homicide in the death of Anna Paxton.

"He did what we call an Alford plea to avoid a trial. When

his old man found out what was in that poor girl's diary, he made Cliff do the plea so the family name wouldn't be splashed across the news media in connection with rape of a child. My boss leaned on the commonwealth attorney so his sentence will be the maximum, ten years.

"Not what he should get, I'm afraid. By rights he should get the right to choose his form of execution. But it's something. Sorry we couldn't help with the other death."

Ambler told him that had worked out without his help. He'd also found an old message from Arturo Lopez telling him, though it hardly made a difference anymore, that Ricardo Diaz's injury was the real thing. He'd been shot in the back, the bullet irreparably damaging his spine. They'd never made an arrest in that one either.

For Ambler, there remained only one unsolved problem, this one a catastrophe.

"She answers the phone. She's civil, polite. But it's like talking to an automaton. No emotion. No feeling. Everything she ever felt for me is gone."

He was talking with his son John at John's small house in Westchester, near the college where John had recently been hired on a tenure-track line in the music department. He was confiding in John because he didn't know how to tell his grandson why Adele, whom Johnny loved like a mother, wasn't with him.

John, going on two years out of prison, was a new man, brimming with confidence, secure and happy in a way he'd never been in his life. Surprisingly, he didn't seem worried about Ambler's predicament. No sympathy. No commiseration. Not even a frown.

"Have Johnny call her," he said.

"You're not serious."

He was. He explained Ambler's dire situation to Johnny in about four sentences. Basically, that Adele was really, really mad at his grandfather. It was all his grandfather's fault. Grandpa tried to tell her he was really, really sorry. She was so mad she wouldn't listen to him.

Johnny went to call her. Ambler waited, sitting on the small back porch with Lola who'd been very, very glad to see him and was now lying calmly at his feet. After what seemed a long time, the boy came out onto the porch and handed him the phone.

"That wasn't fair, Raymond, using your grandson like that." She laughed. It was the first time he'd heard her laugh in forever, the sound as joyful as a host of heavenly angels.

"He said that lots of times you weren't a very good grandfather either and he got really, really mad at you, and that you'd told him yourself you were a terrible father to his father when he was a boy and his dad was really, really mad at you for a long time. And then he said very seriously, 'But we're stuck with him. And it wouldn't be right for me to stop being part of the family.'" She laughed again. "Oh Raymond! Out of the mouths of children . . ."